Daughters are Forever

Other Books by Lee Maracle

Fiction:
Ravensong
Sojourners and Sundogs

Non-fiction:
Bobbi Lee: Indian Rebel (memoir)
I Am Woman: A Native Perspective on Sociology and Feminism
Telling It: Women and Language Across Cultures (co-editor)

Poetry:
Bent Box

Young Adult:
Will's Garden

Daughters are Forever

LEE MARACLE

POLESTAR
An Imprint of Raincoast Books

Polestar Books and Raincoast Books gratefully acknowledge the support of the
Government of Canada through the Book Publishing Industry Development
Program, the Canada Council and the Department of Canadian Heritage. We also
acknowledge the assistance of the Province of British Columbia through the British
Columbia Arts Council.

Text Design by Ingrid Paulson
Typeset by Teresa Bubela

National Library of Canada Cataloguing in Publication Data
Maracle, Lee, 1950-
   Daughters are forever

   ISBN 1-55192-410-2

   I. Title.
PS8576.A6175D38 2001   C813'.54   C2001-910223-2
PR9199.3.M3497D38 2001

Library of Congress Control Number: 2002102384

At Raincoast Books we are committed to protecting the environment and to the
responsible use of natural resources. We are acting on this commitment by working
with suppliers and printers to phase out our use of paper produced from ancient
forest. This book is one step towards that goal. It is printed on 100% ancient-forest-
free paper (100% post-consumer recycled), processed chlorine- and acid-free, and
supplied by New Leaf Paper. It is printed with vegetable-based inks. For further
information, visit our website at www.raincoast.com. We are working with Markets
Initiative (www.oldgrowthfree.com) on this project.

Polestar
An Imprint of Raincoast Books
9050 Shaughnessy Street
Vancouver, British Columbia
Canada, V6P 6E5
www.raincoast.com

1 2 3 4 5 6 7 8 9 10

Printed and bound in Canada by Houghton Boston.

To my daughters Columpa and Tania —
you so deserved the best.

Contents

Part ONE

꙳ ꙳ ꙳ ꙳

Westwind crept. He slid his way across the land. He breathed softly in those moments when, touching new grass, his lust-breath warmed to the newness of plant life stretched before him. The scent of all this green ran red with desire through his being. Along the trail of new life, berries were born of flowering green. He played with them. Brightly coloured lush fruit chuckled, kissed the wispy touch of Westwind. Bees danced above the flowers. Red, white, pink and purple on green painted an easy picture of seduction for bee and wind alike. It took him generations to become familiar with stone, grasses, the four-legged, winged and tree people.

Westwind rustled leaves; moaned wondrous in the spring of earth's beginning. The sea frolicked under Westwind's touch, circling itself into puffy clouds. Vaporous water rose to greet wind's play. Clouds chased Westwind, followed him across hilltops, and then spilled their weight on barren valley floors. Their wet saltless water sprouted more green playmates for Westwind's insatiable desire. He played with the beings that seeded under his touch and so shaped the house of earth.

In the dark above, stars sang. The lights from the north joined the song, touched the stars, and whispered dreams to the woman who lived among the sky beings. *Dream child, dream of being, dream of touch, dream of fire, heat and cold.* They mapped her journey to the physical world below where breath and flowers accelerated at the sight of her. The earth rose, mountains of it. Her magic brought more life and all seemed perfect. On earth, sky woman birthed a daughter conceived in star maps above.

While Westwind played, the subject of his affection-to-be matured. He saw her floating about the flowers whose delicate faces pointed in his direction. His tenuous voice shook; he breathed deep and the grasses around first daughter waved in unison. Their slender bodies rippled about her calves. Sweet green against copper excited him. He exhaled deep, long sighs. She heard, turned to him. Her hair joined with his touch, her body swayed in response; they played together. Then, in the ceremony to which night sometimes retreats, he took her, planted seeds of future in her young, sweet womb. In a moment she was lost to him.

Her sons breathed the breath of this star-nation daughter into the beings they created. This breath stretched from its origin through meteoric pathways of brilliant white light. From the starlight, this breath snatched courage and willful determination and yarned itself around its wisps of air. This breath inspired dreams of life, of newness, of journeys. This breath owned the creative power to engage life and overcome obstacles. This breath spurred the fire of passion from Westwind to gamble on love.

Star-nation woman's breath continued to live here in the bodies of her sons' creation long after Westwind's moment with her ended.

She played with the earth, sky, wind, and conjured plant life. Her children birthed children. Generation after generation of her descendents peopled the Island. East, West, South and North winds played with Turtle Islanders for generation after generation, calling spring, summer, autumn and winter for millennia before the intruders came. Conjured by wind and women, Turtle Islanders built an understanding of the world rooted in the goodwill of safe womanhood. The children of these women felt goodwill in their mothers' touch, heard it in the sound their voices made. They saw it in the eyes of their mothers, the looks their mothers and fathers exchanged.

The winds toyed with the Islanders, breathed the voice of their own breath into their bodies. Like good uncles, East, South and North wind joined in playing with their brother's descendants. The children too came to know the touch of wind and came to derive the song of goodness from their mothers and wind alike. The warm winds inside the women bequeathed by Southwind shaped the softness of their song. Eastwind breathed wisdom and Northwind urged the people to responsive activism. Each wind became a caress treasured by the people. The winds shaped being, growth, movement and transformation.

In the beginning there was only one language on this island. Agreements between all beings were struck. Belief between the beings held them up. The boundaries between beings were delicately maintained. The earth and her winds nurtured the Islanders, flora, fauna and human alike. Sometimes in his yearning for his bride, Westwind called up hurricanes of grief, but his brothers held him in check, turning grief to song. The Islanders learned to sing with the winds. Humans were born and died in the lap of wind-song.

Women were born awake. In their bodies lived the memories of their star-nation mother's moment with Westwind. In their blood coursed traces of old agreements. These traces nagged them until story awakened them. Through story, each generation of women schooled the next to solve crises, to enter into relationship with others, eyes wide open and hearts optimistic. The stories were full of other ancestors who had travelled in aberrant directions and so brought near disaster to their villages. Through these stories the women learned to search the world for responses. They emulated the beings around them, and dodems were born. Helpers were acquired in the dark of huts made of sinew, in which red-hot stones sang extraordinary answers. Systems were born in this way. Successful strategies were repeated in stories, shaping customs and beliefs into systems. The humans gained confidence through their endless discussions about direction and their successful speculation in response to problems. Belief in one another achieved a majesty all its own. Turtle Island women had no reason to fear other humans.

§ § § §

Summer's end brings stillness to life. Weary grasses glisten, limp and tired. Tree sap slows. Fauna rearranges itself, prepares for a long, much-needed winter rest. Storm introduces Winter's steady cold. Autumn gores plant people, stills their blood, and tears the leaf dress off their trees. Their blood stilled, the plant people grow sleepy. Northwind awakes to engage his brothers in a wrestling match. He chases Westwind, clashes with Eastwind, and smothers

Southwind. This man-game is played in earnest. Eastwind tries to protect the younger brothers from Northwind's biting breath. Timid Southwind retreats while the other three brothers collide.

The game of the brothers is rhythmic, dance-like. It pushes back earth life. Northwind will win this dance contest. Plants know. They know to surrender. They still their blood. "Be still," they croon to one another. Trees loosen leaves, sending them flying to the wind in acquiescence. Even in their movement, their internal stillness stands brittle and naked. Animals retreat to lairs. Humans build warm fires and retire to old stories inside the comfort of home. The grasses sing surrender to one another. Trees whistle and whine; the coming cold will be brutal.

Grasses know stillness. Women know the grasses. Grasses feel this knowing. They exchange pleasantries with these women every day. In their modest desire to know these women the grasses listen, learn songs as the women create melodies that urge them along pathways that would help them to ally themselves with the natural world. The sounds are familiar; they engage each other, attending to the need for comfort as the earth transforms. This knowing between them is mature, comfortable. Plant people know something about the living. Any alteration of human breath causes them to stir. Today, the cadence of voice, the rhythm, seemed out of the ordinary. Breath caught unwittingly in the throats of the women. Plants began to whisper to one another: "Something is up. The humans don't feel the same today. There is a pall in the air. Do you feel it?"

Autumn fell as she always does, heavy, raw and cold. She whipped rain into frenzies of snow and ice.

The skin tells stories. Skin feels future. In their vulnerable, safe and open state, the humans open their skin and their ears hear in a much sharper way. Surrendering their vulnerability opens their hearts to belief. Belief opens the skin, the eyes. Sometimes humans see future, transform its expression to song without knowing what it is they sing of, turning future to beautiful music. Sometimes future is connected to lies, but humans have no capacity for understanding that. Sound travels. Water magnifies sound. Those who sense change coming without hearing the words to help them understand it will sometimes sing of it. They just sing what they feel. Damaged future inspires sad songs. The song hummed by one woman seemed unduly melancholy.

While the woman sang, winter rose cold and foreboding and the earth beings prepared for it. Sun rose red and inviting, despite the crackling frigid air. He danced across the ocean's breast and with Eastwind's help he ushered the ships into the bay. The masts loomed tall at the edge of Turtle Island. On the silver-grey jacket of the sea, the ships emerged from under the fog, propelled by sun's early light and the sight of women ashore. Sick with hunger, disease and the misalignment of their tortured spirits, the newcomers spilled from the tall ship into strange canoes.

Dawn's Eastwind breathed heavily, meeting Westwind's lust breath. The brothers danced and played, curious about these men. The collision of winds whirled about the clothing of the women who had sighted the ship. Dancing, the brothers' breath greeted their soft dresses. They played about, ignoring the melancholy humming of the woman, anticipating with joy the acquaintance of the new and the old. Southwind and Northwind were drawn to their brothers' anticipation. They joined the play.

Under the wind-play ships appeared, their white sails billowing on the skyline. The villagers prepared to greet the shipmates from the sea. Food was prepared. Songs were made ready. Women were the first to sing strangers into the village. The ships stopped, small boats were lowered and the men scrambled into them.

A rabble of boorish sound scurried in the direction of the women. The songs in the women's throats halted as hairy faces filled with lice, skin oozing with sores, and bodies caked with ship's filth came into view. The dishevelled clothing of the strangers shocked the women's song into near silence. Ashore, the strangers' swords flashed. Their bodies swung hatred. Woman after woman, confused, fell under the lash of decadent rage carried by these men wherever they went.

The earth echoed the song of the women. This song invaded Marilyn's dreams. Blood oozing, breath choking, the women slunk to the ground, calling something in soft tones to the winds, something Marilyn could not remember. Grace was inside these women. It surrounded them. Light emanated from the acres of bronzed skin now stretched across the open field, so many bodies, all eyes open. They tried to catch one last glimpse of their sky-world destiny as their blood departed, carrying away their life.

In this last moment their minds whirled, projected image after image of their mothers, their antecedents, onto the brightly lit sky, hoping wind would capture these images, make sense of the death happening to them and call out the secret of this moment. No one wishes to die confused. Those women who had not yet birthed a child fought desperately to live. Writhing and twisting ungracefully, their muscles struggled for breath, for wind, for life.

In one spot where grass stood upright under the touch of the early morning wind, one woman lay still alive. Her breath slowed. Her mind drifted. Her body offered itself up to death. Her mind surrendered to the moment. Eagle flew overhead, whistling rage. She called to the woman whose heart had escaped the bayonet, shrieking, "Be still." The grass people cradled her, repeated eagle's song of stillness. "Be still. Be still." The woman heard the echo of the grasses, sighed, then stilled her voice. Her purple light left to join eagle. From the wings of eagle her light surveyed the carnage.

Blood is heavy. It weighted the slender stalks of sweetgrass. Blood is pungent; it drowned sweetgrass' gentle fragrance. Westwind screamed in desperation, darting here and there, touching each woman's bloodied corpse. Eastwind chased him, tried to comfort him. Northwind flew into a rage, gathered the waters from the bay and sent them roaring at the mass of men. His efforts were futile. The men were already too far inland. The birds stopped singing and the very air above the women began to die. Animals retreated under the whirl of the brothers' wind, which collided and wrestled in their desperate attempt to stop the slaughter.

Sweetgrass was stilled. The women's blood stopped the grass from moving. Sweetgrass whispered to the ground below, "Be still," then lay quietly under the women's bodies. She prayed softly for a new tomorrow. The earth did not move. The small beings inside her black soil stilled. Westwind fell onto the bodies of the women and lay there helpless. Eastwind, horrified, returned to the sea. Northwind covered the carnage with his vicious, cold breath. Raven squawked at the men from above, shrieking "Stop!" She was stunned at their deafness, their behaviour, their filth and disease.

Exhausted and unable to fathom what was happening, she too retreated, voiceless, to the base of an old elm tree.

In the blood-filled throats of the fallen women, song froze. In the descendants of the women who bled their innocent perfection onto the breast of Earth mother, a rigid, pain-filled stillness replaced the body's natural desire to move.

The rabble took advantage of the dead and dying women. From between the legs of skirtless bronze bodies shame rose, musty, dank and foul-smelling. The watching woman saw her body misused. In perfect stillness she saw the lout who had taken her, leave her for dead. From above she breathed stillness over her remains. Her lungs relaxed. Her breathless lungs grew still. The next man arrived. He paused, slapped her lifeless body, helped himself to her sex and moved on.

The men saw their women falling from the edge of the village and ran to assist them. Poorly armed and unprepared for the blood lust of the newcomers, they too perished. The rabble killed all but the one whose stillness had rescued her. Satiated, they scrabbled about the land for food, for wealth, for anything. Then they left. It took but a few short hours.

The survivor returned to her body and slept. She woke nearly bloodless. Wolf dragged a water gourd to where she lay. She drank. Eagle dropped a fish. She ate. She slept. She awoke hearing Westwind whisper, "Come hither" in her ear. She rose, wobbled in the direction of Westwind. Between sleep and Westwindward wobbling, this woman with her extraordinary stillness and deadened ecstasy began to recover.

In his retreat, Southwind called other living beings from inland to follow him to the carnage. At dawn, he led men to the meadow of blood. They stood in shock for a moment, heavy with the grief before them. The hands of Southwind lightened the load as the men sought to carry these women to a last place of acknowledgement, of burial, of bidding adieu between the living and the departed. Blood pooled in the grasses. Weeping, the grasses stooped under the weight of their sisters' blood; they bent over and grieved their passing. They would miss these women who spoke to them in a language so tender their voices seemed to call the grasses into being. The trees bent in their direction, against the path of wind. The women's gifts would be missed.

The villagers of the neighbouring nation found the wandering one and took her in. They accepted her strange stillness. They could see the melancholy of the grasses and the lightened shade of purple the still woman's spirit had become. They returned to the ground where the women and men lay dead to bury them. They stared for some time before setting aside the earth to lay them to rest. The men who buried the women remained stamped with the tension of shock that men feel when they cannot accept they were unable to protect their relatives. The barely perceptible chronic tension of these men matched the stillness of the woman who survived. The old ones nodded. It made a crazy kind of sense, given what had happened.

The women's sudden exit created an invisible skin of lonely melancholy above the ground. Earth's skin is not unlike the skin of humans. Her skin holds grief close in much the same way human skin does. Earth now trailed through life with her melancholy feelings hovering lightly above her skin. It was the first time so many young ones had left the world so early. "Something is not right here," ran Earth's lament. "Not right, not right, not right."

The grasses and stones and maybe even the humans could have grieved and recovered, but it didn't end there.

Illness followed. Sometimes the illness travelled ahead of the newcomers, borne on the tip of Eastwind's breath. Horrific decisions were made during the many bouts of illness: "We cannot take care of the aged," and whole hosts of knowledge-keepers died. "We cannot take care of the men," and young men ceased trusting women. Eastwind still felt the guilt of having unwittingly carried the newcomers' smallest beings from ship to shore. This guilt painted the air between land and sky with the memory of carnage, and sometimes little children swallowed the painting. Mixed as it was with chronic grief, this air was sour. This guilt stuck in the throats of children, became part of their being before they understood its terrifying influence. Westwind's lust-breath changed. Repressed, desperate, explosive, disciplined, constrained, implosive, he no longer howled out the names of the unmarried women to young men. He barely whispered romance. He spoke no more of sensual possibilities, of communion with this woman or that one to anyone. He was not quiet, though. He did call out to Marilyn as she slept: "Marilyn. You need to know it's over. We are entering a new era, a new saga has been born."

The headhunters came next. Bounties were put out. Proof of murder required the removal of the black tresses of the men, of the women, of the babies. With every scalp removed, Westwind howled. He wailed a grieving song. The women picked up the stillness of the survivors of each new holocaust. The men picked up the tension of failing to protect. Women taught babies stillness. "Still your breath," they whispered. "Still your body." Crying became dangerous. "Leave howling to the wind, child. Hush. We tread lightly in the forest. We enter silently. No sound when we move. No noise we make." Economy of movement, quiet stealth, entrenched itself in the being of the people during two hundred years of bounty-hunting scalpers. Women, the keepers of cultural survival, passed on stillness as the ultimate way to protect their daughters. Daughters are forever. Daughters never leave. Sons are temporary; they belong to future families. When they marry, they leave. Sons are dispensable, but every daughter is needed to recreate the villagers. The tension of sons went unchecked as they waited their turn to die, neglected by their women.

The newcomers kept hunting. The women hid. They grew silent. This strategy began to show results. The hunting was to no avail. The newcomers found a new strategy. They remembered how easily their illnesses killed the people on those first days after they arrived. Diseased blankets could be traded. These blankets produced awesome results. The newcomers could not seem to stop killing. They killed village after village, until the women gave up their big houses, gave up their extended families, gave up their original being. Softness died in the hearts of these women as illnesses claimed baby after baby, knowledge-keeper after knowledge-keeper, and man after man. Every generation after the newcomers' arrival witnessed the departure of the old, the infants and the fragile. So chronic was the early departure of the Islanders that the grasses stopped weeping for the women.

The still woman eventually bore children. Every now and then the stillness showed up in the woman's children, as though they were branded with it. This stillness became her female descendants' response to life's critical events, the ones that might cause them to grieve, then move on to that magical creative space of change, of transformation. Softness in the woman gave way to the planned grace of stillness and silence.

The earth knows the grieving song of the women, the grasses and the winds. She is neither an unconscious nor uncaring mother. The song haunts. It holds the smell of murder close to her skin. She struggles to remove this scent of murder, bringing wind, rain and storm to bear as she washes herself off. Still, the aroma returns to taint the space just above the earth's skin. Tension invades the men as they dig graves for the dead they were unable to protect. The return of the scent of murder becomes shame as the earth fails to cleanse her of the magnitude of grief. In their tension the men swallow her shame. Their every breath returns it to the space next to her skin. They can't seem to let it go. They cling to it as if it were an invisible blanket made of jewels from the past. There is a perverse pride in having survived all that carnage and felt all that shame. They wallow in the putrid scent of shame that layers the earth on Turtle Island and fills the bellies of the people. The tension of shame kills their courage a shovel-load at a time.

Dead courage opens the door to fear. Fear is an old shrivelled snake lying in wait, a snake that pounces inappropriately. These snakes are shape-shifters. They are invisible. The humans swallow them in bundles. The snakes hide in the bellies of the humans, slithering about inside and propagating at will. They can't get out. These snakes have lost their minds. Crazed, they rear up, biting the heads off their own young.

Momma Earth weeps. Wind echoes her grief and roars at Turtle Island men. Fearful, the men shrivel and close their ears to windsong. Although they need to listen to their uncle's howl, the male descendants of those first fallen dare not hear the wind. Declining to listen to the optimistic potential of love, of romance, they loll about the earth waiting until their turn to leave early rolls around. Apathy dulls the light inside them, disconnects them from future star paths. The layer of shame blanketing their mother's breast dims their light; listing in an uneasy perpetual fog, they cannot fire up their passion. Life has become a dull moment in which the loving expression of Turtle Island men is an unwanted, hated thing. If these men heard Westwind's song, their own song would want to well up, to find its way to that old duet men and women once sang to honour wind, breath, origin and future.

Grace has left their bodies. They are rendered stiff and tense by the knot of shame that sits stuck in their throats. It needs to be expressed, pushed up and out so they may sing again, but five centuries of "Hush, don't cry" holds the expression of their shame still. Under it lies a dangerous grief. They now tread heavily on the back of their mother. Lunging from place to place, they plant seeds but don't bother to watch them grow. They water nothingness as though this water will somehow recreate life without their participation. Many have acquired the jerky movements, the bad skin and the hard, strident song-less voices of the newcomers. Their world has lost its future. Cut off from considering their past, they list in the momentary context of the present. Consideration requires a spiritual sensibility, one that sees life from all its jewel-like angles. The men don't see life; they barely feel their existence. They avert each other's gaze. The reflection of grief and shame in the eyes of others mirrored back at them is too terrifying to contemplate.

They mark time. Time is the enemy of the dispirited. Those who dare not make use of it mark time for death, for murder. These men wander aimlessly, killing time in small pieces. They bellow ominously from barstools, party houses and booze cans in every impoverished urban centre. They float from one woman to another, leaking manhood into wombs, some of them belonging to women who are too young to appreciate the gift of life. Other women are too numb to feel this gift, too raw to enjoy it, or too near death to wonder during its giving. Some are too still to deeply feel the presence of life in the gift. Some of the men do not bother to seek the women's consent.

Turtle Island women's homes have become revolving doors where men enter then leave in dawn's quiet, sometimes without bothering to ensure the women who served them remember their names. Open, close, the door invites entry and exit but not staying. Always the house is missing, missing the scent of men, and missing the quiet resolve of men who listen to women and children. Long ago, men were awed by the sound women and children made in homes. These men once listened and wondered at the voices of small children and the busy talk of women. They once planned future from what they heard. They braided their dreams together with the women's and children's lives to create a symphony of forever in their hearts. Small acts engaged in over and over by successive generations of women and children are intended to inspire the awe of foreverness in men, but only conscious men reared in the lap of original promise can derive this symphony from the sound of family. Men who cannot hear women and children in an awe-inspired way cannot appreciate the "foreverness" of these small acts.

Normal is the roller-coaster ride of desertion, stillness and bloodletting. Turtle Island women almost expect it. The wind of desire holding promise still whirls around inside, but it is drowned by the sound of songs of desperate bloodletting and desertion. "Oh no," women wail as partners desert them. We can all hear the banging on the walls in the houses and apartments next door. Another woman, another child's blood, is let. Some women are killed in this way. Some know death is too common for anyone to feel the depth of the shame we should feel for murder by lovers.

Risk-takers are born of peace, not war. The old shrivelled snake of doubt now nests in the throat of the women. The snake creates snap-drawling yo-yo sounds in the throats of the women. Snake then shrivels into his nest, recreating more snakes until doubt consumes the sound women make. Softness is a gamble and these women dare not wager. The women no longer hear themselves; not hearing themselves, they have nothing to invest and so do not gamble.

We are all born screaming. Smiling and laughter are cajoled and curried from us. Our mothers must spend months squeezing our smiles out from between the language of our tears. "Open up. Open wide. Yeah. That's it. Good girl. Good boy." These instructions become familiar now only in perverse contexts. Instead of conjuring the feeling of forever, the art of child-rearing defiles our spirit. Babies feel the absolute goodwill of their mothers in the sound of their voices. They also sense its absence. The conversation still goes on, month after month, child after child, but the sound of motherhood has changed. There is so much threat in the voice of motherhood now. The babies fear it, writhe under its menace. For weeks on end, the children fight to bend tongue, throat and mouth, trying for the breath that will inspire the sound of forever in their mothers' voices. Babies so want to be good.

Children hear what is said, see what is done, and are moved to become us. Their bodies carry memory. This memory is forever. They remember what ought to be said and done too. They feel what is said in the rhythm and tones of the speaker. The body memory of origin invades their present, before language can explain it to them. These are the really dangerous gifts children possess. The women who died on the shores of Turtle Island so long ago knew this intimately, deeply, automatically and practically. So intimate, so deep and so automatic was this knowing that they could not have told you how they came to know it. They knew too from the looks they did not exchange that love was a constant, not a variable.

Children feel love as the absence of chronic spiritual hunger. The world must hold up promise as a reality; promise must be reachable, attainable and realizable or spiritual hunger will dog them and shape their character.

Generation by generation, the original promise became some strange and painful foreigner. Westwind continued to pick up this promise, binding it to desire and carrying it desperately to all corners of the island. Over the centuries, the promise became twisted into a double-headed snake: one head twisted into promiscuity, the other head carefully cradled the memory of the original vow. More blood was shed than anyone can safely remember. There was so much bloodshed it became the norm. Now children make games of bloodshed. Blood is shed in drips and drops. A broken foot, a broken nose, slashed arms, wrists, legs, cigarette burns, blackened bloodied eyes. Pieces of us are punctured and the blood leaks out chronically.

There has been no relief since the Turtle Island women first graced the earth with their first untimely passing.

Westwind's song became a shame-based grieving song when the outsiders, the foreigners, eased up on killing Turtle Islanders and the Islanders began to kill themselves. The song tears at doorways trying to be heard. It disrupts gatherings, rips its way into hearts. Mis-translated, the mournful sound sparks anger grown in gardens lush and bountiful. This anger ignites and finds expression at the oddest moments.

Westwind is restless now. Frustrated with the deafness of Turtle Island citizens, who have no way to translate his song, he sometimes howls inappropriately. The air just above the earth is heavy with chronic assault and unexpressed grief. Westwind is crazed by his own need to cleanse it. He spits out storms much more often than ever was intended by Earth. His brothers work feverishly to keep him in check. Sometimes, this has the effect of creating the very storms the brothers seek to prevent.

Part TWO

§ § § §

Eddy heard the song. He heard it one night when his mind was polluted with beer. It reached him at the same moment as his twelfth drink. The amber swirled, magnified the sound as it curled its way to the lips of the bottle. Eddy tasted the amber, felt the sound, jumped up, slammed his fist on the table, knocked over the chair and tore the lamp from its moorings. In a strange moment of delusion his body believed the noise he made would drown the sound. It didn't. Screaming desperately, in an insane bid to outrun the sound, he ran from the house onto the highway and collided with a transport truck.

The driver wept in fits and starts, volleying between grief and grim shock as he stared at the very flattened body of Eddy. "What the hell?" he kept asking over and over to no one. Window curtains across the street moved slightly. The viewers took the time to recognize Eddy then returned to their beers and their own effort to drown the sound of Westwind. Three more "What the hells?" and the driver called the police. His last "What the hell?" changed from the sound men make when they cannot for the life

of them figure out what you were trying to do, into the sound
they make when they're wondering what is going to happen to
them, their jobs and their life.

"Emergency? I just killed someone…"

·"No. It was an accident…"

"Highway 10…"

"I think I'm on the Indian Reserve. Well, he's an Indian and he
came from some old shack here. He appeared outta nowhere.
There was no way to stop." The driver was no longer responding
to the dispatcher. He continued to babble defensively for a time,
"Outta nowhere. Just ran in front of my truck. I couldn't possibly
see him," he finished, then dropped his phone. He sat staring cata-
tonically out the window until the ambulance came.

The lamp Eddy knocked over struck Anne, knocking her
unconscious. The sound woke Marilyn. She crept off the bed. Her
tiny feet gingerly swept the floor in front of her as her eyes struggled with dark. Her feet searched for a clear path. She picked her
way through the debris to the half-lit kitchen door at the end of the
hall. Her eyes could not adjust to the indirect light from the
kitchen, which crossed the hallway at the end but did not spill much
light onto the pathway in front of her. She felt her way along the
hall with both hands and feet. Her hand touched the electric outlet,
and then she snapped her fingers back as she remembered her
mother's voice barking, "Don't touch that." She halted at each new
sound explosion from Eddy. She urged herself forward during those
moments when her Daddy's voice did not puncture the silence. Her
heart beat too fast when she moved, slowed down as she froze at the
entrance to the kitchen just as her Daddy bolted for the door.

Blood still gushed from her mother's nose. Around her mother's body, which lay curled up on the floor amid the tangled mess of beer, blood and lamp glass, lay the odd bits of paper that seemed to create so much tension between her dad and mom. Broken bottles and supper leavings accented the physical chaos.

The door gaped open. Marilyn thought she saw the heels of her father disappear through a wall of black night somewhere beyond the door. A quick glance around the kitchen: *Daddy's not here. Mommy's on the floor.* The images of her father's feet fading to black and her unconscious mother unlocked a scream inside Marilyn. Her mother stirred, pulled at her consciousness. Marilyn ran after her daddy. She stopped dead at the edge of the yard just as the truck swallowed Eddy. She knew he had been swallowed. She saw it. Her skimpy little nightie flapped in the warmth of Westwind and the night died. It died heavy. Night fell flatly on Marilyn. Her little hands covered her mouth. Her eyes stared at the truck. Nothing moved.

Marilyn's mother, Anne, staggered into the carcass of night. She pushed through its heavy lifeless black and scooped Marilyn up before the police arrived. Otherwise, Marilyn would have become an orphan.

In her grief, Anne shuffled about the kitchen without speaking. She poured water in a jug and mixed instant milk powder with it. She reached for a spoon from the drying rack where the dishes from the night before still stood upright untouched. She grabbed a bowl, filled it with puffed rice and placed it in front of Marilyn. Marilyn took the spoon and began feeding herself. She offered a soft smile to Anne, but Anne had already headed for the window. The window drew her attention away from Marilyn like a vacuum sucking the joy out of the room. Marilyn toyed with the food and then, hungry, she wolfed it down.

She jumped down from her seat, went to the sink and rinsed her dish and spoon and placed it in the drying rack. She returned to the table and drew a picture. She trotted to Anne: "Look, Mommy." Anne glanced at it. She almost smiled, then said, "Go clean your room" and she turned her back on Marilyn. Marilyn mimicked her mother's silence. She shuffled about quietly, practising Anne's stillness. She took up keeping vigilance at the window. Maybe Eddy would come back. Maybe someone would pay attention to her then. She needed attention. Westwind saw Marilyn. He remembered his affair with a human woman. Marilyn so reminded him of this woman even in her child state. He summoned the voice of wisdom from Anne's ancestors: "Children are a gift, a loan. Appreciate this gift." On the wings of his changing breath he fought to fill Anne with the desire for growth and transformation. "Pay attention", he murmured with care. "Children need attention. Courage is cultivated by the nature of the attention we pay to children. At some point humans need to face themselves. To do so requires the courage to become conscious. This courage is not born, it must be nurtured."

Anne did not hear him. All she heard was the din going on in her own mind. Brittle phrases filled her head. "That is just like Eddy, to leave me to raise his child alone." These phrases repeated themselves over and over. Anne's phrases robbed Marilyn of the nurturing she needed to become herself.

Stillness filled both mother and daughter. It became their governess. Their bodies adjusted almost automatically to it. It felt old, familiar, so right in the dead night of Eddy's death, which was too strange to truly contemplate. This stillness surrounded them. It fit like a halo. Its heavy presence weighed down upon them. The thickness of it stopped their skin from acknowledging their own presence. Their skin lost its ability to feel its way through life. Their skin grew blind. Their muscles atrophied under the stillness of their bodies and the blindness of their skins.

"Don't move" became the command of Anne and Marilyn. Their response to all crises and irregular phenomena was slow, shallow, almost imperceptible lung movement. "Don't move" guided both women like some terrible secret. Neither would ever discuss this trademark stillness, but it was there in the way they sat, the way they economized every move of the hand, eyes and mouth. Even the internal cellular movement of their bodies was too thrifty. Their graceful resistance to movement was mistaken for stoicism, for grace, for conservation, for wisdom, for just about everything but what it was: residual shock.

This hangover, this bottled secret shut out the world. This hangover is constructed of the shattered glass on the kitchen floor, the shattered glass of the transport-truck lights, and a dead Eddy weighting the night. It fogs their desire for peace and freedom — breath-song. This weight, this shattered glass, triggered a dream-song memory of the first women murdered in the field when the newcomers came and of the lone survivor who stilled her movement. It silenced Westwind's lustful breath. It denied Marilyn and Anne access to their dreams and the truth these dreams bring.

Night is so imperative. In her aliveness she brings dreams of future. Night is the playground of our hope for tomorrow. In the night, deep ceremonial thought over our day's sacred being happens. Without nightlife, humans are only half here. Alive, night moves humans and their children gently through change. Alive, she governs dream-paths toward change. Night gives shape to change. In the dark of the dream world, the path toward transformation is brightened. In the absence of aliveness, night brings dead air. The dead air arrests memories of change and threatens to push up memories of carnage. The humans have not had the opportunity to exhale the breath of carnage and so cannot reconcile with it. There is no resolution without reconciliation to their dilemma. Humans fear night dreams. Dead night plagues humans who are emotionally paralyzed. Nightmare-plagued dreams are the destiny of dynamic humans whose nights lay dead. Those humans whose nights have died feel compelled to choose a path of emotional paralysis.

Marilyn tossed and turned. The dream-song tried to reach her. It hummed about in the thin layer between her muscles and her skin but could not reach her unwilling mind. The stilled woman who left her body spiritless so she could survive the carnage and procreate, haunts, but she cannot communicate with Marilyn or Anne. Dream-song memories can be cruel. This one assumed governance of Marilyn and Anne's bodies before it registered in their minds. Neither woman could have told anyone what her stillness represented. Both would have denied its odd existence.

§ § § §

Outside, Southwind played with the city. He tapped at windows, clicked awnings together, snapped canvas against aluminum frames and engaged trees lining the streets. Southwind brings this rain, moves the peace and dead quiet of the cold to a messy orchestra of movement and sound to create a wet and wild chaos. Cold recedes under the breath of Southwind. At first Northwind defies Southwind's breath. Southwind pushes at cold, presses upward to the skies, rolls it back from the soil. The cold resists. Northwind captures it and invades, is pushed back and one last time fights mightily against cold's eradication.

Southwind breathes deeply, retreats to the ocean, and engages his brother from the west. Together they recollect their strength for another push at winter. Northwind is older, chillier, more knowing than his younger brothers are. He is infuriated by their impetuous intrusion. He rears back, slaps at them. They entangle. Eastwind joins the fracas. They retreat, regroup and surge forward, whirl and parry, waking up the thunders. The thunders settle it all. These old men who have seen so much change, whose voices are so dangerous to provoke, slap all four brothers, then usher in Southwind's healing warmth and drive the cold up and out.

Winter retreats. His retreat is not all that peaceful. No one likes changing so much they hurtle themselves forward, reckless of consequences. When one being moves forward someone else has to take a step back to make room for their presence. Taking turns being in the front or centre is not easy, especially for these old and powerful men. Westwind yearns for Turtle Island womanhood and so hesitates to step back and give Southwind room. Northwind mocks Westwind's lament. They wrestle a little more.

Westwind threatens to seduce Northwind. Northwind grows fearsome. Vehement, he entrenches himself in his cold, brittle breath. He holds fast to yesterday. Season to season the body of Earth changes. Not even Earth is sure of the outcome of the transformation from winter to spring, spring to summer to fall and finally winter. There are too many variables. But like all loyal mothers, Earth presses on, calling up change from within. It is she who awakens the thunder beings. Together Southwind and the thunderers force Earth's progeny from sleep, hot-housing spring's awakening. It takes an entire spring of wind and rain to wake up the earth and call life into being.

Westwind is the bellows of Earth's transformation. He summons the strength to repair the damage life can wrought on the body, so earth might move gently toward old age. Earth understands that mothering is a state of attrition. Children ought to outlive their mothers. Still, they are variable. One child may threaten another. Sibling rivalry is dangerous to familial being. It could get out of hand. This happened on Turtle Island more than once, long before the newcomers came. Spiritual cannibalism, opportunism and incest were the by-products of this war in the days before Raven, Eagle and Earth ended it. The cannibalism, opportunism and incest were prevented with much human-woman effort, in story, song, dance and teaching.

Westwind follows Marilyn. He whispers old story as he tugs and nags at her coattails. He is always beside her. He pleads with her to listen. But Marilyn has no memories of reassurance, no cultivation of thought processes that would guide her to hear Westwind. Her courage is an elastic band with very little stretch to it. The wind, the breath required inside her body to bring about the chaotic images that, when examined, would point her to the

road of transformation are crunched back by memories she
should never have had. She pays no attention to Westwind except
to clutch her hair and coat when forging through it from automobile to office and from automobile to home. She does not hear
the Westwind-borne voices of her ancestors whispering in her ear.

ﬅ ﬅ ﬅ ﬅ

For someone as still as Marilyn, university and social work
seemed the best option for employment.

She sat at her desk now, a file folder staring at her, still and
stark. The blood inside Marilyn pumped unevenly. She drew in a
breath and exhaled before the air reached down into her lungs. She
knew about breath, how it should float across the lungs, scour
them, pick up bits and pieces of dust and such too small to see.
Breath should plunge itself into every nook and cranny of her
lungs. Sometimes though, like today, it simply refused. She had
long ago convinced herself that perhaps it was the air-conditioned
room, the absence of natural air. When outside, she persuaded
herself that her breathlessness was related to air pollution. In
spring, it was ragweed allergy. In summer it would be the humid-
ity. At night it was fatigue. Early morning, it was the absence of
coffee. At midday it might be because she smoked too much.
Rationale after rationale helped her to avoid wondering why her
lungs did not work. "Mind over matter. Talk yourself into it." She
instructed her treacherous lungs to breathe. "Inhale even, deep
breaths," she nagged, to no avail. The rapid, shallow sighs thickened the pumping blood, giving it weight, slowing the mind,

making her feel lightheaded. She thought it odd that heavy blood made the mind feel light, giddy.

The file continued to stare at her. Forget breath; she must begin her day. She watched her fingers appear on the desktop, saw them move in the direction of the file folder, opening it as though the hands did not really belong to her. The nearly foreign hands opened the file of their own volition; they did not require instruction.

One hand left the file the moment it was open to stroke a thick mane of darkened hair, the other covered the photos in front of the documents. Lady Clairol coloured the grey, staving off the image of premature aging for a while yet. The thickness of it, the texture, relaxed her breath. She took the time to examine the tips, orange-red atop dark brown. Where did the orange tips come from? Her hand moved the photos out of the way. She chuckled, then read the file: Elsie Jones. Age: 23. Live births: 3; children: 2. Cause of child's death: pneumonia. Extenuating circumstances: neglect.

There was a paragraph following the vital statistics. Marilyn read them every time before she had an appointment with Elsie. She was looking for something, though she didn't know what it was. Maybe she believed that some hint of what happened to Elsie, to herself, to Indian motherhood was buried between the lines.

On April 24, 1989, social worker Madison arrived at the home of E. Jones. Marsha Jones, aged eighteen months, lay in her crib, soiled diaper unchanged, wheezing and coughing (a dry hacking cough). The other two children played about quietly on the floor. James, aged three, was without clothing; Theresa, five, appeared to be feeding James breakfast cereal from a bowl without milk. Elsie Jones lay on a soiled easy chair, her hand clutching an empty beer bottle; strewn about the room were children's toys and soiled clothes, and on the kitchen table adjoining the living-dining room were dirty dishes. Ms. Jones was not awake.

April 24, 9:42 am: Marsha A. Jones, aged eighteen months, James L. Jones, aged three, Theresa Jones, aged five, were apprehended. Mindlessly, Marilyn reached for the photos under the sheet of statistics. There were several large black-and-white eight-by-tens. Each shot gave Marilyn a picture of where Ms. Madison must have been standing. The companion taking the photos opposite Ms. Madison told Marilyn what they both had seen.

Each black-and-white shot had a matching Polaroid colour shot. In some strange way, the black-and-white shots were more damning. The black-and-whites had a sense of morbidity about them. They showed the absence of emotion and the depth of suffering in the children's eyes much more clearly. In the one angle shot of the living room a photo caught Elsie, flopped into an easy chair surrounded by magazines, a spilled ashtray, butts dribbling to the floor at her feet, a damning beer bottle in her hand. Marilyn stared hard at Elsie's face. The lids of Elsie's eyes were not fully closed even in her passed-out state. Marilyn stared at the eyes under the half-closed lids.

A claw caught hold of Marilyn's belly. A five-fingered beastly thing wrapped itself around the muscle that was supposed to ease her breath in and out, sure and deep. It held tight, shortening her breath supply. The claw seemed to be connected to Marilyn's gaze on the photo holding Marsha's eyes. The photo

was beastly. Marsha's inclusion in it was more a perverse twist of
fate, an accident, than a deliberate act on the part of the photographer. She just happened to be in it when the worker directed
the photographer to take pictures of the room. The series was
intended to provide proof of Elsie's negligence, thereby justify-
ing the apprehension of the entire family; it was not intended to
capture the desperation in Marsha's eyes. The more Marilyn
stared at the photo the more aware she became of the emptiness
of the gaze that was Marsha's one last plea for life, for rescue
from the disease tearing at her lungs, the tighter did the claw's
grip become. As the depth of the emptiness of Marsha's eyes
registered on Marilyn's consciousness, the picture began to move.
It swayed idiotically in the beginning, then the photo stilled and
the child inside the frame moved.

Marilyn started. Her breath stopped. She thought she saw
Marsha's eyes blink. Marilyn shook her head. She could not have
seen that. Next, Marsha's hands reached up and out to unseeing
people, who ignored her. This isn't happening, Marilyn told herself. She fought to get a grip on reality, to look away, but her eyes
were riveted to the moving picture, held captive by the moving
photo. Mesmerized, Marilyn watched. The photo became a moving screen of the events surrounding Marsha's last moments.

Marilyn told herself to leave them alone, but she couldn't.
She strung the photos into a cinematic representation of what
had happened. Inside the little screen Ms. Madison moved in
clinical fashion, swift, emotionless and confident. Her companion shot the first photo, moved to another spot in the room and
shot again. The camera rewound automatically, she whirled,

repositioned herself and shot again. The child that was Marsha lifted up her hands in the direction of the strangers. The hands moved so slowly. Beads of sweat formed on her forearm. Her thin little fingers shook. The strangers' reedy, sure bodies ignored Marsha. That was when Marilyn saw Marsha's eyes change. The blankness left them. A tiny spark of light appeared in their blackness. Her lids blinked heavily. She almost fainted with the effort of blinking, lifting and getting the light in her eyes to shine. Her tiny mouth almost formed a smile. The smile she hoped would charm the stranger into tending to her need for breath, for wind, for voice, for life.

Marilyn side-glanced the photo, not believing what she was seeing. She didn't want to see this. She tried hard to lay the photo down. The photo clung to her fingers. She told herself to let the photo go, as though that would stop the moving images of Marsha or force her fingers to open. Her hand would not obey. Her eyes continued to stare. Her brain itemized what she saw.

The Madison woman was tall, brown-haired and thin. She wore glasses. These glasses heightened her impersonal air. A wide, flowered skirt flowed against her movements; when she turned left her skirt swung right. Her hands had long fingers, one of which bore a diamond engagement ring, but no wedding band. Her shoulder-length hair was wavy. The thinness of Madison looked well fed, her plainness seemed well manicured. Marilyn pictured her working out at the gym on weekdays — aerobics, likely. She would be one of those modern, yogurt-eating, health-conscious young professionals who expected to do well, marry well and live well, the sort of person who already has a retirement fund.

Oh, gawd, spare me. I'm hallucinating, Marilyn pleaded inaudibly to no one. She placed the photo on the table in front of her and again told her hands to let go. They would not obey. Southwind had hold of her. He continued to carry her through the moving picture of Marsha's last movements. Marilyn finally surrendered to the scene. She watched, horrified, as Marsha's head tilted upward, her eyes wide now. The hand moved. Sweat beads appeared on Marsha's forehead. Her eyes lolled backward into their sockets with the strain of her hand's movements and then she rolled forward, collapsing with the effort. Ms. Madison's companion shot another photo while Madison took copious notes. For a second, Madison stopped, looked right at Marsha, and then carried on. It had taken at least an hour for the workers to oblige the law, snap the pictures and write the notes on the condition of the home. Madison finished off her notes with the short quip: "The child known as Marsha collapsed." Then she called an ambulance.

Marilyn collapsed at her desk; unable to endure the grizzly scene, she lost consciousness for a moment. She came to, mumbling, "What right have they, what right have they, what right?" Then she stopped. Fully aware now, she looked about her office. Flushed with embarrassment, she checked to see that no one had seen her. She didn't want to think about what had just happened. Stupidly, she looked for something to distract her thoughts. Nothing in the office caught her attention. "Change the emotion, change your response," she repeated Lindy's phrase to herself. Sympathy was all she could come up with.

"Oh gawd," Marilyn's body heaved. Her sobs were tearless.

"You poor baby, your last desperate plea for caring was made to a heartless stranger."

Those poor little beings: the pathetic five year old trying to mother the younger ones; the desperate Marsha wheezing her last breath under the glare of a camera whose photograph testified to her mother's neglect, and a photographer and social worker who failed to rescue her. The photo released Marilyn.

Marilyn's mind wandered around the logic of the whole mess. Apprehension meant, among other things, to frighten, to terrorize; yet the rationale for child apprehension was protection. It made no sense. The worker did not bother to tend to the well-being of the children. The handbook governing the apprehension of children by government social workers clearly states: first take photographs; make copious notes; speak to the parent (if one was present); assess whether or not the child was in danger; collect clean clothes, toys, bottles, diapers; then round up the children. Mindlessly, sightlessly, the worker and her photographer carried out their jobs in accordance with the dictates of their procedural training.

"I carry these bones," someone whispered in her ear. The photo's landscape changed. Forested hills in full colour pushed through the debris of Elsie's home. A funeral pyre raged in the background. Women in aprons were picking through ashes. The women were singing about carrying bones. Marilyn had no idea how she knew this song. It was not English, but she knew it. Eastwind breathed words all over her: "Men are ostracized, not children. Ostracism is the terror only men face. Men who terrorize women will suffer ostracism." Northwind joined him, carrying a different basket of memories. Sparks flew. Marilyn lolled her head back and forth like an old bear trying to get a bead on the picture of threat. The old image died.

She moved on to the rest of the photos. There were four wide-angle shots of each corner of each room. The other two children must have been eating in one of the corners of the living room floor because they appeared in one of the angle shots. The shot caught them head-on, little bowls of cereal in front of them. Both Theresa and James were as gaunt and sickly looking as Marsha. It looked as though the boy had been counting on Theresa for all his care for some time. His thin hair was matted, his nose was runny, his shirt was dirty and he had no clothes on the bottom half of his body. The darkness on the soles of his feet indicated he hadn't bathed for some time. A tiny voice inside Marilyn's head whispered, *I was never quite this bad.* She loathed the cheap comparison she made to exonerate the feelings of guilt that rose up whenever she looked at the pictures. *Cut it out*, she snapped at herself. *This is not about you.*

She was looking for something she had no name for. She could feel the invasion of memory. "Mommy makes us eat grass, that's what she told me." Ms. Wong is standing behind Marilyn as Marilyn harvests her wild mint patch. "Who are you?" asks Marilyn. "The school social worker," the woman answered. "You look Chinese." The woman winced slightly, then raised an eyebrow and answered: "I am." "Then you must know how these people feel about any food that is not theirs. Remember the controversy over your barbecue pork. My children's classmates call our food grass. My daughters copy them because they find the ignorance of their classmates amusing."

Marilyn's eyes hang half opened. She cringes. *Don't go there,* she tells herself. Cigarette butts insult her floors. *No, this is about Elsie.* Behind Elsie's photo she could see feet heading for the bush. She watches the feet. Her own feet grow cold while she watches. The photo holds her still. She manages to hold Elsie's body in the photo frame, but the backdrop changes. Bush-lands replace the filth-ridden room. She can see feet disappearing from the frame. They are so cold. Must be winter. Whose feet are disappearing? She stares hard at the soles of the feet, trying to recognize them. They reshape themselves into a basket. Out of the basket poured old memories.

Marilyn sitting alone on a stone by the river, water rushing by, and she entranced by the water. Marilyn sitting alone in the dark, her mother sleeping on the couch, passed out, really — dishes everywhere. Marilyn is hungry. Her mother looks faded in colour and size. Marilyn's little hands feel the air in the room. The room seemed so lifeless, as though its energy had been drained. "Was that it, Momma? Were you too tired to wash a dish or hunt for food?" Her feet jumped out of the basket, shivering with the cold. Was it Marilyn that was tired, or is it Elsie? *What is this nameless thing I seek?* The namelessness of it made her feel so completely overwhelmed by the pictures she stared at. Marilyn watched as she waltzed over to the basket with a large butcher's knife and imagined herself slicing this wake-dream-illusion completely in half.

Marilyn closed her eyes. If she closed her eyes and sat really still she could return to reality. Elsie had been hysterical in court. Theresa had fought hard and the baby, James, had called out "Teesa, Momma, Teesa, Momma." So read the court records.

Breathe. Hysterical: hysteria, hysterectomy, of the womb. Marilyn's womb tightened. Her armpits sweated. Her breath grew hot and short. The other images crowded her focus on Elsie and she disappeared.

Marilyn had lost her eldest daughter to these people, just once and only briefly. It was the first time the passionate wind of her western breath had burnt the stillness from her body. Westwind cracked the armour holding stillness in place and invited the icy breath of Northwind — busy, cold and active — to fill her up. Together the winds spawned willful, calculated movement. Movement calculated not just to be heard, seen or believed, but movement designed to fight and win.

Marilyn was young then. She remembered tearing up her house. She hit her husband. She broke her furniture. "They aren't going to steal my children," she screamed. "They won't beat my baby," came on the heels of smashing the dresser drawer that served as Cat's bed. "I will kill them first."

She engaged a lawyer, then bought a gun in case she didn't win. Her husband spent hours trying to talk her out of purchasing the weapon. Marilyn grew stubborn, she secured documents and reference letters from well-placed individuals, but she still insisted on the gun. "You don't understand. I will die if I do not see her from birth to maturity. I will die." He settled on a commitment from Marilyn to try peaceful means first. As one of very few Native women university students, Marilyn knew some important white and non-white people. She secured references and went to face off with the child protection agency, but she took the gun with her as well.

She remembered the day she got Cat back as though the memory was ensconced in a specially lit altar, an altar separate from the clouded place old memories usually live.

The worker told her Cat wasn't there. Marilyn's skin was so alive then. She knew Cat was in the other room. She could feel her. They asked her to sign consent papers. She read the papers. They gave the society permission to keep her for three weeks, despite the fact that they had only had her for ten days. "Give me my daughter and I will sign." Marilyn filled her body with threat, and then softened her voice to emphasize the deadliness of the threat it contained. The woman in front of her quivered with fright. "Wait here," she said. Marilyn's husband told her it was best to sign. She glared at him, put her hand in her pocket where the gun lay resting. He knew it was there and sighed. "Okay," he said. The woman returned with Cat. Marilyn supposed that the society thought poorly of tangling with a student who was studying social work and had garnered such an array of extraordinarily well-placed white references. Marilyn imagined them fearing her. In had only been a brief ten days and Catherine was returned. Marilyn signed the papers and they left.

Catherine had been only ten months old. She returned still, austere and lacking in vitality. Marilyn remembered how magical had been the feeling between her and Cat before the apprehension. From the day Cat returned, the two unconsciously fought their stillness to meet on the same arc of shared light. Their love for one another grew more urgent and desperate as they failed to connect on the arc's strongest point. An invisible bridge divided them. A kind of whimsical distance coloured their interaction.

Sometimes Marilyn could almost see the ramparts to the bridge that neither knew how to cross.

Marilyn contrived to restore Cat to her original self. But her effort never seemed to completely erase the thin, sticky web of distance between them. Sometimes Marilyn thought she saw Lindy watching the tense dance between herself and Cat. She believed Lindy understood what was happening between them. It disturbed her somewhat, this other kind of seeing Lindy seemed to possess, but she rolled with it. "Ride the wave"; Marilyn would repeat Lindy's favourite saying. The colour from both women arced, danced and strained to touch, meet, and then was repelled. They invariably failed to win this fight, but they never gave up trying. Even today, twenty years later, a hint of tension rises up between them when a discussion moves in the southern direction of intimate wind.

Marilyn opened her eyes. Elsie's face looked completely defeated. It sagged. There were heavy, dark circles under her eyes. A look of bewildered helplessness could be seen even in the eyes' half-opened, drunken state. Terror slowly replaced the bewilderment. It filled her eyes and Elsie's life seemed to drift into a maddened, senseless, wasted state of being from which there didn't appear to be any return.

"What right have they?" Marilyn whispered out loud. The energy drained from her body and the question emerged without punctuation. Someone had broken Elsie, Marilyn decided. Marilyn felt the brokenness, saw it in Elsie's eyes, but she could not name the culprit. Her eyes hurt. She couldn't look at the pictures anymore.

§ § § §

Marilyn received Elsie's case file after the fact. The court case had already gone through. Apprehension: to terrorize. It had taken all her strength to move, but she'd managed to launch her own investigation at the time of her first dealings with Elsie. She remembered the resistance put up by her board of directors at the mention of investigating the apprehension. A great souring in her stomach came up at the intrusion of this memory. She ignored the souring and continued to remember. Maybe it wasn't quite resistance. More like a deep barrel of inertia — a tense, quiet stillness. An overwhelming feeling of "Be still. We will all get into trouble." "Residential school hangover," she had once glibly remarked to someone while standing at the back of a Chiefs' conference. "What's that?" her friend asked. "That's what I call the tension that arises when some courageous man utters words of encouragement or self-assurance in the face of colonial authority." The woman laughed. "Oh yeah. That's why the room feels like it has been sucked dry of all desire to move." They both laughed. Marilyn was sorry now that they had laughed. Her stomach no longer felt sour.

She took her memory in the direction of Elsie and her children. Marilyn had first spoken to the attending physician at the hospital. He sighed, threw up his arms and said he could not state for sure that the hour or more it took between the worker's arrival and the ambulance call would have made a difference between life and death for Marsha. Then, softly, he murmured that he was prepared to make the recommendation that a coroner's inquest be held. He explained the purpose of such inquests: They cannot assign blame, but they can make recommendations to prevent further mishaps such as the fate Marsha had suffered.

"Mishap." Marilyn had been barely able to repeat the word. "The child died of neglect, first from her mother, then from this worker. You call that a mishap?" Dr. Mathews ignored her words. The doctor had meandered across his own memories of the case file. It was too thin, but at the same time, something was very wrong inside the pages of this case. Something had to be done and he reached for the least he could do, because it was the surest.

"It may be worthwhile if the recommendation of the jury is to have the order of business procedure reversed so that the first concern is to ensure the children are not ill, before the evidence is collected." He stared hard at her. There was not much else to be done in his mind. "It is the best we can do," he said. Marilyn felt they both ought to shoot for better than that. She felt obligated to come up with something more than this thin response, but without his support the shot would not hit a target. "No," she admonished, "that is the best *you* can do." She understood why the physician was hesitant to take on the bureaucracy for which Ms. Madison worked. It was a law unto itself. She opted for the inquest.

During the trial, the court had made it clear that they held Ms. Madison blameless. After all, she was not a nurse, so how could she know how little time Marsha had left? She had followed standard procedures to the letter. Marilyn could see that the inquest was a losing proposition from the outset, and she planned her response to it.

After the court case was over, Marilyn held a press conference: "Neglect: oversight, whether deliberate or not; omission of an essential act, whether intentional or not. That is the meaning of neglect. Ms. Madison's failure to see the seriousness of Marsha's illness was at least an oversight, whether deliberate or not. Ms. Madison's failure to call an ambulance for at least an hour was an omission of an essential act on behalf of Marsha which may have changed the outcome for this child." The newspapers had quoted her directly.

Marilyn almost lost her job. The board became hysterical over her press conference. "Fences will need mending. Bridges will have to be rebuilt," they said. Marilyn tried to talk her way through it. "Something more has to be done to prevent the untimely death of Indian children and the tragedy of the horrific conditions in which Native women are forced to bring up their children. Apathy is killing us." The response from the board was universal. "Don't bite the hand that feeds you." Meeting after meeting, she held her ground.

It looked as though she would lose this skirmish with her Board of Directors, but then the Children's Aid Society's Regional Director asked Marilyn for her personal input at a conference discussing "the implementation of the inquest's recommendations and ways and means of sensitizing workers who deal with Indians." She read out the invitation to everyone. They became quiet. They did not fire her. They did, however, pass a resolution that the press could only interview board members, and they said no more to Marilyn. Marilyn thought it was a lousy win.

Until the inquest and the press conference, Marilyn received case files of mothers who were charged with negligence after the fact. After the conference, she received case files before they went to court. This was too late for Elsie, and it made Marilyn's job harder, but it was something.

§ § § §

Marilyn finished reviewing the court records of Elsie and her children's trial. Extenuating circumstances were noted: Elsie's fourth pregnancy had ended in premature natural abortion. The court noted that she might well have been in a state of malnutrition, which precipitated the miscarriage and partially accounted for her inability to clean the house and care for the children. Nonetheless. Nonetheless, there was evidence of alcohol abuse. The one beer in her hand and the six bottles at her side, all of them empty, crucified Elsie and locked the judge's ruling to the apprehension application made by Ms. Madison. In his magnanimity, the judge restricted wardship to temporary care and ordered Elsie to seek counselling rather than grant the society the permanent wardship they requested. The society objected: Marsha died of neglect. The judge reminded them that they had been on the scene for an hour while the child was still alive. Their objection dissipated. Marilyn could not help but feel the pomposity of the judge's magnanimity, considering the weakness of his response to that last hour.

How do these people sleep at night? she thought. *It's a bloody stupid question: the same way as everyone else, just crawl into bed . . .* She stopped, blanked out, then returned to her file.

The air in the room softened, muffled itself and relaxed. In the quiet, soft air, she recalculated the time it took to complete the investigation, sighed, and then turned to the window. It was a rather useless exercise. Some anxious piece of her wanted to reverse the demise of Marsha.

Just deal with Elsie, she told herself. Fix her up. Get her to see that she must take care of her children, feed them, clothe them and love them. She can't be spending her days drinking while her children waste away, hungry and cold.

The solution to the whole mess was so much more complicated. Marilyn knew it. Elsie's condition had taken over one hundred years to create. Just under Elsie's file folder was the file containing Marilyn's master's thesis, the work from which she derived all her current speeches. She had taken it out in preparation for her trip to Toronto. It would take time and effort to resolve the historic condition that had birthed massive child neglect among Native families. The blueprint of the effort she outlined in her paper seemed straightforward and sensible, but the flogging of the theory to make the authorities recognize its viability and its desirability would, it seemed, take forever. "Give us the time, the resources, to explore our own solution," she thought.

Strangely, she came into opposition with her own people in trying to make her theory work. To be fair, it was not that anyone actively worked against her. The opposition was more passive than that. It was more that very few worked toward the goal of reclaiming the absolute right of Native people to rear their children. It was as though, after one hundred years of siege and prohibition, no one had the energy to fight another political battle against the various forms that prohibition took. In the first place, it took money and huge patience and a host of dreamers to raise a child; those things were pretty scarce in Native families. Furthermore, it seemed as though every time one prohibition ended, a new one replaced it. The very moment they shut down the residential schools, the government went on a child-raiding spree. People seemed to be convinced that some new prohibition would just come up to replace the one they laid to rest.

"Scoop-ups," Marilyn sighed. Every win was followed by a new loss. In the meantime, children were continuously robbed of their mothers' love, such as it was, and taken to some strange place where strange people "integrated" them into their family life. Just as often, they did not bother to try to make the children part of the family. Marilyn was coming to realize that more often than she cared to know, these foster children became exploited playthings in the homes to which they were sent.

ʃ ʃ ʃ ʃ

Jeezuss, get a hold of yourself, Marilyn instructed herself as she closed the file. She jumped up from her desk and moved to look out the window. Elsie would be here shortly. Marilyn cast a sidelong glance at her calendar on the wall. It spoke of her upcoming trip to Toronto. A feeling of strange relief rose within her. Images of highrises, freeways, faceless, lonely crowds, busyness, and people chasing words ping-pinged about senselessly inside her mind. She watched herself catch the activity of preparation, saw herself lose herself in lectures, in moments empty of connection. Her body acquired a more upright posture; her mouth articulated words much more carefully. The words dribbled from her lips, divorced from meaning.

Her presentations seemed stupid just now. Time was killing families while she trod the lecture circuit attempting to stop the clock and turn around an impossible situation conjured from attitude, condition and history. Right now she wasn't sure whose attitude was at the root of the condition, but she knew that no mother chose to neglect her children. No mother sat down, pen in hand, and empowered Ms. Madison to apprehend her children. It was so base. The listless eyes of Marsha as she wheezed helplessly, her little body gasping for breath, continued to tug mercilessly at Marilyn's emotions. She needs to respond, to hate someone for Marsha's death. Madison was an easy target, yet she was not responsible for the condition that led to Marsha's death. Marilyn didn't like the direction in which her argument was leading her.

What happened to us? Confusion is a tornado. The direction of thought is a wind. Southwind moves us to heal. Northwind calls us to action, Westwind to passion, Eastwind to intelligent being. Wind's breath darts about inside the humans. He resists travelling in any one direction. His breath is erratic. He quarrels with breath choked back by stillness. When wind wrestles with internal breath, confusion is born. Confusion is incapacity to settle on the direction breath needs to take to see deeply, effectively, completely and forever. Marilyn knew what had happened. This was the wrong question. She needed to know how to unravel the effect of what had happened, but she never seemed to get past this first question. Each uttering of the phrase brought up the war between her breath's desire for movement and her mind's old, still direction. Her stillness was older, bigger and much more familiar than action. It got in the way. So normal did this still-ness feel that Marilyn convinced herself that her desire for action was the culprit causing her discomfort? *I'm too impatient.*

What happened to us? Over and over Marilyn asked this question with a growing sense of cynicism. Her hands took hold of the sides of her hair, pulling at the question, trying hard to force the ordered answer from her usually agile mind. This could have been her file. She knew it. She had neglected her children. She had drunk away her lonely hours and been unable to wake up in the morning and motivate herself to carry out the simple chore of feeding her two daughters. She had sipped wine privately, in the dark, and then secreted the bottles in garbage bags, neatly tied so the children would not know. Drunk, she had opened the window slightly so the scent of the wine aged by her own breath would leave the tiny, dingy apartment before her girls awoke. The lie only served to help her, while her girls slept inexplicably lightly and the wind disguised her drunkenness.

Night, she sometimes comes fast. Husky breath brings her neatly, light to dark. A rush, a torrent of black silence; she hurries her deep quiet to overpower day. She folds her light, caresses the lines of seeing then fills the corners of day with her urgent black. Night, she sometimes cons the day out of bright moments, holds them in soft, dark memories, captures the remembered wind of voice in her folds, then still and muted, she holds everything immo-bile. Memories await the holder to unleash them, release them and free them. Nothing happens without a spark to catalyze freedom.

In perfect darkness the imagined memory achieves a crazy drama, a wild perfection, false in night's gorgeous dark folds. Night's skin is soft — silky soft, impossibly soft, soft beyond words. In night's electric silence, in its swift movement, it stretches, encases, haunts and pushes up memory. Memory finds its way to this soft fold.

ⓢ   ⓢ   ⓢ   ⓢ

As Marilyn read about Elsie's court scene, memories of her own nights intruded. Pictures that had held no significance for her during their unfolding pushed their way forward. Fetid and still as they had become, lying encased in the dark folds of her night, they returned to remind her to look from some angle she dared not think existed.

In the middle of the night, the smell of burnt toast awakened her. She lugged her half-drunk body out of bed and staggered into the kitchen, feeling her way along the hallway walls, tripping on shoes and toys. *Gawd, have I done this before?* Instead of answering her question, she cursed herself for not cleaning up before she'd gone to bed. She came into the lighted kitchen. Smoke was everywhere. She could hear Catherine whimpering. Just barely whispering, Cat's little Cousin Alfred was comforting her as best a three-year-old boy could: "Don't cry, Cat. I fix. Don't cry. Cat hurts?" A wall of shame dropped over Marilyn. She opened the window, unplugged the toaster then reached under the table. Both children stared wild-eyed in frightened anticipation of how she might react. Cat was holding her injured arm. Alfred kept urging Cat to keep her crying quiet.

On top of the table, a blackened slice of toast continued to smoke. Two steel knives protruded dangerously from the toaster. The children could have been electrocuted. Marilyn unplugged the toaster, then bent down and pulled the two children out from under the table. Alfred murmured, fearfully defensive, "Cat was hungry." Marilyn could not speak. She just held them on her knee and sang softly to them. It was probably the last time she was sweet to them after waking up to some awful surprise. She sang until the shame inside her drifted away and died. They fell asleep before they had any toast. That must have been the first time she began using the children to serve her.

Night wanted to retreat. Marilyn fought so hard to forget her nightlife; her dreams fell wasted and useless to her days. Weary of its own fruitless being in Marilyn's life, night wanted to sneak away to some other place where its value was felt, was seen and heard. It hesitated to conjure a dream world. Marilyn lurched toward her days, bit chunks of living off them as though they, too, intruded on her body somehow. Night half-flooded the whiteness of day until the distinction between the two worlds blurred in Marilyn's mind. Day died pale grey under night's hesitant waltz. Spiritually bruised, Marilyn lumbered mindlessly in day's direction. Emotionally sorrowful, she swallowed light's last ray of thoughtful protection.

In the half-light of her life after that incident, guilt and shame shone grey inside Marilyn. It blurred under the prison of her insobriety. She held up the bottle, fought, and most often lost the battle, but she never completely surrendered to the crushing half-light of her drunkenness. She told herself to put away the bottle after each sip. She scolded herself after the instruction failed to produce results. Each sip was followed by a firm knowledge that her girls deserved better. Each swallow was met with *What's the use?* Wild, frenetic dreams followed her passing out: image after image of social workers clutching the small hands of her little girls as they ushered them away. Small, frightened, quizzical looks on her daughters' faces as they cried out, "Mommy, we'll be good."

Her own madness and hysteria, in and out of court, accused her chronically. On those nights when her dreams ran thus, she awoke early. She punished herself by madly cleaning the apartment, fighting like hell to get the ancient grime off the walls and scrubbing the toilet until her whole body ached with the effort. On those mornings, the eldest girl would appear at the door to the bathroom, holding the hand of the smallest, and in a voice that pleaded intently for some sort of sanity from their mother that would diminish their fear, Cat invariably asked if Mommy needed help. Somehow that line broke the treadmill Marilyn felt she was on. She would reach for both girls and hold them so tight that Lindy sometimes whimpered with pain.

She remembered the last time she drank like that. The kids weren't very old. Night emerged, a black comforter cloaked in translucent skin. It two-stepped above her day and danced her in the direction of a lazy kind of dream, one in which not a lot happens. In the dream they had been playing in a park. They started to play a game of rhymes. First she rhymed, then Catherine, then Lindy. On the second pass she could not dream up anything for the girls to finish their rhymes. The pool at the park reflected her image back at her. Her face took on a ridiculous look of sympathetic lip-synching as she tried to help them finish the lines, then her reflected face began laughing at her real face, jeering, "You don't know them well enough to imagine them playing a game in your dreams." She leapt awake. Sitting straight up, she brushed the sweat from her forehead, groaned and then finished the night in fitful sleep.

The next day was predictable, mundanely so. Night returned as it always did. She wrapped herself in a black lace negligee of negligence and opened her familiar six-pack. The silence was velvet in the beginning. Somewhere along the trail it gained a rough sharpness as she poked back the beers. No argument took place in her mind as it usually did. She grabbed each beer as though it was some person, some enemy she meant to whip, almost punish, by finishing it. She awoke the next day feeling like today was going to be different. It didn't begin all that differently, but the feeling hung about her anyway. Both girls slunk into the bedroom, one carrying a bowl of cereal, the other a half-full coffee cup. The night before, Marilyn had left her shoes in the narrow aisle between wall and bed. Lindy slipped, tripped and fell, spilling the cereal.

"Sorry, Mommy," she pushed out softly. Fear crimped her breath and stretched her voice into thin streams of barely audible, wary words. "I'll go get some more." Her body pleaded for forgiveness as she flailed her nervous, empty hands, looking about for something to wipe up the milk and cereal. The negotiation, the desperately timid hopefulness and the diplomacy in her voice were intended to ward off terrible imagined consequences.

"Imagined consequence is born of experience, of memory, of reality," Marilyn said out loud. It was so clear to her today. She could still see her child flailing her nervous empty hands. Marilyn stopped breathing as she reviewed the scene. A lead weight seemed to be driving the air from her lungs into some dead spot in her belly. Lindy kept looking about for something to wipe up the soggy mess. *Fuck you, Marilyn.* There was nothing in sight for Lindy to use as a rag. Lindy's hands swept the air a couple more times; her eyes darted back and forth, still desperate for a rag. None was forthcoming. Finally, Lindy's small hands settled for picking up the corn kernels very carefully and placing them back into the bowl one at a time, while tears of failure fell across her moon-shaped face. *How could you? . . . fuck . . .* Marilyn wanted to hate herself, to hate someone, but she couldn't. Lindy's little shoulders rounded in anticipation of the expected attack from Marilyn. She had failed to please Mommy. There were consequences for this particular failure.

Catherine looked from Lindy to Marilyn. She was so familiar with the consequences of her own failure. She sucked wind, announced that she would run for the rag. Lindy's whimpering shocked Marilyn, as though it was the first time she'd heard it. Prior to this moment, whimpering had annoyed her. But now the sound made her hands grip the sheet. A wave of unfamiliar emotion swept over her. *Oh gawd, my children are taking care of me; it should be the other way around. How the hell did I ever get things so upside-down?*

ᛞ ᛞ ᛞ ᛞ

Time is slippery in the West. It floats. Days slide into nights, into dark, without much notice. Light is thin inside the human body.

The dark is so pervasive it is almost black. Sunshine passes across the skin, penetrating very little of the surface. Distance rather than time becomes the standard measure that keeps memory separate. To the inside of our bodies, the difference between moonlight and sunlight is negligible except for the fact that images conjured under the light of the sun are more easily recalled. They stay with us longer. Light helps to stretch the distance that memories travel. In the darkness, the emotional intensity of shame erases distance. Distance and time disappear.

The sun popped out and Marilyn could no longer reference the events running amok inside her. She lost her capacity to differentiate between past and current time. Today, yesterday, tomorrow all melded into one another. Thoughts of reconciliation became real as she visualized them happening. Yesterday's images pushed up today's emotions, sharp and painful, then coupled themselves with images of potential resolution until she was not sure what was real and what was not.

Time is a critical illusion. It is necessary to separate our dream world from the real world, from what is hope and what is planning, from what is desired and what is executed. The separation of moments in time defines sanity. Marilyn searched about for a way to locate herself somewhere in time. She needed time's clarity and differentiation, but it eluded her. She began making a grocery list of the information she knew to be in the past. She remembered taking Lindy to the window, remembered her own clawing for breath as she had fought to name the things of life outside to Lindy and Cat.

Marilyn had been barely able to see the grasses through the meager light offered by street lamps. They had seemed so unreal, coming up at her through some kind of blur. Still, she had fought to name the plants growing below the old quadraplex. She'd managed to differentiate each weed, naming them and encouraging Lindy to repeat the words. Catherine joined them. Marilyn put an arm across each girl's shoulder.

"There is power in naming," she uttered mindlessly to the girls. "There is power in naming."

Time resolved itself. It settled on the past and indicated to her present self that all this had happened yesterday, years ago. Somehow these words "There is power in naming" broke a bitter, destructive cycle going on inside her. If she could just figure out how they had done so, she could help Elsie.

❦ ❦ ❦ ❦

The knock came too soon.

Janet popped her head in the door, saying, "Elsie Jones is here."

"Tell her to come in."

Elsie sidled through the door, minimizing her imposition on Marilyn's time. In the three months since she had first walked in, Marilyn had not been able to get Elsie to relate to her in any genuine sort of way. Well, perhaps that was an unfair way to put it, Marilyn chided herself. She wanted Elsie to relate to her in a powerful way. Yet try as Marilyn might, Elsie deferred to her in the same way she did to any other person with authority over her life. *She defers to me like she would any white woman,* Marilyn thought, pushing back the bitter feelings this last thought evoked. Elsie's eyes darted about, unable to make contact with Marilyn's. Her shoulders folded forward. She wrung her hands. She answered all of Marilyn's questions with monosyllables and punctuated the answers with question marks, as though she were guessing. After speaking, Elsie looked up as though hoping she had got it right. Marilyn decided to throw the textbook therapeutic approach out the window and just chat with Elsie.

Elsie stood in front of the chair waiting for the usual "Sit down, Ms. Jones, tell me about your week" from Marilyn.

"Elsie, I was just thinking about needing to get my hair done. I'll be leaving for Toronto tomorrow and my hair wants a dye job."

"I can come back." Elsie turned to leave.

"Actually, I was thinking you might want to join me."

Elsie nipped back a bit of breath and looked away too quickly.

"At company expense, of course," Marilyn lied. She knew the money would have to come out of her own pocket. This little lie entitled Elsie to hold onto a much deeper truth. Marilyn would not have to suffer; Elsie could maintain the illusion of independence in her relationship to Marilyn. "You shouldn't have to do without your appointment to see me. Have you ever had your hair done?" Elsie shook her head.

That she had misread the meaning underlying Elsie's intake of breath did not occur to Marilyn. Reaching for her coat she turned to tell Elsie, "We will have to deceive Janet." Marilyn paused, then resumed: "We really aren't allowed to carry out our sessions at the hair salon. I will have to tell her we are heading out for a luncheon meeting." Elsie shrugged and chuckled. She seemed to like deceiving Janet.

They walked a little ways together. Then Elsie said, "I don't like anyone fiddling with my hair."

"How come?"

They both stopped for a traffic light.

Elsie stared at her hands. They stopped fidgeting. Her small brown fingers gripped one another, then relaxed and opened up. Elsie seemed to be looking at them for the first time. Her hands moved gracefully, trying to conjure up the answer. Her face changed from a blank stare to quizzical wonder at what her hands appeared to be trying to tell her. Marilyn, too, found herself looking at Elsie's hands, wondering what they wanted to say.

"The last person to fiddle with my hair made my hands do horrible things." Her eyes slowly filled with water. They seemed to take forever to fill up completely. None of the water spilled out. The eyes just filled up, and then the tears rested there, surface tension holding the water to her eyes. Marilyn had seen this before among Native people. She thought it odd. She stopped staring at Elsie's hands. Once Elsie's eyes filled up with tears, her hands dropped and she hid them at her sides.

Purple-mauve, barely perceptible colour filled the space between the two women. It was round and clear, shiny like plastic. Inside, some entity seemed to be breathing, creating pictures of some other person's reality. Marilyn could see this purple-mauve light play with some other woman's hair. Marilyn appeared to be running across flowered fields chasing the purple light — or was the light following her? She couldn't tell. The light took shape and then dropped its purple facade. It was a man. The image of both beings sunk into the grass and the bubble popped. Marilyn was horrified by what she saw next. The male entity was looming over Elsie. No. This was definitely more information than Marilyn wanted.

The traffic light turned red, then green and was about to turn red again, when Marilyn felt a tug.

"The light keeps changing. Are we going to go?" Elsie asked, as if to say that standing there waiting and watching the lights change from green to red wasn't all that bad a way to spend the afternoon, but then again, Marilyn had seemed to want to make it to the salon, so maybe they ought to go.

"Do you want to tell me about the horrible things?" Marilyn's breath slowed. She had taken to breathing in deeply, holding the breath, then letting the air out quietly as though it were being strained through a filter. It altered the sound of her voice. Unconscious as she was about wind, voice, passion and compassion, she did not notice that the warmth in her windless voice had left. Elsie had no name for what she did not receive from Marilyn's voice. She could not have said that she even felt it, but her response was to hold back as though she didn't feel like this would be a good person to unfold her private thoughts to.

"Do I have to?"

"No." Then quiet.

Marilyn was uneasy about letting Elsie slide away this easily, but she was also slightly relieved. "How about you sit with me and get a manicure?" Compromise. Marilyn felt like she was floating without direction, and it unnerved her, but she continued to float.

"What's that?"

"Well, that's when a woman fusses over your fingernails, chatting in your face about nothing." Elsie stared at her for a moment. Her lips parted in disbelief. A soft sound arose from her throat, and as she let it go her lips stretched into a winning smile.

"Why?" She giggled. Marilyn wasn't expecting this. She laughed. Elsie was jarred by the laugh. She seemed to cast about looking for some place to hide.

"No reason. It's supposed to make you feel beautiful, I suppose," said Marilyn.

"My Gramma used to say I had pretty little hands. That was before other stuff happened. I hardly remembered her till now."

"Do you like remembering your Gramma?"

Elsie looked up. She nodded. Her eyes welled with tears again, but none escaped. Marilyn noted that it was the first time Elsie had looked at her and made eye contact. Marilyn wanted to give Elsie's head a shake. Elsie looked like a child for that moment, a child no older than Marsha. *Odd*, Marilyn said to herself as she tried to meet Elsie's eyes without betraying her desire to shake off the image of Elsie's child-like face. *Sometimes deception is the fastest way to truth*, she muttered, repeating an old saying of her own Gramma's.

Grandmothers understand breath. They feel wind-song and know its caress. They can discern the direction song comes from and know where it is leading when they hear it. "Grandmothers are doorways to different points of view," Marilyn's mother used to say when she felt somewhat exasperated with one of her children. With a tight little expression, she'd send the child off to talk to Gramma, pushing them on their way.

Marilyn tried to recall if her mother's strategy had worked.

The answer wouldn't come; besides, Elsie was still staring at her expectantly. It didn't occur to Marilyn that to pay attention to her grandmother's counsel she had to be able to discern between the need for stillness in order to contemplate direction and the need for stillness to avoid the necessary contemplation required to determine direction.

"Maybe you want to watch pictures of your Gramma in your mind while the hairdresser does your nails."

Elsie smiled. Marilyn imagined Marsha's smile. Then her image of Marsha changed into the smile of her own daughter. As a young mother Marilyn had not fully seen or appreciated Catherine's beautiful smile. Now, in memory, Cat's face was so clear. Marilyn savoured the innocent image of Catherine's small mouth opening up, eyes turned up, head cocked to one side. She wished she had been able to appreciate it with the same depth and feeling she was now experiencing. *Catherine. I must tell Catherine what a horrible fool life has made of me. How did I miss that gorgeous smile?* She erased that thought right away. Catherine would think it weird. Marilyn couldn't portray the context clearly enough to explain it to Catherine. She could not explain it without making Catherine feel like she was being invited to take a ride on a bus that picked up passengers with names like unloved and neglected on the way to guilt station.

They continued to trundle in the direction of the salon, a sort of female odd couple, Marilyn in her serge suit, Elsie in her best sweats. Marilyn began to wonder why she kept going to this salon to dye her hair. At first, she had gone because she thought having grey hair at thirty-five was a liability when looking for a new man after her divorce. As the years went by and no man appeared to save her from work and worry, she slipped into a pattern of dyeing her hair every two months without thinking about it. Remembering the "looking-for-a-man" plan nearly made her laugh now. It had been years since she'd actually believed she needed one. These days she just liked the feel of Noreen's hands scrubbing her head clean. There was a pleasant sense of something she had a hard time naming. It was the way she enjoyed the senseless chatter about the trivial things in life. It had become a ritual. That was it: ritual.

The winds got excited. Ritual. The dead, the living, the whole spirit world required ritual. Marilyn was so close. They took turns whispering in her ear, "Love is of the spirit. It is all about mutual rituals romancing stone, earth, fire and water. Love is about desire and its breath is fueled when we mount the ramparts to reach the top of the bridge separating our spirits. Love is the spirit breath whose rituals bathe us in courage." Marilyn heard only her own breath, slow, deep and soft.

Sometime after she relinquished the dream of being rescued by a man, it dawned on her that she was more attached to this little ritual than she had ever been to her lovers. The more men she came in contact with these days, the less inclined she was to want to bring one home. Five years had passed. Now she relished the rhythm of heading for the salon every two months, trying out this or that combination of dark brown, red, burgundy and black, seeing the effect each new colour combination had on her looks and paying for it easily out of wages earned on her own. The very triviality of hair colouring for effect wound itself around her need for ritual so comfortably these days. Her breath returned to normal. She was oddly cognizant of it. She cocked her head to one side. She listened to it as it eased in and out, slow and smooth.

The winds continued to whisper softly between the buildings and in the scant spaces between the trees planted in cement buckets here and there along the way. The sun warmed her skin. Her overcoat rustled with dignity between her legs.

She was aware of her stately middle-aged good looks. Her body still worked well. Her walk was lithesome, her legs still somewhat agile — jaunty, even. It was spring: a good time of year for a jaunty stroll. She glanced warmly at Elsie. It was the first time she had ever invited anyone to join her on her trip to the salon. It altered her deception of Janet from a simple secret to a joint conspiracy. For no reason at all, this felt good. It also opened the door to the significant, creating the semblance of ritual from a practice as ordinary as getting your hair done. She smiled. Elsie returned her smile. An arc of pale light danced between them.

"I like spring," Elsie said softly. "Reminds me of Choklit Park."

"Choklit Park? The one above False Creek, kind of hidden between two apartment blocks?" Marilyn knew it wasn't there anymore, but Elsie started recounting the joys of Choklit Park. It had taken so little to get her on a roll. While Elsie went on about the park, Marilyn located it in her memory. It was a barren little spot, perched on a bluff above False Creek, peopled with wooden toys, challenging climbing devices and one great swing. Elsie's words painted a picture of a not-so-well-manicured park; rustic, almost ill-kept, small and exciting. She ended the description of the park and her many after-school moments spent there with the beginning of a story:

"Once Georgie, my youngest brother, fell off the monkey bars and hurt himself bad.

"How so?"

"Poor Georgie. Daddy was drunk and I didn't know what to do. His little balls swole up big, real big. I kept saying, 'Daddy, Georgie's gone and hurt his balls.' Georgie lay there doubled over, trying to scream, puking, and Daddy tried to get up and think of what to do." This image struck them both as inappropriately funny, perhaps because they both knew Georgie survived — well, at least it seemed as though he must have, or Elsie would not have rattled on so without saying something about the outcome. "Funny, when Daddy was really drunk like that, he looked, talked and acted like a kid." This last remark opened no doorway inside Marilyn. She shook it loose of the attention needed to grab the thought and do something with it. Marilyn slipped into a moment of reverie, just enjoying the street, the walk and the wind. Marilyn could hear the heels of her shoes clicking back at her. It was an easy, expensive sound. It lulled her into replaying Elsie's story to the rhythm of her clicking heels.

"What happened?" Marilyn finally asked, remembering they had left Georgie and his injured little balls kind of hanging unresolved.

"Oh, Daddy straightened up when Georgie finally got a scream out." Elsie laughed sardonically at the picture of her father. "Sobered right up. He told us to wait there for him and took Georgie to the hospital. They were gone till well after dark. We hid in the tunnels till they came back — they came back so late." Her voice trailed off.

❧ ❧ ❧ ❧

The door of the salon lay before them, no time for Marilyn to process this last image and get nosy. She wanted to know more. She had questions about Elsie's age: Was she the oldest? How long had they waited? Were they scared? She feared asking too many questions out here in public. She decided to frame her curiosity in innocuous questions stretched out over time and disconnected from the story she had just heard — more deception. "Eastwind's deception weighted with Southwind's patience can sometimes mother truth," Westwind murmured to her. Marilyn imagined these words coming from within her. *This talking to yourself is getting to be a scary habit, Marilyn,* she admonished herself softly as she opened the door and ushered Elsie in.

After the arrangements were made for hair colour and mani-cure, both women settled into chairs, side by each.

"Are you the oldest?" She began her inquiry into Elsie's journey.

"Yeah. Then come Ethel, Joey and George. We call him George now." She laughed again. "He never liked being called Georgie."

"Georgie, porgy, puttin' pie." Marilyn began reciting the reason why.

Elsie laughed out loud, letting a squeal of delight push through, then she finished the rhyme, adding, "Boy, that used to make him mad."

Marilyn giggled along with her. "Must be awful to be the youngest and have a name like George."

"Not near as bad as being the oldest and a girl," Elsie's mani-curist added.

"Amen," Noreen interjected, lamenting being the oldest girl by five years and a stepdaughter to boot. Marilyn understood this last remark more deeply than she cared to. She closed her eyes; just behind her lids a moving screen formed and images from her own stepdaughterhood rolled up on her. She stood at the top of Snake Hill not far from school and some three miles from her home. Another detention had cost her a bus ride home. Her legs quivered. School confused her. She couldn't seem to make it through a day without getting a detention and missing the damned bus. Marilyn watched her small child's body running helplessly behind the old '52 Ford belonging to her stepfather, screaming "WAITT WAI-AIT." She watched the car slow down, saw his head turn, recognize her, smile that horrible wicked smirk, and then saw his head turn away from her. Her feet hit the road and sped up, her quivering legs dragging on her feet, slowing her down. She almost reached the back end of the black Ford. Her hand shot out. Just as her hand almost touched the trunk, the Ford picked up speed. She ran harder, screamed louder. Her screams seemed only to assist the old Ford in accelerating. The car bent the corner, disappearing out of sight. Her run slowed to a full stop.

The ribbon of black highway took on a treacherous attitude. Empty of all traffic, it seemed to reproach her desire for a ride with smug meanness. The emptiness of the roadway seeped inside, not quickly but slowly, like a steady, thin stream of cold water. Marilyn shuddered in the salon chair. The longer she stood there staring, hoping her stepfather was kidding and any moment now he would reappear, the deeper and rougher became the texture of the emptiness. The richer the texture, the more still her breath grew and the colder her feet became. She stood there staring dumbly at the roadway until she was filled with the emptiness. Her body chilled. That was when the damn dog came roaring out from the driveway beside her, growling and barking.

She climbed a tree and hid there. The dog jumped up, attacking the tree, trying to climb it. From her perch the barking, leaping, arcing and falling of the dog became a crazy kind of dance, of chance, of danger, of safety and fear. The dance stilled her. Her stillness reduced the fear, but it chilled her feet. Cold feet or fear, her choices backed her into some kind of narrow framework. Her chilled feet pulled her breath from her lungs toward her ice cold feet. Her breathlessness numbed her body. Numb, she became entranced by the dance of the dog. Apathetically, some piece of her felt seduced by his dance. Seeing it from this place of no emotion felt powerful, safe.

"Tell me if it's ever good being someone's daughter, sister or mom," the manicurist laughed. The laughter popped the image of the dog out from behind Marilyn's eyelids. The screen blackened. She thought the laughter cheapened the complaint somewhat, minimizing it, but she welcomed the cancellation of memories that had called up old feelings she had no way of putting into context. She laughed along with everyone else. Emotionally numb as they all were at that moment, their high, tinny laughs bereft of breath bounced around the room, off the walls and finally settled into a silent void.

"I don't know why we're all laughing," Marilyn said between chuckles.

"Beats crying." Noreen helped them dodge getting any closer

to the subject and they laughed again. "Tightens your belly in a good way too," Elsie interjected. This brought silence down from above their heads like an uncomfortable fog. It was about to settle into some awkward unfinished position when Noreen changed the subject.

"Your hair at the back is getting greyer."

"Great. I really wanted to hear that. Every now and then I picture growing it all in white and silver, peppered gently against the black. I imagine it looking distinguished, then I wake up." Marilyn's grey has been around since she was thirty-five. Too young. Her mother had nagged her till she dyed it, convincing her that it looked so out of place on a young woman. It did. The harping from her mom brought up old doubts about the way she looked and made her feel not quite acceptable. Rather than wrestle with the doubt, she dyed her hair. Acceptable for what, she neither asked nor answered. She had just dyed it one day and hadn't stopped since. She was forty-five now.

"Well, your silver won't look mousy against the tanned skin." Noreen was scrubbing at the scalp. It relaxed Marilyn.

"That's no tan, honey; this old body came with that brown." Why do white people do that, she wondered, refer to the colour of your skin as a tan if they like you? A tan is something you get by working in the sun, or sitting outside bathing in it. Natives are born brown. A tan makes us dark red-brown. Yet somehow white folks have this need to refer to our natural colour as a tan, as though this weren't really the way we are, as though we had browned our- selves on purpose and underneath it all we are really white. It's their way of humanizing us to themselves. Maybe it helps them to like us without too much justification or wrestling. It's so annoying. It makes liking them so difficult.

"Well, there ain't anything worse than not being able to tell where the white of your skin ends and the white of your hair begins," Noreen whispered close to Marilyn's face, so close Marilyn could feel the wisps of Noreen's dark auburn hairbrush against her temples. They both crunched back a hearty laugh. Nettie, the manicurist, and Elsie wanted to hear the joke. Noreen leaned into their faces to repeat it, and both stifled a laugh. All of them scanned the room looking for an old blonde lady. Vicious, but some place inside Marilyn felt satisfied at the nasty implication her mind dreamed up of the image of blonde hair slipping to white and the colour melding with skin.

Nettie couldn't leave well enough alone. "Blondes wrinkle more severely" she carried on, describing in detail the murderous effect age has on fairer women as opposed to brunettes. Nettie and Noreen were both white girls — Irish, in fact. The reality of their dark hair sunk in. Most of the Irish Marilyn had known in school were blond or redheads. She had read somewhere that the occurrence of black hair among the Irish Celts had something to do with the occupation of Ireland by the Moors of Africa. She wasn't sure she believed this, but when she read it she had told herself that that was probably why England gave Ireland such a hard time. In a peculiar way, these two Irish women and Marilyn there identified with one another. The identification had a slightly vengeful anti-blond edge to it for all of them. Marilyn had never thought the "blonde obsession" of the white world as oppressive toward other white women. After all, at least they were white. The vengeful glee they shared seemed particularly puerile because the advantages for blondes were dubious at best. They married sooner, which, given the nature of marriages and their effect on women these days, didn't seem much of an advantage at all. Marilyn knew married women died sooner than single women did. The glee at the horrific wrinkling of blondes seemed all the more vicious since the focus on youthful expectations placed upon women only was unfair all around. The alternative to aging was death. Marilyn was aware the glee they shared as brunettes accentuated the unfairness of the rules governing women and aging, and she hid the realization that in order to be acceptable, they must all prevent aging. To successfully prevent aging women would have to die early. Die early or die unacceptable.

There aren't many windows at a beauty salon. The windows are at the front and the salon chairs are always facing the walls. The walls are covered in mirrors. For the brave and the self-confident it is a pause long enough to assess the self; for Marilyn, the mirrors accused. She wanted a window.

What is happening to me? Her mind seemed bent on rushing toward some dreadful logic full of foreboding that led to despair more and more often lately. In its quest for despair's dark corners, her mind stretched logic beyond normal limits. *My life does seem to fit the pattern of dying alone right now.* She didn't bother arguing much against the stretch. It was just curious.

"Do you want a facial?" Noreen asked.

"You better give me one after that," Marilyn giggled.

"Oh, c'mon, Marilyn, your skin is the envy of everyone here." She doubted that, but hearing it was pleasant. Besides, it got

Nettie extolling the virtues of the colour of her skin, which she needed to hear from someone. "Brown sugar," ended her comments. A brief discussion followed on the origins of the song by that name. Rumor had it that it was written for a half-Indian, half-Spanish beauty. They discussed the thrill of having someone famous write a song about you. Everyone was careful not to mention that the songwriter divorced his love shortly thereafter. He moved on to wed the blonde model he had been seeing during his marriage, even while the song was still fresh on the turntables. Story of my life, Marilyn told herself.

The women wrapped up the business of painting the first coat of polish on Elise's nails and applying the last touches to Marilyn's hair, arranged them in their chairs, got them each a cup of coffee, then left to do work on someone else.

"I always wondered what went on in these places," Elsie murmured, the awe dancing in and out of her voice.

Elsie suddenly looked pathetic. Marilyn felt herself to be absurd. Dyeing her hair would not change the reality of time's march. It just gave the world a false impression of who she was, cheated them of the truth of time. But she was forced to admit she really liked coming here, being fussed over by the same woman, indulging in the same old bitch-and-complain wheel they always got to spinning on. The complaints changed but the subject never seemed to: Women are a bit of a sorry lot and the world is so unfair. They never approached their life dilemmas with any sort of urgent need or even a desire to alter their lot. It seemed doubly absurd for Marilyn, the daughter of a bush-widow born to abject poverty that spanned thirty-five of her forty-five years, to have only this little bimonthly sojourn to the beauty parlor as a reward for the meanness of those years. The whiteness of her hair was a testament to the intensity of the meanness. Her gorgeous black hair was whitened by hardship before the world recognized her beauty. Some piece of her wanted the world to know just how mean it had been to her. She wanted to rinse all this crap off her hair and just walk out. Some other, more stubborn sentiment kept her locked to the chair. *My hair stays black until someone sees it as lovely*, she told herself, her lip forming a slight pout.

Pathos. Elsie was no more pathetic than Marilyn was. The invisible table separating them became a slender wedge dividing the truth of each from the other. Both women sat at the wide ends on the outside edge of the wedge dividing them. At any moment each could choose to slide to the centre where the wedge became the same point.

A slow smile of satisfaction curled around Marilyn's lips. Elsie looked at her nails. She grunted a couple of times. "They do look nicer," she admitted. She took a look around the place. "It'd be nice to work here, around girls every day. No men," she mused to Marilyn. Nettie returned and Elsie asked her what it was like to work with just women. Nettie carried on about how it made you appreciate yourself in a strange way. "Appreciate men more, too," she quipped, though she didn't say how. Her remarks were so quietly serious that none of the other women dared to query further. The conversation between Elsie and Nettie was as thoughtfully sensitive and intimate as any Marilyn had ever heard among women. It dawned on her that she too worked among women only. Unlike Nettie, though, she had no man to return home to and appreciate. She picked up a magazine and buried the emptiness trying to be born inside.

From outside, Westwind felt Marilyn's emptiness. He crashed against the window, trying to get inside. "You are my desire, my breath, my moment with this island." He could picture his breath running gently across her skin. He pushed against the glass. The glass was unrelenting. Frustrated, he whipped at the world outside the little shop. Gum wrappers and empty coffee cups that disrespectful citizens had dropped onto the sidewalk jumped about. Dust licked at passing legs. Hats flew off. Women clutched coats and frowned. Westwind heaved hot breath against the windowpane. If he could just get her to turn and look, he knew she would hear him and respond. Westwind went unnoticed by Marilyn. Westwind stifled a scream and retreated to his lair beyond the ocean sky. Inside, the radio was on. It hummed out meaningless tunes, helping the women to waste time.

Noreen returned, shampooed and rinsed Marilyn's hair, then lowered the dryer over her head while Nettie began putting the finishing touch on Elsie's nails. Marilyn picked up a magazine and settled into reading. The pages floated.

The street appeared. She was on it. She saw something that wasn't there. Her head snapped right, then left. Westwind waited on the corner. He leapt in her face, whipping Marilyn's new hair. It felt good; she laughed. She recognized the wind. "You're a little brassy today." Her response excited him. Pirouetting in the middle of the street, he leapt upward through the city and flew in the face of Northwind's direction, bragging about his connection with Marilyn. "It was do-able," he howled to his elder brother.

"If my kids could see me now," Elsie said and sighed. Marilyn jolted. She looked at Elsie; wonder still registered on Elsie's face. Elsie was staring at her own hands. I must not have said anything out loud, Marilyn decided. Time slid out from under her grasp again. Beads of sweat crawled about her forehead, drawing itchy little patterns. She wiped them away. Elsie turned to Marilyn. "You finished with the magazine?"

"The magazine?" She looked at her hands holding the magazine as if she had just discovered something really odd about her body. She looked around; surprised they were still in the salon. "Oh yeah," she said, and then she passed it on to Elsie.

"You've never told me what it is I have to do to get my kids back." Elsie was trying hard not to make it sound like an accusation, but Marilyn couldn't help but feel the sting of the question. The court order had named a number of conditions that Elsie had to meet if she was to have her children returned. One was the successful completion of the counselling process of which Marilyn was in charge. Elsie had to meet some standard set by Marilyn. Elsie had figured out who held the key to her children's return, but the rest of the temporary court order's language was foreign to her, escaped her. Elsie's inability to derive a picture, a pattern of actions based on the words contained in the order, had moved her to challenge Marilyn.

Marilyn was bound by her Western ethics. Holding to the discipline these ethics called up sometimes meant betraying mothers. A social worker was not entitled to serve up a blueprint for reunification. She was not at liberty to coach Elsie. Marilyn was supposed to work with her, help her to change her lifestyle, her attitudes, without telling Elsie that that was what she was supposed to do. This seemed altogether mean, like laughing at blondes who wrinkle so badly, when aging is such a horror for all women.

"Let's do lunch, Elsie; we need to talk."

The quiet between them lay thick. It sped up Marilyn's blood. She gave Elsie a sideways glance. The fingers clutching the magazine acquired a small tremble. In her discomfort, Elsie too cast furtive glances in Marilyn's direction. Both of them waited for Marilyn's hair to dry. Elsie acted as though she really was reading the magazine. Marilyn tapped her fingers unobtrusively, wishing for time to rush on. Time doesn't rush; it doesn't stand still. It doesn't really do anything, but Marilyn had not been able to figure that out. Losing time, gapping, as she called it, intensified her belief in time, making it an obsession. She had to know she had a grip on time.

Her hair dry, Marilyn paid the bill. She and Elsie headed for a cozy little lunch place Marilyn loved.

៛ ៛ ៛ ៛

Wind-play can be erratic. It will sometimes sing without rhythm. Wind's vision is to move weather patterns through time and space, to alter the stagnation of air, to create the energy push for rain, the surge that will lead to rebirth. Sometimes wind's play is an adventurous run at failure. Wind sometimes calls you to play, at other times to hesitate. It can force you to yo-yo through life, to jump hoops, to stretch, to fail, to succeed, to play host, to play

guest, to restlessly confuse movement and to clarify dispassion-
ately the direction of movement completely. Failure to engage
wind can lead to premature death. A wind gust caught Marilyn.
She lunged into the street to dodge its grasp. She lunged too
soon. A car came at her, its tires squealing. Elsie grabbed her and
pulled her back to safety just in time.

Marilyn was both shaken and relieved. They hurried to the
restaurant, clutching each other. Inside the restaurant Marilyn
breathed easily. The food was great, the prices light and the service
efficient but not indulgent. No potted plants to inflate the cost of
food. No dim lights or old dark wood to confuse or cause some
false emotion; just clean Arborite tabletops and unadorned chairs.
On one side wall were a half dozen booths. You could vanish into
a restaurant like this and no one would be the wiser.

Marilyn stared at Elsie as Elsie scanned her menu like she
was studying it. Marilyn's job was at risk. She couldn't decide
whether to tell Elsie the truth or not. Elsie was asking the
impossible; Marilyn could get fired for answering her. It seemed
mealy-mouthed and petty to worry about her job instead of
Elsie's children's return, particularly since Marilyn's children
were grown and gone; still she had worked so hard to be in this
job. Marilyn moralized that by answering Elsie's question, Elsie
would have a head start. The changes could be conjured, not
genuine. She ought not to be giving Elsie a cheating start on the
whole process. What if no change occurred, just a semblance of
it, and in the end the children were returned to the same
suffering? She was tempted to say, "I need to be satisfied that
Theresa and James will not suffer Marsha's fate. I need to know

that you understand the depth of caring and commitment that children need." She resisted.

She looked hard at Elsie and asked, "Are you satisfied that you gave your children the best possible care you could?"

"No," Elsie said softly. "No. Every night I go to bed, but I don't sleep. I keep seeing Marsha, her eyes staring at nothing, her body shaking all the time with fever. I keep seeing myself sitting there staring dumbly at Marsha, getting mad, and then I see myself run to the liquor store, drink away the fear. One night she started choking. I just sat there staring. She was lying on her back — flat-like — coughing and turning red. I never moved. I was too drunk to move. Theresa had to get up and pick her up. Marsha screamed, coughed, cried, screamed and coughed and I never moved. Theresa looked at me with them big eyes, beggin' me to do something, and I just sat there. For a minute, it was like being in Choklit Park. Theresa was me and Marsha was Georgie. Except, I'm not like my dad. My dad moved. I didn't. Why didn't I move?"

Elsie's face became childlike again. The question popped out of nowhere, as though it were not intended for anyone in particular. She stared hard at her hands as if the answer was in them, but they wouldn't tell her the answer.

"You and me, Elsie, we're going to find the answer to that question. And when we do, you'll get your kids back," Marilyn said.

They finished eating and left one another on the street. Elsie looked liked she wanted to say something else. She leaned into the words then retreated, mumbling a soft goodbye. "Thanks for the nails."

It was a short walk back to the office. Marilyn wanted to kick herself. Somehow she had found the key. It had happened so easily. Why had it taken so long? What ended Elsie's silence? What changed? What happened that encouraged her to unlock the door? Marilyn went back over their conversation, searching hungrily for the key. She needed to know, lest the door close and she could not open it again. It never occurred to her that the answer lay in what she had not said.

✿ ✿ ✿ ✿

Sun plays with cloud in the west. It never really settles into any sort of routine of rising and shining. Westwind pulls up clouds from the massive breast of the sea. He rolls them about like balls for a while, and then gently escorts them to coastal mountains where the winds begin a playful push-me, pull-me game with them. The games are endless. Wind, sun and cloud enter into a triangular relationship of cool sun and cloudy days. The game ends in windy rainstorms. In the passionate play, they can create all manner of weather conditions in a matter of hours.

Today the winds step lightly between cloud and sun. Cloud shrinks under sun's insistent glare. The winds break the clouds into small, wispy ribbons that skitter across the vast expanse of an apathetic blue sky. Sun burns through the wisps, vainly trying to evaporate what little is left of the clouds' vapour. Days like this speak to the skin. They speak of hot touch against sweating skin cooled by wind-dance. They speak to the very conflict within the human spirit — hot touch against cooling, emotional breath. They speak of the body's need to frame the picture of freedom before permitting the spirit to imagine it within the moment. They warn of too much passion and not enough cool, clear thinking.

Underneath sky's wind-sun-cloud-play, the ocean drapes almost flat, with the barest of ripples that merely hint at being waves. The ripple tips glow like hot diamonds. Children reconfigure the diamond tips into fantasies of beauty, power and sensuality. The ocean sparkles with crystal light and cool air in those moments when wind scrapes against its diamond-backed surface. The children dart back and forth between the edge of the sea and its thin plate of tide, trying to pick up the diamonds.

Marilyn took the time to walk down by the sea and watch the children at the skirt of the ocean. The odd rhythm of hot, cool, cool, hot, warm, hot, cool, light wind movements against the skin enlivened her body, touched her soul and awakened her heart. Days like this were made for conjuring, for imagining and reinventing others.

Clutches of small children, some red-legged, others tawny, others dark, moved about in small circles doing a Mexican hat dance along the tide's edge. The circles of children were ensconced in a dome of high-pitched giggles, full of wonderment. On an old dead log in the foreground, a small child sat. His red shorts were too large and his long hair scrabbled its way to his shoulders. He had no shirt. His warm chestnut skin sharpened the red satin of his shorts. His fingers trailed over the journey of worms through wood. He was alone.

Marilyn stopped and leaned in his direction. The empathy wrapped itself around words that slipped away. She halted, looked and then hurried away. The moment fell.

❧ ❧ ❧ ❧

Marilyn was late returning. Janet glanced at the clock and reminded her of her one o'clock appointment. It was one-thirty. Marilyn looked over at the morose face of a teenaged woman slouched in the chair nearest the door of the waiting room. *Another fine piece of work. Reminds me of my own ridiculous youth,* Marilyn murmured to herself. Out loud she said, "Send her in."

"Hello, Miss Evans?" She glanced at the file and motioned Carole Evans to sit.

"I ain't your damn puppy you can make wait then order to sit." The words cut through the air, full of hate. Despite them, Carole sat noisily into the chair.

"I apologize for being late. I was with another client."

"So Janet says."

The interview went by the book, smooth but for Carole's attitude and Marilyn's constant struggle for breath. She wanted to tell Carole she was an ungracious brat who had no idea how much power Marilyn had over her life. Carole's was one of the first files Marilyn had received since the review of Elsie's case; she was seeing Carole before her kids were lost to her. Marilyn wanted to tell Carole that if she chose not to deal with her, she would lose her children, possibly forever. Carole was likely aware of Marilyn's power over her future as mother and likely resented this fact. The insolence was probably more resistance or resentment toward the right Marilyn had to that power rather than any real feelings of hate; after all, she didn't really know Marilyn. They worked out a schedule of regular visits. Marilyn assured Carole that she wouldn't be a "no show" next time. It came out sounding forced. The constraint in Marilyn's voice did not go by Carole. She left, slamming the door as she went.

⑨ ⑨ ⑨ ⑨

Marilyn was preparing to leave for Toronto. In a strange way, these out-of-town lectures were welcome breaks from her work. She did not get very far with the women on her caseload. She felt stuck. This spawned a kind of hopelessness she tried not to acknowledge. It was just there, like a nagging bill collector. The lectures, on the other hand, always left her with a feeling of hope. The future continued to look brighter as long as someone in the audience heard. From a thousand different angles, Marilyn's message was clear: leave us to do this ourselves. She now felt nauseous, unsure of the wisdom of her message. Logic told her that because the problem had been created by the outside, the solutions had to come from inside. Nazi camp guards, she reasoned could not be counted on to solve the impact that the concentration camps had on the inmates. Likewise, the perpetrators of the terrorism on Native children could not be counted to ease the fears of Native mothers. The principle was logical, but the case files stared at her. A dead little girl kept nagging her, and now Carole and her willful hate would become another one of her many unresolved cases punching up doubt. Maybe she didn't have any real solutions. Perhaps she was talking to the wrong people about all the wrong things. Maybe she should be looking for Indigenous people who were doing similar work and together they could try to figure out just how to resolve the dilemma they and their clients were in. *Clients. Clients? People. How do people become clients? How do clients become people? Oh fuck.* She slapped her files in the cabinet.

"Leave it alone," she chided herself aloud. She gathered up her papers, her coat, hat and purse, took a quick scan of the room, flipped the light switch off, then opened the door and quietly closed it as she left. Janet was nearly ready to leave. As usual, Janet had packed up her papers, cleaned and tidied her desk and locked the doors. She looked to Marilyn as though none of the problems facing Marilyn's "clients" mattered to her one way or another. Marilyn pondered the absolute lack of curiosity Janet showed toward what went on between Marilyn and the women who came to see her.

It dawned on her that she and Janet had never really had a conversation about anything other than who was here, who had an appointment, and the hectic scheduling, rescheduling and calling people that Marilyn's trips required. Marilyn wondered what mindset it took to come to work every day and not be curious about the people you work for or with. Marilyn caught herself staring at Janet's back and realized she wasn't curious enough to break the pattern of unconcern. She turned to look through the glass doors that emptied out into the lobby of the building. Her reflection caught her eye. The face was clearly lonely. She urged herself to speak to Janet, failed, conceded defeat and joined the staff in the hall outside their offices. She watched the various people from different offices as they all left their jobs. They exchanged pleasantries with one another just as Marilyn and Janet did, but their faces looked like Marilyn's. Marilyn sighed and turned out onto the street and headed for her car.

"Walk me through this paddle song, walk me through like soft wind." Marilyn did not react to Randy as he breathed these words out to her. She just recognized Randy being randy. She saw him every day. He passed her office, smiled, waved and generally made some odd comments like this one. She cracked her face enough to grin acknowledgement, but rarely stopped to chat. He always had a couple of lines for her at quitting time. She was never sure what feeling he was trying to inspire in her. It never occurred to her that he had no ulterior motives, that maybe he was just being. She tipped her hand slightly, smiled and turned away.

The air swished loosely about her Burberry, the wind sang low and soft, an old paddle song. She cocked her head to one side to hear it. There weren't that many trees in the city to echo the voice of wind. She had to strain somewhat to hear it. From atop the hill above False Creek she could see the water below. It was almost smooth, evenly inundated with tiny ripples moving swiftly to shore. It looked as though today the wind could easily carry a great canoe across the water. Paddle songs are fashioned after the rhythm of wind in the trees during a good seafaring kind of day, she decided. *Smart, we were so damned smart. How did things come to this? Maybe Randy knows something.* The light changed. Randy dropped from her mind the moment her foot reached for the sidewalk pavement, and she thought no more about him. She reached the parking lot, got in her car and drove out into the traffic.

She hated driving. She felt the omnipresent danger of sinking into reverie and thought about the danger of having an accident in those slips of time when she gapped out and disappeared from whatever her reality was. So far she had not gapped out too badly while in her moving car, but she worried at the effort it took to stay in the present. Behind the wheel, she dug in. It made driving tense and unbearably tiring.

Memory doesn't always stick when vision is too hung up on the immediate. Memory comes from some other process. It arises from the sum of our perception of reality. It is tempered by the emotional angle from which we are looking at reality. The stretch we apply to significant memory is funnelled through our emotional filters. We hold up memories that validate our perceived totality. In this way, all memory is slightly false. Depth, breadth and accuracy of perception can be hampered by narrow emotion. Marilyn's filters were grey. She committed to memory only those moments that appeared to accent the grey light of her emotional apathy. She sometimes got lost on days when the grey was so intense that she could not recognize the markers that located her in the city. Today, she missed her street. She missed it by a long way. She came around on some strange end of town she barely recognized. "Damn." She took a look around to see if anyone had noticed. This time, she laughed. "Oh, like the world is actually giving a shit and watching you," she said. This seemed to pop the grey and clarify the streets for her. She finally made it home late.

She was barely in the door of her townhouse at False Creek when the phone rang. It would be Catherine: she always called just before Marilyn left for a trip. Marilyn made sure her two daughters knew where she was at all times. It was an old habit left over from her Mom. "I don't care where you go, just let me know where you are" was about the only discipline her Momma exacted upon Marilyn and her six brothers and sisters. She guessed her brothers and sisters had used the same rule with their own, but she wasn't all that sure. They had never been encouraged to talk to one another, so communication between them was scant, sparse even. Maybe communication wasn't all that simple for them. Maybe, after suffering what seemed like an endless run of shoeless, coatless, cold winters and year-round hunger, they wanted the fullness of their bellies in recent years to be their only memories. It struck Marilyn just now that reminiscing with her siblings might be dangerous for all of them. They would be forced to remember the sound of Willie screaming as their step-dad bounced him from one wall to another for infractions they, the younger children committed.

Guilt, grey and cold, chilled her. They would be forced to remember staring blankly at each other's eyes, each of them looking so deeply sad at the plate as it emptied itself before their bellies were full. They would be forced to remember ... Marilyn slammed the door to her coat closet and kicked the bottom of it. This always cut the remembering short. She took a sharp breath and dialed the phone.

Catherine was excited about school, her friends and a new boyfriend. Had Marilyn heard from Lindy?

"Not for about a week," Marilyn answered softly, a hint of trepidation in her voice. Lindy had just moved out a few months earlier. She worked with a local theatre group. The hours were long and the pay poor. She wondered how Lindy was faring. Neither of the two girls had any idea about the cost of setting up house for themselves when they moved out of Marilyn's apartment, but the whole notion of living on their own had been a moving one for both of them. *I guess it is the only way kids know they are grown up and capable,* Marilyn said to herself, sighing. In the end, she had helped Lindy settle into her apartment. She chased whatever doubts she had to a dead file in the back of her mind and waited for Catherine to continue.

"She's going to be in a movie." Catherine sounded excited. Not a feature film you go to at a movie hall, but an independent film. Still, they were going to pay Lindy. Catherine chattered on as though she were the one who had the golden opportunity to be in a movie. Marilyn resented that Catherine always found out what was up with Lindy, then passed it on to her. A wave of sadness passed through her. She was destined to know about her younger daughter through her elder sister. Lindy never phoned her mom with her news first. Marilyn wanted to be first. Being last had peopled her life. Last in class. Last to sleep. Last to marry. Last to be chosen on white school teams.

Her stomach churned. She leaned against the gym wall, one leg crossed over the other. She stuck her left hip out and shook her right foot rapidly. Her right index fingernail clicked against anxious teeth. Her mind was deliberately blank. All her emotions were in high gear, working overtime to hold her stillness intact. Her head tilted up and her eyes peered out from under the tilt. Patience registered on her face. It never helped to know they didn't want her because she was Indian and they were ignorant, and not because she was a poor athlete, unworthy of being chosen. She was an excellent athlete, but they didn't want her. She knew it. They knew it. Being last created a desperate hunger to be first. Being last was her only experience. She had no idea how to make first-ness happen. She wasn't even sure she would recognize first-ness if it happened to her. Not any of that was seriously true. She had never taken the time to figure it out — which was true. She sank slowly into a chair.

The sadness got thick for a short while, then a sharp stick cut a slice out of her empathy for herself. She caught the image of the first time she told Lindy she was good without following it up with "but you could" . . . Lindy waited for the rest. She waved her hands, indicating that Marilyn should finish. "That's all," Marilyn whispered. "You're so good."

"Oh my God," Lindy squealed loudly to the crowd of strangers attending the reception for her play's opening night. "My mom just gave me my first clean compliment." She yahooed for what seemed like ages. The crowd disappeared from Marilyn's consciousness. She felt so alone, like the scraggy-haired little boy tracing worm trails in wood. Her eyes wove their way through the room, skimming the surface of faces in snake-like order. She felt a stone settle into her guts. She scanned her mind, looking for its origin: was it shame or guilt? No? Well, maybe it was shame — shame of realizing she had never paid either girl a compliment without some sort of "do better" qualifier. The crowd seemed to be smiling. They seemed to get caught up in Lindy's joy without wondering at all why this moment was so pitch-thick and sticky for Marilyn. You could see the thickness of the moment, feel it, and almost touch it. It clung to you. Marilyn floated through the scene, detached. She could feel her face smile but her eyes were dead. Now, she replayed the scene as she listened to Catherine bubbling over the phone. Marilyn couldn't think of a time when she had said anything like that to Catherine.

"You're marvellous, Catherine." It came out raw and without context.

"What?" Catherine's voice sounded confused.

"You're marvellous"

There was a moment of silence at the other end. "You're not sick are you, Mom?"

Marilyn suddenly wanted to cry. Sick had been the word she used for hung over. Sick was what she feared when she gapped. Sick was revolting to her. Hadn't Cat figured that out? She hated the lying years. She hated the hiding. She swallowed her tears, breathed, and said no as calmly and sweetly as she could. Another short silence, then Catherine mumbled thanks and asked Marilyn about her trip to Toronto. While she answered Catherine, Marilyn promised herself she would phone Lindy late that night to get the scoop from the girl herself and offer her congratulations. The conversation ended shortly after Cat asked her if she was excited about the Toronto trip.

"It is such a golden opportunity, Mom. I'm proud of you, Mom." She said it softly.

Marilyn couldn't help answering, "That's funny, Cat; shouldn't I be saying stuff like that to you?"

"Mom." There was a sweet scold in the voice. Catherine was altogether too mothering toward Marilyn and Lindy. Marilyn knew it. She tried to open the door to some discussion of the past, discussion that might alter the way they related to one another, but Catherine as usual ignored the entranceway. Would she ever walk through? Marilyn could think of nothing else to say so she told Catherine she was proud of her too, for what, she didn't really say. The "thanks, Mom" was flat. They both said I love you and good night, then the dial tone sounded. There is nothing worse than the uninterrupted sound of a dial tone after a reasonably empty conversation. Marilyn stared at the phone for a moment, then carefully placed it on the bar and sighed.

She sank into the chair next to the phone and let her energy fall away. In the half-light of her living room, the energy drain seemed mystical, almost magic. She couldn't afford to let herself relax too much though; she still had to wash up the morning's dishes, throw in a load of laundry and pack for tomorrow's early flight. She draped her hands on her lap and drew her legs apart while her mind searched for some small place inside where the energy she needed to pack might be hiding. Her breath came in and out steadily. The room stood still, the air in it slowed, became comatose; she stilled with it. The air felt as though it were dying. She picked up the phone and dialed Lindy's number.

Lindy was thoroughly modern. She saved every penny she could and bought herself a host of technological toys. Her little apartment was filled with cameras (for her hobby), including a video camera, a computer laptop complete with fax modem and printer, a Xerox machine (for her writing), and attached to her telephone was an answering machine. It was the answering machine that greeted Marilyn.

"Hi, guess what, I ain't answering (some music) but I am sooo curious about who is at the other end of this here line that I'll die if you don't let me know your name. I'll be plagued with insomnia for at least a week if you don't leave your number so I can get back to you."

"Hi, babe. It's your mom. Call me when you get in, no matter how late it is." She tried to pick up her voice. She couldn't figure out why, but she felt like a vacuum had sucked the joy of life out of her when she wasn't able to get Lindy on the line. The call hadn't done much to renew her energy.

Jeezuss, is that why I called, to renew my energy? A torrent of admonitions set itself into motion. She battered herself, asking why she couldn't call her children out of concern for them. *Why the hell is it always some petty need of my own?* She dealt with all kinds of mothers in her job; they all swore they lived for their children, but she knew it was a crock.

All evidence pointed to children living for their mothers. She felt like one of the mothers. Image after image poured through her mind; each picture snatched the years from her grown daughters as she searched for evidence that she at one time might have lived for them and not vice versa. There were moments: when the girls were sick or had contracted lice, the scourge of poor people, and Marilyn had girded up her loins and gone to work fighting the disease, laundering every piece of cloth, scrubbing the entire apartment and delousing everything with a fury. But in general, her youthful motherhood was haunted by near suicide and destructive drinking. The girls had paid.

℘ ℘ ℘ ℘

Marilyn recalled the first day she signed up with the wagon of partygoers; that's when she first stepped onto the treadmill of consistently robbing her children's right to be children. She was twenty-three; her husband had disappeared again. Lindy, the baby, was staring out the window late on a Friday. It was dark. Neither of the girls wanted to go to sleep.

"Daddy's wirkin', right Mom?" Lindy asked cautiously, like she was afraid of the answer. Marilyn realized Lindy was sitting at the window waiting for him to arrive. His sojourns back into the world of alcohol had been few and far between before the first child, and then after Catherine they increased month by month. The frequency of disappearing acts shot up again with Lindy's birth, until he'd finally disappeared altogether. Prior to today she remembered all this without really thinking about it. It was a memory like some news clipping might be. Until now it had no significance to her or her life.

The memory of five years climbed up on Marilyn. She grew weary of working off the upset of wondering when he would bother to arrive, worrying about whether he would have any of his paycheque left, and worse what mood he would be in when and if he arrived. She had spent five years carefully monitoring every penny they spent, saving coins for big ticket items, shopping with intense caution, calculating the cost of every item she bought, wrestling with every coin, saving five cents on necessities, browsing sales with diligence and doing without anything new for herself. She recalled applying for school. She had to go through an oral interview. The instructor asked her what she read. "Pardon?" she responded, not quite catching the question. She heard the words, but the meaning did not seem to stick.

"What sorts of things do you read? What books, magazines, newspapers?" the instructor trailed off.

"Read? I read…" She paused. Then answered honestly. "Ads. I read ads." She wanted to laugh at the look on the instructor's face. It was pathetically humorous. "It's okay," she said. "The ad-reading has all been to little or no avail, which is why I am here." The instructor squirmed in his seat, cocked his head to one side, trying to get a bead on what she was talking about. Marilyn knew the rest. The family didn't even own a table after five years of her scrimping. Her husband's alcohol consumption, then hers, had invaded the stability of the home. It continued to wreak havoc with their lives long after he had left. She declined to let the instructor in on her private world.

In the end, she winked and smiled. The instructor laughed and went on to the next question.

Marilyn's mind retreated to the middle of the old room they had all tried so hard to live in. A drum squatted with a square board over top. It fought desperately to be a table. She covered it with a sheet, not even a tablecloth, to hide the hideous thing they ate from. As a twenty-three year old, she had failed to see the sad little picture painted by her anxious child, fingers clinging to a window, waiting patiently for a dad, unmindful of the dreadful conditions in which he forced them to live. Now she saw the smallness of Lindy, the anticipation and the worry. She saw the small round face pressed up hard against the window as though by pressing hard she could will her dad to come home. She heard the unconditional love of father, rich with promise, in Lindy's voice. "I promise to be good, Daddy. I promise to be good, Mommy. Don't hit me, I'll be good." Then Bobbie's pleading, loving, eager, terrorized little voice begging his stepdad to stop layered itself over Lindy's voice, obliterating it. Earl picked Bobbie up to toss him against the wall. The very moment Earl grabbed Bobby, he sucked wind and held until Earl let him go. He would hit the wall in silence, land. Bobbie's screams and begging would only start up again if Earl advanced on him for another go at the wall. Once he didn't scream or beg at all. Marilyn only heard the thud of Bobbie's body hitting wall after wall. Then the picture changed. Marilyn loomed over Catherine, a wooden spoon in her hand.

"Bend over, bend over, or I'll hit you anywhere I can." Marilyn's voice was a horrific shriek. She hated herself while she was shrieking and determined to follow through with the licking. "I promise to be good, I promise to be good, Mommy. *Please don't hit me*, I'll be good." The begging, pleading, loving, eager, worried, terrorized little voice begged Marilyn not to hit her.

A ball of cold air filled Marilyn's stomach. Her hands shook with the coldness of the rage that seemed to be shooting into them from the ball inside her belly. Her heart sped up. She watched Lindy. She saw her scurry here and there. She heard her make grunting, fearful soft sounds. Lindy's face looked as though she were trying to find some answer, some bit of truth that she hoped lay somewhere on the floor. She crawled first this way, then that. Marilyn swung, caught Lindy on the backside as she crawled. Lindy's back arced under the blow. Cat rushed to save her. Marilyn swung again, catching Cat's hands. The hands retreated to Cat's ribs. Cat jumped toward the wall. Lindy froze in the middle of the floor, her whole body just shivered. Marilyn thought maybe Lindy just wanted to find the road out of this horrific moment before it was too late and the wooden spoon and the hateful, maddened eyes of her mother fell on her or Catherine.

Marilyn heard her mind tell her to walk away from terrorizing these poor little girls. Her mind was disconnected from the
hand holding the spoon. The hand was being controlled by the
cold air splitting off from the ball in her belly in shafts of ugly
rage. Her hand rose, the spoon landed on Catherine. Catherine
skipped away, making an odd squeaking sound of trepidation
and hurt as she went. She didn't get away though. Another whack
connected with her little body. Cat jumped up on the bed, managed to get out an audible, "Please, noooo, Mommy." Catherine's
breath came too fast. She kept her eyes on the spoon as she fled
from its blows, dodging, ducking, jumping and running all over
the room. Once in a while she got away. Lindy was frozen.
Whack. Lindy was too terrified to move. Another swing. Lindy
flinched, but remained still. The words in Marilyn's head sped up.
Stop. Don't. Quit. Walk away. Put the spoon down. These are your daughters.
The words kept going off in her mind as the spoon rose and fell.
The words of admonition seemed to drive the hand to continue.

Catherine's eyes became serious. They matured. She grew intent
on dodging the wicked spoon, bent on escaping the beating.
Determined to survive, Cat became cleverer, more agile, and swifter.
Lindy's eyes clouded and remained frozen. They were full of sus-
picion, wary of Marilyn's every mood. One day Lindy did not
whimper or scurry, she just looked up at the spoon and waited for
the blow. Finally, the voice in Marilyn's mind gained the upper
hand. Marilyn stopped, turned and left the room.

Now, Marilyn needed to cry. The urge was overwhelming. It
pushed up from her belly with tremendous force. Her neck

tightened, her hands formed a fist and her face muscles locked. She pressed her fists against her face, hit herself a number of times, then with a fierce will she pushed down on the ball of tears now welling up in her throat. The picture of Cat and Lindy died as she pulled back the first image of Lindy at the window.

"Yeah, he's working," she answered to her empty house. Her voice was thick with resentment, then and now. Her voice scared Lindy and Cat. Lindy started to whimper. Years ago, when she terrorized her daughters, Marilyn had not seen the terror. She had seen only herself. She had seen her husband's desertion. She'd seen his refusal to come home and help her raise their children. Now all Marilyn saw was her children. She barely saw the resentment of a twenty-three-year-old mother.

"Get away from the window," she had snarled at Lindy. "Isn't it your bedtime?" Lindy grew quiet, slid noiselessly away from the window ledge. Cat moved to rescue Lindy.

"Come on, Lindy, let's go play dolls." The words came out softly and carefully, lest Marilyn become upset. Cat took Lindy's hand. At the door to the hall Cat turned to tell her mom, "She's just scared, Mom." Then the room at the end of the hall swallowed them both, swallowed them just like the truck that had swallowed Eddy. Marilyn left the girls to resolve their terror alone. Catherine and Lindy hugged each other and cried themselves to sleep while she sat in a chair in the kitchen, eyes vacant, looking for the source of all the hate eating her insides and driving her to destroy her children. Not once, but over and over again.

From her chair, Marilyn's hands reformed that old fist of almost twenty years ago. "Oh gawd, please roll the clock back.

Lindy, I didn't mean to scare you. I never wanted to scare you. Catherine, I never wanted to hurt you. I never wanted to hurt either of you," Marilyn said out loud. The loudness of her voice jarred her momentarily. She couldn't stop. "I was so tired, so weary. Don't you see? I just couldn't be any more heroic than I was at that moment. I'd had it." She excused herself. She wanted to relieve herself of the horrible truth of what she had forced her daughters to live with. She wanted to fix it. She wanted to remove whatever ugliness lived inside her before she brutalized them. Somehow this ugliness had distorted her character before her children were born. She couldn't remove it retroactively and there was no excuse. "But I was so tired." She pleaded for some kind of mercy.

No, it wasn't that. It wasn't just plain tired. She was so much more than just tired. It wasn't a normal kind of tired. It was a wasting-away tired. A snake filled out of control, a murderous tired. Her breath stilled. Memory is fragile. It comes to us in delicate wisps, layer upon layer of image-filled sound. It hooks itself to present being. Filtered by thousands of experiences, the truth underneath memory sometimes cannot quite pierce through all the layers. Memory melds with the present. Past tense, future and the moment unhinge, float about ill-disciplined in the mind of those too fatigued by their emotional senselessness to decipher meaning.

Eddy jumped out from the back of Marilyn's mind, sandwiched between her layered memories. Her father bobbed and weaved, trying to get through. He seemed to want to help her name this strange stillness. If only she could breathe. She could see him, but her breath eluded her. It slipped by her lips and nose unnoticed. It was barely tangible. It slid into her lungs, filling very little space, and just sat for a long time. Her mind stilled, directing nothing.

Spiritual energy is the power source directing thought. There seemed to be a huge spiritual vacuum sucking the energy out of Marilyn. In this stillness, random thoughts flashed, etching pictures without connection or reason onto her mind. Eddy popped up, his heels swallowed by night; the rest of him swallowed by a truck. Then the stillness came.

She could not imagine the movement it would take to change the relationship with her children. Stillness wrapped itself around her. It choked her imagination, blunted her sense of future movement. Tiredness cemented itself to the space between future and past. It was the kind of tired that is so deep, so long and so old that seeing aliveness is painful. Children are so alive. Some piece of Marilyn hated their aliveness, their very optimism. She hated hearing her children's unconditional love for their father, who was out sleeping with who knows whom, drinking who knows what, spending the little money they had. She had so little love to share and the little she had was twisted and hidden underneath this terrible hate, which froze every morsel of affection she had for herself and her life.

Still, she felt the love inside. She grabbed her belly where she imagined this love lived, all wrapped in a ball. It seemed to bang around the walls of her belly; it bounced between the moving pictures in which moments delivered action and other moments delivered stillness. Action was a hated thing. Action brought terrible consequences. Sometimes, though, it beat the deathly stillness. Carefully, she chose those sorts of actions whose consequences were trivial or completely acceptable: cleaning, scrubbing and cook-ing. She had not wanted to challenge herself, to move away from the edge that delivered her to madness; she just wanted to stop beating her children. The cleaning kept her from being violent, but it also became the log that fed the fire of paralysis inside. She experienced aliveness between old pictures only when she cleaned.

Her weariness was beyond that. She was weary of making excuses, exhausted by the sound of her unanswered screams and cries day and night. She had no will left to try and be anything more than she was. She justified the absence of will by naming it "tired." She had been heroic. She had fought. She did the best she could. Her teeth gritted at the old familiar prattle she used on clients. She didn't buy the "did the best you could" counselling line. She had not been victorious. It is incumbent upon mothers and fathers to engage in life victoriously at least over their own per-verse direction. Marilyn's failure ushered her children into the world of emotion ill-equipped to engage it. Her failure coloured their every move. It defined the absence of movement, spawned a sense of hopelessness, and the refrain "tired" made it all justifiable. She hated the phrase "did the best you could" with a passion. When she used it, it came out of her mouth tinny and hollow.

The alternative seemed to be to live a life driven by guilt. Guilt is an impossible ghost to feed and satisfy. Guilt is a night-mare. Guilt sucks the life out of night, rendering it windless. Guilt drags failure along with it like they were old friends. Together they turn the dream world into an insane nightmare. This nightmare spurred the incessant battle inside Marilyn's body between what she did and what she believed. Belief was so much more fragile than her body's hatred of movement. Marilyn repeated her efforts to stop, despite repeated failure. Her efforts to stop were barren. She carried on under a dome of excuses that snatched victory out of the jaws of defeat. The internal war raged on and her children became the enemy. Her crimped voice began with her five-year-old scream. Marilyn heard herself utter it. She screamed for her mother to come up with some mature feeling for her, to imagine something different for Marilyn, something beyond the expectations Anne had of herself.

"'I'm doing the best I can' is a response from a mother to a child, not a mature response to anything. Our responses to the calls of children have not grown in the direction of victory." The words from her presentation dried in Marilyn's mouth. "Dumb catchphrases of defeat," she whispered. She opened herself up to seeing how all those phrases silenced any reckoning inside. Some web of understanding tried to take shape inside her mind. It grew large, into a wheel. The words seemed to fog the wheel; or were they blocking some possibility? The wheel was made of possibility. The words rimming the edge of the wheel wanted reconciliation with her past, not acceptance of it. Acceptance leapt from the rim razor sharp, cutting off the possibility of reconciliation. She watched as the wheel rims of reconciliation were slashed by a perverse acceptance of what she had done.

Her behaviour lined up with an unimaginably perfect beast with which she shared a crazy kind of link. This beast negated any furthering of who she could be. She stared at the beast. It was she, and at the same time it was not. It was as though her beast had been conjured by her own will in those moments when guilt could not lead her to an almost comfortable, apathetic acquiescence.

No, that wasn't it either. Someone — many someones — had filled her life with pain and hate. It was all she had to share.

Wrong again. It wasn't that. She felt the love inside, wrapped in a tight ball. It banged around the walls of her belly, bouncing between moving pictures of moments that delivered action from some place outside the ball — action she hated, like hitting her kids. It beat the deathly stillness, the paralysis she was bound by. Her children's aliveness challenged her paralysis, accused her stillness, as though her stillness were somehow guilty of conjuring her hate. She had no other pictures of aliveness but her violence. This realization calmed her somewhat. Her fist relaxed. She was breathing again. Her mind slowed. She sighed heavily, comforted somewhat by naming the cause.

ჰ ჰ ჰ ჰ

Magic moments peel themselves from the mind like children's stickers. They can sometimes unglue memories and stop them from travelling in the normal direction of the mind. These moments fall from the sky, like people that cross your path when you are desperate for them. Sky people watch humans. They alone own time. They collect it in balls of starlight. Every now and then they toss it to a human they believe needs to catch something. Stuck humans are desperate. Starlight draws attention to locked memories that keep humans stuck. The unstuck memories would change Marilyn's direction, but she had yet to experience that change and so paid little attention to the magic of the moment.

She told herself it didn't change anything for Lindy. Lindy didn't deserve to be a little girl staring out the window waiting for her drunken father to return, hoping he would rescue her from her mother's wrath. Cat did not deserve to age from a child to a protective adult with a body too small to be successful. It had begun then, this terrible tiredness born of Marilyn's nearly futile struggle with terrorism. The tiredness arose from her inability to rise above her violent emotions. Failure to break the crusty edges encasing the love inside her body had robbed her youthful eyes of sight. She failed to see the sadness in Lindy's and Catherine's little faces. Her failure shrank the empathetic response she now felt filling her body. Twenty years later the picture looked so horribly, horribly different.

How could I know I would feel so differently now, so unforgiving of those youthful days of hot rage, uncontrolled and misdirected?

The dam broke. The tears came. Huge wracking sobs followed. She could hear herself. She saw herself standing in the kitchen watching the girls furtively skulking to their room, their small backs curved with the weight of their fear. Lindy kept looking back, eyes big with fright, face filled with confusion, tears leaking down her lovely moon-shaped face.

Oh God, what have I done?

The picture slowed down of its own accord. The girls' trek to the bedroom at the end of the hall seemed to take forever. Marilyn saw herself run after them. *No. I didn't mean to scare you, Lindy. Come back, wait.* The picture suddenly changed. Again she was running down a highway, terrified, chasing her stepfather's car, screaming, "WAIT ... WAIT ... DAD, WAIT, I'M SCARED."

Again, she watched the car slow down, saw him turn to look at her. Just as she approached the car she watched it speed up, bend the corner and drive out of sight. Again she saw herself cast a terrified glance about her, felt the cold creep into her bones, noted the coming dark, saw headlights coming toward her and watched herself head for the bush.

"Why didn't anyone care about me?" She wept long and hard.

From beneath the sound of her memory she could hear the phone ring. She wanted to reach for it. Her hands wouldn't move. She stared at them. They didn't seem to belong to her just this minute. They looked small, childlike. *What's happening to me? Please, someone help me answer the phone.* She ceased talking out loud. *I'm losing it again. No, I can't afford another breakdown — not now. Please, not now. Answer the phone.* Her voice wanted to push out wind, to greet the room with sound. It wanted its sound to wrap itself around her ears. She could break the grip of this moment if only her voice could be heard. If only she could move some part of herself. She stared at her hand. *Move, hand. Damn it! Move.* No sound. Her little hands just sat there limp and cold. She was still in the bush, catching her breath. She could see this self, this small child, as her mind kept pleading with her: *Stop. Not now. I can't afford another breakdown.* At the same time some rational part of her mind listed old arguments, while some other piece of her acknowledged the chair, the living room. It was too dark. No, that wasn't it. The image of her, hysterical in the bush, was too big. The word breakdown was too loud. None of it would go away.

Marilyn wanted her mom. She could see herself: six years old, crying for her mommy in the growing dark. The damp, cold dark squeezed her smaller than she was. The phone kept ringing. Her body was rocking in her easy chair, trying hard to reclaim her forty-five-year-old self. She could hear the phone through the noisy chaos of her splitting mind. The person rocking in the easy chair felt like herself, rocking in the bush next to fern and cedar. She surrendered to movement, to the rocking, to the sweet smell of bush. "Don't fall asleep" came next. Mommy says people who fall asleep in the cold die. *Wake up. Get up. Put one foot in front of the other.* She sang it softly, rhythmically, until finally her hand reached for the cedar's wet branch. In her hand was the phone. She stared at it in disbelief. She was back in her living room. The voice at the other end was Catherine's.

"Mom, Mom, are you all right? Mom, shall we come over? MOM, answer the phone, Mom."

"I'm okay. I'm just trying to get out of the tub," she heard herself lie. Her voice was amazingly calm.

"We were worried. You sounded so down on the answering machine." It was Lindy. This surprised her. Marilyn thought her voice sounded pretty chipper. Now she wondered privately how conscious she was of her own voice. She heard herself speak, but she had never heard the emotion the sound was delivering, and she barely felt it either. "Did I sound down?" she asked Lindy. *Am I feeling down?* she asked herself, not listening for the answer. It occurred to her that she only heard one sound when she spoke, as though her voice had rhythm and volume, but no emotion. Lindy must know something about voice and the emotion it expresses. I should ask her, Marilyn thought, and then corrected herself. *Christ, Marilyn, can you never quit misusing your girls?* She guessed the story behind Lindy's phone call: Lindy must have phoned earlier. Not getting an answer, she had phoned Cat. Cat insisted to Lindy that she knew that Marilyn was at home. They phoned again. Scared (though she called it worried), Lindy went over to Cat's. Together they phoned a third time. This was a recurring story too.

At some point years ago, Marilyn had decided she would rather die than hit them anymore. At the time the only other response to their miscreant behaviour that she could come up with was to succumb to a strange catatonic state. When angry, she retreated to her room, stopped breathing and lay staring at the ceiling — sometimes for hours. Lindy was the first to ask if she was all right. Then Lindy would call Cat. Cat would enter, asking if they could have something to eat. Finally both would appear together and try to get Momma involved in some game. Sometimes it worked. Marilyn would get up and go through the motions of playing the game, doing papier-mâché, artwork, or some such thing, but Marilyn knew her heart wasn't in it. Her involvement was coldly clinical, emotionless. The girls tried to be happy, but their nervous laughter made it clear they were afraid of their Momma. The human being who ought to have been the safest person in the world inspired fear in them day after day, year in and year out. It had the effect of pushing up their tenderness, their caring for her. It was all so upside down.

Marilyn felt panic fluttering about, teasing the walls of her stomach as she wondered how long these drifts into the past took. They seemed to be happening more often. More and more they occurred in the company of others. Picking up her voice after such sojourns required a huge effort. *They must know*, she thought. *Know what? Know there are pauses. Of course they know. What do they think it is?* she wondered. *Stop it*, she ordered. *Respond. Say something.* "It's not supposed to be this way," Marilyn finally managed to say. The panic fluttered faster, scraping her stomach lining thin as she wondered how much Lindy and Cat knew about her drifts. What did she look like when she was boomeranging back like that?

"What way?" Lindy's voice was laced with caution. She didn't like treading down the hallways to intimate conversation with her mom any more than Cat did. Disaster was too often the result. Marilyn could feel Lindy preparing to hang up. Marilyn never could figure how to say things to Lindy without making Lindy feel like she was accusing her of wanting to hurt her mother on purpose. Lindy had had enough of feeling like she had consistently ill motives toward her mother. She behaved as though her mother believed that Lindy lay awake at night scheming up ways to unsettle Marilyn. Lindy had not said this to her, but Catherine had. Each of her children was free to talk to her sister about how she felt, but neither of them felt free to tell Marilyn directly how she made them feel. They had this practice of trusting only each other. If Marilyn said anything to either of them, the fragile circle of trust between them would be broken.

Neither of the girls knew how frustrating this was becoming for Marilyn. Unless the girls accused her directly, Marilyn could neither alter the old course nor account for herself. She felt like she should do something, say something to end the parade of terrible memories that stood between them, but every suggestion inside her mind seemed to be power-packed and charged with guilt. She was in a corner. She had no idea how she arrived here and no idea how to get out. Outside, a tree snapped. Northwind grabbed hold of it. He knew that sometimes humans are jarred out of lying to themselves by sharp sounds. He wanted Marilyn to become conscious. He knew she had plenty of ideas about how she arrived where she was, but no single one of them seemed big enough to justify it. Further, he knew there was no justification; but there could be redemption if she actively accepted what she had done. The trick failed. Sighing, chilly and sad, Northwind withdrew.

Marilyn was horrified. She had backed her girls into this crazy corner with her as though misery really did love company. Lindy and Cat were still on the phone. She fought herself to keep the conversation light.

"I'm the one who is supposed to worry about you," she said, and she chuckled. They all laughed at this — comic relief. "I have a feeling this trip is going to be different," she blurted after the laughter.

"Oh," both said in unison. "Owe me a Coke," Lindy said, and they laughed again. Marilyn could feel the effort they were making to keep the conversation light. She decided to respect their effort. What a crock.

"Oh, I don't know. I have been having a lot of erotic fantasies lately." They laughed heartily at this. The girls could not picture their mother actually having erotic fantasies and they said so.

"What? You think forty-five-year-old women don't have sexual fantasies?"

"No. It's just hard to picture someone as awesome-looking as you having to rely on fantasies."

"You're right. I lied. I haven't had any fantasies yet. It's just that I have been hankering after company these days."

"Ooh, Momma's on the prowl. Look out, Taranta," said Lindy. "Be careful, Momma. I hear tell they are all barracudas and sharks out that way."

Lindy told Marilyn about her opportunity to make a movie and her desire to move East to further her career some day. They had a comfortable three-way conversation that ended in good spirits. Marilyn felt better when they finally hung up the phone. The crying helped, she knew. She just wished someone had been there to hold her. She finished up her packing then turned in, and drifted easily into sleep.

Part THREE

༄ ༄ ༄ ༄

Marilyn woke on automatic pilot. She had been through this same routine so many times before. Put the coffee on, throw the suitcases in the car while she waited for the coffee to perk, hunt for the ticket, check it twice, make sure it is in order, check the briefcase, make sure she had her speech. (She never used any of her speeches in the written form, but she always prepared one. "You never know when words will escape you; better to be safe than sorry." Another one of her mother's maxims that Marilyn lived by. *Too bad it did not give her a longer life*, were the words that crossed Marilyn's mind.) Check to make sure she had the phone book with Gerri's number. She didn't want to be alone in Ontario with foreigners; even Indians were included in the foreigner category when they were all Ojibways with long names and strange ways. Wolf a coffee; pour another in her 7-Eleven to-go cup and bolt for the airport. Park the car in the Econo-lot, shuttle to the Air Canada line-up, get the boarding pass, make sure the agent had her Aeroplan number, pick up a magazine, go through security, then head for her seat. Sigh and fly — that was all that was left. Four hours without a smoke. That was Marilyn's only worry.

She bought gossip magazines for plane rides: *National Enquirer, People* and *US*. Mindless gossip was all she could handle without a cigarette. Not much was going on in the world of the performing elite except divorce, scandal and affairs. Ms. Ravishing went off with some friend of her future husband's, got caught, and her fiancé declined to say their affair was over. Meanwhile, Ms. R. swore the sortie into the night was innocent; they were just friends. No one dared to say, "Yeah, but the rest of the world doesn't fuck friends, Ms. R. You obviously do." The magazine was as enthusiastic about the sortie as the couple that had indulged in it. Marilyn liked looking at the pictures, marvelling at the faces, the clothes. The world of image-construction and reconstruction was so far from her world of creation and recreation. She indulged herself in making up stories about them — performers were an intriguing bunch. She had spent so much of her life in total invisibility, but at sixteen she had landed a lead role in George Bernard Shaw's *Pygmalion*, which landed her an opportunity to audition for a television series. She had flopped. The lights, all those people staring at her, white people telling her to relax. ("You'll be fine, you're beautiful, just be yourself.") Be yourself? Her self was wide-eyed, perfectly still and shell-shocked. Her self was a long way from relaxed.

White people had never looked at her so seriously, so intently. The cameras were rolling. The lines she was supposed to say were staring at her accusingly. She bolted. She couldn't do it.

She wondered how Lindy managed it. Theatre is so different from film. Of course, Lindy hadn't tried film yet. The director of the film had cast her without an audition. Maybe she would bomb, too. *Oh, quit, Marilyn. How can you say that about your beautiful daughter*

Lindy? Things were different now. She wanted a smoke. Her hand went to her forehead; an old anxious gesture left over from her childhood. It used to help to block her eyes from watching Bobbie's face as he screamed. Her forehead was perspiring. She wondered if it had perspired in her childhood. She let the magazine drop in her lap and looked out the window. Best not to remember. They must be over the Prairies, she told herself methodically changing the subject of her private world. The land didn't stretch out from this point of view the way it did in all those novels about the Prairies she had read. It was a giant patchwork quilt made of uneven squares coloured in different shades of green to yellow and deep black to light brown.

"We're approaching Winnipeg," the man next to her said. Her eyes registered private surprise. *Am I wearing a friendly welcome-to-my-world look?* she wondered to herself, her brows furrowing with this question. She turned to answer him.

"Yeah?" was all she said. She looked at him for a while. He looked like he might know why the earth was all different colours down below. She decided to ask him. "Do you happen to know why some of the dirt squares are brown and some black?"

He did know. He told her that the colour depended on how long the earth had been lying fallow: black is recent, light brown meant that the ground had been fallow for about a year. In crop rotation, the different colours of green and blond signified different grains, or poor quality crops, sometimes drought. Marilyn loved that story. She stared at the patchwork quilt of colour the earth had created based on its thirst. Parched dry land was grey. Dark brown was well watered. Good crops were emerald or greens with a hint of blue; thirsty crops were blond-green. She smiled at the blanket below.

"Manitoba and Saskatchewan have been plagued with drought for some time now," the man said.

"Really?" Marilyn wondered why that wasn't bigger news. She found herself easing into a conversation she was not at all interested in having, and the desire for a smoke died.

§   §   §   §

Gerri was waiting at the rail just outside the baggage room. Marilyn was glad. The man had been taken by her and was hinting at seeing her sometime in Toronto: "Maybe we could have a drink or something?" To which she smiled and said, "I don't drink." Just as she dodged a direct decline to his question, Gerri's ebullient voice called out to her. The conversation with the man ended. On their way to Gerri's home, Marilyn told her about him. The story made Gerri laugh. "What do you expect, darlin'? You are looking more stunning by the day. Divorce has been agreeable to you over the years." They laughed.

"Gettin' rid of a hundred and eighty pounds of ugly will do it every time." Marilyn was surprised at the foulness of her own remark. Where did that come from? Gerri found it amusing. Marilyn corrected herself. "No. I think it has something to do with me being on the prowl. I'm looking, Gerri."

"Well, that's good, because a friend of mine wants to meet you."

Marilyn was curious, but Gerri didn't say anything further and Marilyn's Salish sensibility forbade her from asking. It wouldn't be modest. They exchanged pleasantries about people they knew in Marilyn's home province. Both women had originated there, some two hundred miles from one another. They weren't the same nation, but their colonial history and national responses had been similar so they felt like they had a lot in common. Conversations centering on their common history usually kept people friendly with one another for a long time. Besides, there was something about all the different Nations west of the Rockies that bound them together. Perhaps it was the mountains that invariably surrounded them and gave them a different perspective on things. It seemed that the Indigenous people from those nations who grew up surrounded by mountains had a gentle laissez-faire way about them, without knocking the initiative out from under their feet. Marilyn found that the Eastern and Prairie Native peoples who were assertive were also somewhat callous, and many of them were just plain predatory. *Some of them are barracudas and the others are sharks,* Lindy had said. *Yeah, and the barracudas are always trying to put the sharks into a feeding frenzy,* Marilyn thought to herself. There was something about them, though, that fascinated her. Eastern Natives seemed to be much more glib about white people and their ways than Natives in the West. They seemed to know them more intimately, in an emotionally distanced way. The antics of white people, their meanness, didn't shock them. Fascinated as she was at the prospect of meeting Gerri's friend, she reminded herself to be cautious. *You don't understand these people, Marilyn,* she told herself.

Compared to Easterners, she came from a village of people who had an unsophisticated and naively hopeful attitude toward people and government. It always seemed to work against them.

Still, she understood her own. She knew where the boundaries began and where they ended, and there was a warming comfort about that. Marilyn had a clear picture of the givens with her own people, an intrinsic knowing about where to tread and where not to, how to say things and how not to, what was courteous and what was not. She was not familiar with Easterners in the same way.

"Aren't they the ones about whom the old people say they always have their coats off?" Marilyn said. Gerri looked puzzled. Marilyn continued, "You know, they're always fighting — fighting the government, white people, fighting each other, fighting whoever they believe is getting in the way of whatever their personal sense of justice happens to be."

"That would be T.J.," Gerri said, and she smiled.

In the West, everyone who did not grow up in a bowl surrounded by mountains was essentially an Easterner. Having an Easterner interested in her was slightly scary. It was exciting, because he would likely be intellectually and politically astute, but scary because he would just as likely be shark-like. Maybe she wasn't all that ready to share her life with someone.

Gerri started to tell her the story of how her friend had asked her if she knew who Marilyn was. Gerri told him she did know her, that in fact Marilyn was headed for Toronto. He asked if Gerri thought that maybe Marilyn might be interested in coming out for coffee after the gathering.

"Does this invite to coffee qualify as a date?" Marilyn interjected.

Gerri didn't answer. She just laughed. They were quiet for a while. Toronto had an unreal quality for Marilyn. It always made her feel a little odd, as though she were not actually located in any particular place in the world but rather floating along just above the city. Marilyn had no real interest in being in Toronto beyond making this presentation. She was curious about none of its landmarks or the city's characteristics. She was aware that the city was big and cumbersome and at the same time very compartmentalized, but these things were nothing more than words. The area of the city that hosted gatherings featuring Native people as participants and speakers covered about a square mile. Marilyn had been called to speak to one group or another once or twice a year for several years now. She had never been outside the boundaries of the square mile.

Marilyn could hear Gerri chatting away again, reporting the news about the people she worked with to organize the gathering, the difficulties they had had and the sorts of attitudes Marilyn would be up against. Marilyn made mental notes about it all without responding emotionally. She was completely apathetic about the problems of organizing people in Toronto; after all, what did she care, she didn't live there. She listened to Gerri's monologue enough to make some intelligent comment every now and then, while still drifting off into her own space. While Gerri carried on, Marilyn floated above the city along with the car, which was riding the freeway, a few stories higher than the landscape from the airport to near downtown where Gerri lived. The urban sprawl below took on distance and seemed so much less threatening than when you were in the middle of it. She was saying this to herself as Gerri pulled off the freeway and plunged the car into the city. Shit. Not long afterwards, they arrived at Gerri's.

Gerri rented a duplex in some place called the "Annex." *Must be expensive*, Marilyn thought to herself, but she had never found the crassness to actually ask Gerri what the place cost her. It was an upstairs two-bedroom with the landlord living below her. This was never an ideal situation for any tenant, and given Gerri's activist, gregarious nature, friction was beginning to build between her and the landlord. Gerri seemed to take it all in stride, as though it were inevitable that a landlord should try to give an Indigenous tenant an unfair shake. She took him on, was well within her rights and was winning, but the fool seemed to be bent on foolishness; he was threatening to take her to court. Gerri was all set to go — sometime next month they would have it out, once and for all.

Marilyn was curious that this did not upset Gerri more than it did. Marilyn always moved when landlords got finicky. She had started to realize why: when she was younger, she had raised two kids, and they might call the welfare office on her. *Who might call the CAS? Who might . . .* Oh God, she had hated raising those two girls under the gun. She was always terrified of being reported, being checked up on, and losing the kids. She had to tell herself not to think about it. Gerri was going on about her roommate. *Focus on the roommate*, Marilyn instructed herself. *How can I?* she asked herself, *when I have never seen the woman.* They lugged Marilyn's bags up the stairs, huffing and puffing.

"I got to drop some of this excess weight," Marilyn quipped, bringing up a who-cares kind of chuckle. After she had hit thirty-five, Marilyn found she struggled with weight gain like a lot of her fellow Salish women.

"Keeper genes," Gerri commented in a matter-of-fact tone.

"Keeper genes?" This brought Gerri's man friend back into the conversation. Now how the hell does someone get up the curiosity level to explore genetics enough to know about keeper genes? Marilyn wondered whimsically without dwelling on it or making a note to ask Gerri. Marilyn found herself wandering through the sound trail made by Gerri's voice. She relaxed into following its cadence, rhythm and accent with a pleasant satisfaction. The accent had dimmed after decades of being away from home, but it was there, and somehow hearing it in Toronto was particularly sweet, she supposed because it was incongruous to hear a Shuswap accent here in this strange town. She drifted.

As she drifted, an image of a man sitting across from her in the room took shape in her mind. The image made her want to sit up. She felt her body awakening; cell by cell, it began to warm up. Weird, she thought, but didn't pay it much mind. Instead, Marilyn waited for a break in the conversation, and then described the man she was imagining to Gerri. Gerri's eyes opened wide, her mouth dropped and she leaned back onto the couch.

"My gawd, have you met T.J.?"

"I must have," Marilyn said, knowing full well that she hadn't. This reminded her of the photo that had become a moving picture of the child Marsha's last breath. What was happening to her? She could see the man as though he were sitting there at this moment. She could almost hear him speak. His eyes had a kind of gotcha smugness about them. Small beads of perspiration formed themselves in Marilyn's armpits. They tickled her uncomfortably as they wended their way across the sensitive skin to the outer edges of her ribcage below. She leaned forward to escape the trickling sweat. She had no idea why her body was carrying on this way. It was like being immersed in physical fear without experiencing the emotional terror of it. Weird.

"Oh, you'd remember him if you did. He is extremely unique," Gerri said. Marilyn thought about her failing memory; she had a lot of days that she remembered very little about. Over the years there were a lot of gaps. Some of the gaps stretched over long periods of time. Lost memories. She must have met him and forgotten; otherwise, this other thing was becoming too real. She didn't want to tell Gerri about either of these two things — her memory loss or her drifting images. The memory loss was an aspect of herself she had kept secret from everyone and she wanted to keep it that way. The other thing seemed unreal and unnameable. She shrugged to avoid flushing. *I must have seen him somewhere before*, she repeated to herself. *Where would it have been?*

"Did you meet him during Oka?"

Lighten up, Gerri. "No," Marilyn answered, her voice as bland and matter-of-fact as she could make it. She didn't like the line of questioning Gerri was pursuing and she decided to deflect it. "But I have heard of him over the years. As a matter of fact, people have been telling me that he thinks just like me since I was about twenty. I'm not sure I want to meet someone who thinks like me." The subject was sufficiently altered. The best deflection was a piece of truth.

"Why not?" Gerri had those eyes, those eyes that seemed to see forever. It made Marilyn always want to tell her the truth. She liked Gerri. She was aware that to like Gerri, you had to trust her. Well, not exactly. It was more that you had to trust that your real self would always be good enough. Outside, Westwind heard Marilyn and whistled approval. Marilyn had no way to know that she was being affirmed, so she paid little attention to her own words.

"I'm a pest. I tend to say what's on my mind without much regard for tact and, generally speaking, Salish logic is inarguable. That would be all right if I could mellow out my comments with tact, but mostly my mouth gets into gear while my brain remains disengaged. I'm arrogant in those tactless moments, and consequently, I tend to piss people off. Could you imagine two of us like that bumping up against each other?"

"Well, apparently T.J. read some article you wrote for the *Womanist* and he liked the clear thinking in it."

The image of him disappeared. "How odd, a man who reads the *Womanist*. That was actually a speech. They taped it. Someone else must have transcribed it and submitted it to the *Womanist*."

Gerri had an amazing mind for detail and order. She rarely let some side comment slide if she thought it needed challenging or clarifying, like the one Marilyn had just made, even if it was punched up at the beginning of a paragraph and followed by a change of subject.

"T.J. comes from a matriarchal culture, so reading feminist literature is not odd at all."

There was a sharp edge to the sound of Gerri's voice, some faint hint of who do you think you are, or maybe it was a scolding for assuming the worst in men. Marilyn felt the hint but refused to query Gerri about what was underneath it. She preferred to keep her cognition secret. This way she could stew over it in private. In any case, the conversation was sufficiently far enough away from any intimate place that would force Marilyn to release a piece of her secret knowing. They slipped into the old habit of dancing on the outer edge of life.

Marilyn was becoming comfortable again. The trials of the last day at work were light years away. While she didn't like the idea of meeting this man, it seemed sweetly romantic that someone would travel nine hours by car to meet her because of that speech. She remembered its first lines: *Peace, freedom from strife, freedom from war, freedom from conditions that annoy the mind. We have not known peace since the Europeans first came to this land. It annoys my mind . . .* She recited the words to herself then laughed.

"What's funny?"

"Well, the whole article was rooted in definitions of words. I took the meanings right out of the dictionary. I used to think we had a hard time understanding this language. Now I am convinced that people do not pay much attention to what they are saying or do not understand the meanings of some very common terms. Not even white people speak this language with any disciplined understanding. Later, scads of white people told me that my definition of peace was so powerful — almost poetic."

She remembered how emotional the delivery of the speech had been. The tension was so thick it felt difficult to move. Every nerve in her body had stretched itself tight for every single day of the crisis. Everyone she knew, Native or non-Native, worked furiously to resolve the Oka crisis peacefully but without actually asking the Mohawk people to give up. The tension had intensified, it gained weight, became obese like an invisible oppressive monster that lived outside in the air, inside her heart, her mind, her body and spirit. Every cell in her body had seemed to push up on the tension, which gained weight minute by minute. The army was seen only on television, yet it felt like the little green men armed with assault rifles and waiting in their camps amid the tanks and heavy artillery were getting closer and closer to one's own doorstep no matter how far away from Oka one was. Minute by minute, her emotions wrapped themselves tighter around the tiny numbers of people inside the treatment centre at Oka, until they became more significant to her than her own relatives. Some strange and ethereal significance had claimed them, her, and thousands of other Native people, had clutched at everyone until they were like fragile heroes and heroines who refused to see that taking on the Canadian army was absurd.

"And ...?" Gerri encouraged her to finish.

"Well, I took the definition straight out of the dictionary."

That was years ago. The memory still hung in the air like an invisible dome of pressure even as the murder of a young Ojibway at Ipperwash passed without response. For so many people, time was measured by Oka. So much heart had been invested in it. The absurdity of this — clutching at the memory of Oka as though it were yesterday — seemed insane right now At the same time, it all seemed so entirely sensible in a crazy kind of way.

"Where do warriors go when the battle dies?" Marilyn asked, not really expecting an answer.

"Oh, T.J. hasn't given up. He goes back and forth between Ipperwash and the Confederacy trying to drum up support for the Ojibways. For some reason the Ipperwash incident doesn't seem as sexy as some Mohawks on the bridge standing off against the Canadian army, but he hangs in there."

§ § § §

During Oka, even Westwind had grown quiet with the weight of the emotions every human child was feeling. There were those white people who panicked; in their hysteria they cast rocks at Natives as they crossed the bridge to their homes. There were those white people and Natives who pleaded for mercy in tones unrecognizable to the rock throwers. "Isn't this Canada? Isn't this a free country? They threw rocks at our Elders and our babies. Our Elders. Babies."

§ § § §

Birds sometimes buck up against Westwind, running into him, chasing their hopes. In a storm, Raven runs into Westwind. Raven is calling to his grieving lost love with lust-breath gone wild. Westwind is unsympathetic, caught up as he is in his own lonesome song. Unmindful of birds who fly into his face hoping for a glimpse of passion endless as the night air, Westwind buffets them about, ping-pong style. When humans hold their breath, Westwind has no voice to draw. He is attracted by the smooth tones made by the breath of First Woman's relatives as they utter tribute-language to life and love. He yearns to connect with these women. When there is birdless, breathless tension,

Westwind retreats, quiets himself and sings not a word.

Bluejay sees Raven bucking the wind. It calls up his romantic desire for adventure. Like a cat he crashes in Westwind's direction, sings to his crotchety face, whispers his yearnings on the tip of his own blue-winged movement. He tries to waken the father of passion. Bluejay's romantic will is legendary, the stuff of dreams. The pumping blood of romance moves the voice of the past, melds it with future, and changes the face of wind, earth and sky. Its journey from beginning to end brings breath, voice and our winged spiritual origins together. Romance, after all, most often has a finish, Bluejay whispers to the wingtips of Raven.

Some finishes are fine, honed of warm wood colours, Raven responds. Others are honed, adzed but not planed, Bluejay recalls. Slightly burnt, weatherworn and unpainted, the finish reminds humans of unwanted breath-word-memories sounding off in the backwaters of the mind. Finishes such as this are difficult to face, Bluejay moans. No matter, Raven quips.

Marilyn was no different than anyone else. She hated to face a rough finish. Just because she hated to face it, Westwind was going to make sure she had to. Bluejay conspired with Westwind, shaving all the fine markings of a romance story, preparing it, and locking Marilyn to T.J.'s trail even before they met.

Marilyn didn't recognize the quiet of Westwind. The soundless skies, whose birds could not enjoy flirtatious play, the awesome stillness of sea, land, water and trees escaped her. The stillness of life seemed like such a relief under the dome of tension that it went unheeded, and so not understood.

Marilyn remembered the day the Quebec police invaded Oka and no one retreated. The present standoff at Ipperwash was inspired by the Oka crisis. Everyone was fed up. There was no way to say, "Be peaceful" anymore. At Oka, shots had rung out on both sides, but no one had surrendered. The army had replaced the Quebec police. "Well, now we've finally gone and done it," she had said to Catherine, who was sitting at the table with her. "Now there is going to be a war. "

"Done what?"

"A cop is dead and they have called in the army and no one is retreating."

"What are we going to do?" Catherine had asked. The assumption between them was that they, two Salish women who knew nothing about the issue between Quebec and Kahnesatake, had to do something.

"Whatever we can. We exchanged a talking stick for a wampum belt a long time ago. One of our ancestors went to the Confederacy during the recitation of the Great Law. We have tribal obligations to their law." Marilyn called her younger sister, who was always closer to such political sorts of things. She would know what to do. Under Sherri's tutelage, Catherine, Lindy and Marilyn did what they could. Everything from letter-writing, to making petitions, to speaking. Both she and Catherine travelled to Oka. Drawn there like moths to a light, they had experienced the tension in a way they never would have, had they stayed at home. Marilyn remembers standing at the Peace Camp outside the army's razor wire wondering how the men and women inside could stand it. She could barely hold up her own weight under the tension she felt in front of the wire. It didn't seem possible to be able to hold up your body from behind that wire. As it turned out, some of the individuals couldn't hold it together, but others held them up. It all convinced Marilyn that human beings are quite incredible.

✿   ✿   ✿   ✿

Marilyn was staring at her hands. She noticed a tiny wet spot on them. She looked up to see that Gerri's eyes too were filled with tears. No words passed between them for a moment, and then Gerri began talking about her friend T.J. again, how the post-Oka blues were destroying him.

The community needed to deal with the post-traumatic stress syndrome that the siege had created, but the various governments refused to recognize the syndrome existed. Not recognizing it, they saw no need to hire the necessary counsellors to help the communities work it through. Those Iroquois who cared about and had money before the crisis were now basically broke. The two Iroquois communities were popping and cracking at the seams and it seemed there was little that could be done about it. Gerri's friend did what he could, but as usual, when humans implode or explode they reach close by for the nearest enemy to scapegoat, and T.J. was all too handy for too many people.

In retrospect, the whole Oka situation seemed unreal. On the Canadian government's side, the premier of Quebec, the Prime Minister of Canada, both provincial and federal ministers of Indian Affairs had all worked to disarm the Mohawks of

Kahnesatake and Khanawake. Some sixty thousand Canadians had worked to disarm their own army. Some thirty-seven Native nations had worked to promote Mohawk sovereignty. The citizens of Chateauguay had continuously rioted against the Mohawks who had occupied the Mercier Bridge. The irony of the bridge occupation was that the structure was slated for closure due to repairs. Furthermore, the bridge had been built with loan money made by the British colonial government from trust accounts belonging to the Iroquois Confederacy. Neither Canada nor Britain had ever paid back those loans. Lastly, the Canadian government had declared that no pre-1867, pre-Confederation land or financial issues would be entertained for settlement — and practically all of the Iroquois Confederacy land and financial issues were pre-Confederation. The whole of Quebec and Ontario were pre-Confederation. Canada was not built nor settled after 1867, but prior to that date. The same was true of most southern Ontario Ojibway treaties. Marilyn wondered why there was so little support for these men trying so hard to reclaim dominion over a tiny piece of their original national soil.

Gerri's radio was playing a song by Tracy Chapman about domestic violence. Images of Bobbie bouncing off the wall, a crazed Marilyn with a wooden spoon, drunken husbands finish the song. Nightmares of violence, and women organizing, marching, phoning others, and building a future without any let-up in their ghoulish nightmare-life flooded before Marilyn. It all came together in one image. In the centre lay the terrible truth: Oka was about defending our dead. Ipperwash was about supporting men.

We don't feed men. They are the last to be cared for during an epidemic. It was likely that all the organizers of Ipperwash had been victimized by some man or other in their lifetimes. Although they could write letters, collect dimes and march for the dead, no one was inspired to hold up living men.

It seemed odd to Marilyn that Native leaders didn't remind Canada that if no pre-Confederation treaties were valid, then the whole of Canada, especially Ontario and Quebec, still required some sort of permission to settle the country. The settlers gained their initial permission to be on the land prior to Confederation from the same source with which Native people negotiated treaties — a source that Canada steadfastly chose not to recognize, namely Britain. What works for the goose, works for the gander Marilyn let that notion go. It reminded her too much of the Area Board she belonged to, the board that governed the monies for Native service organizations. She had been lobbying with the Native board members, saying that in order to have even a semblance of equality, both white members of the board and Native members should have to submit a budget for approval.

The money belongs to the whole of the Canadian people, including us, she argued. The government gets its revenues from royalties, stumpage, sales, liquor and tobacco, and land taxes. The lion's share of water rentals, royalties and stumpage comes from non-ceded land. It is primarily ours and we ought to be requiring them to practise prudent fiscal management of that money and insist that it is spent effectively, fairly and appropriately in accordance with our values, cultural concepts and notions of prudence. Let them stand with their proposed budgets and face our Elders.

That would be fair. Or let us stand separately, face our own governments, receive approval from our governments, and receive transfers based on self-government approval, just like them.

The logic was too radical and terrifying for her colleagues; some of them shook when she merely mentioned such things. None of them actually believed they were colleagues with the white people, equal in every way, and her notions of cooperation with white people seemed to scare them. Behaving as equals requires that we believe we deserve the same things, that the same rules apply. Most of the board members were so grateful for every penny they squeezed out of the budget meetings, in the end they were prepared to enable white people to make Indigenous people pay more for whatever services they received. And they seemed almost glad to receive less money for doing the same work. It was kind of a rule of thumb for the colonial process. Marilyn sighed. Somewhere along the line we lost our sense of logic.

Eastwind interfered: "Logic is a spirit-to-spirit question of relationship, not a math question." Marilyn heard this. The voice was male, unrecognizable. She shook her head back and forth, squinted her eyes like an old she-bear trying to recognize the body in front of her, the one making sound. No picture came.

⑤ ⑤ ⑤ ⑤

Gerri talked more about her friend T.J., the loss of his family and wife, his aloneness and the attacks some of the key people in the crisis were making against him. She defended him. She had watched him work day and night, without sleep, and so forth.

This seemed to always be the bottom line criteria for goodness among the Salish nations. *You can busy yourself doing the wrong thing, but as long as you are busy someone will defend you to your death.* Marilyn scolded herself for the nasty remark. She really ought to give the man a clean start. She decided to turn in.

I must be getting cranky in my old age.

Marilyn and Gerri exchanged "good nights." They had this habit of saying a last line or two from their beds, like two sisters facing one another from their bedrooms and exchanging a few last thoughts before finally turning in. Marilyn liked this little ritual between them. Silence fell in pieces shortly after.

⑤　⑤　⑤　⑤

Night, sometimes she falls restlessly. She adorns herself in the sickness of the past, reshaping old images without their old outcomes. On those nights the body dreams fitfully, it awakes with a start; it peers through the blackness trying to catch a glimpse of the familiar. If the body is not at home, momentary terror stops the eyes from seeing. Sitting upright on the strange couch, Marilyn tried to remember where she was. She felt the thing under her: a couch.

Whose couch? Ah, Gerri's. Her mind grappled with the faded dream. A hallway, two little girls, a thin woman reaching for them, unable to catch them before they retreated into some dark opening, then the feeling of being hurtled through space, the sudden jar of landing somewhere and she awoke.

The picture got her mind racing again. What is she going to do about it? She had to think it through. Every time she tried, the memory of herself as a child invaded and she found herself chasing a car screaming, "WAIT." Then it changed to a smaller version of her slipping and sliding in snow, wearing rubber boots that served only to freeze her feet. She fought to keep up with her mom, who kept barking at her to hurry amid threats of never taking her anywhere again, while Marilyn cried "Wait!" in a painful whimpering voice. She managed to kill the memories, begin thinking again, only to have them push up, interfering with her ability to reach some sort of plan to change the condition she had created for her daughters. Some sort of accounting had to happen.

Breath, wind, voice, excuses. Fatigue, slow shallow breaths, oppressed breathing patterns. Lindy.

Arguing with the self.

Burnout: when what you're doing contradicts your beliefs. Belief is old, coded into the memory of every cell. Tribal consciousness, lineage memory, old beginnings were pushing up at the new layers inside Marilyn.

"I was sick," she pleaded for herself, "near to death." She begged the taskmaster inside for forgiveness.

Illness in the mother has its own terror for children. The ancient Salish law says: adults are responsible for their own care and the care of children.

"But I didn't know anything then."

That doesn't help the children. She brought children into the world filled with a tremendous absence of understanding about what is involved in staying alive, in being, in living. Somehow her world went from a condition of knowledge to a condition of ignorance. Somewhere along the line, the most fundamental and basic living skills had not been handed down. It dawned on Marilyn that while illness enabled her to forgive herself, it did not help her daughters free themselves from the chains of fear that held them to caring for her and worrying about her, even now that she was well.

Time spent mothering and nurturing Marilyn was time her daughters did not take for themselves. Since she had authored this condition, she was responsible for altering it. First, she had to get past the guilt and pain of remembering how she had been as a mother, then maybe she could think herself clear to resolving the fear she knew must plague her daughters. As the mother, she was responsible for establishing the atmosphere, the spirit, the nurturing with which her children were raised.

What the hell does responsible mean, anyway? she asked herself. She looked about her, listened for Gerri, decided she was asleep. Then, carefully, she slid out of bed, turned on the kitchen light and quietly looked up the word. Responsible: ability to respond appropriately. Defensiveness and guilt would help no one. They were inappropriate responses. She felt lighter, energized, and even hopeful. Everything is fixable. She returned to her couch and slept peacefully.

৯ ৯ ৯ ৯

Time is a critical illusion. It demarcates the difference between the physical and the spiritual world, between sanity and insanity, between life and death, consciousness and coma. Consciousness requires a deep appreciation of time. Marilyn was losing the system for calculating and marking it. She did not feel inspired to live within the boundaries of its illusion, make reality spring from it, or hook her being firmly to it. She was losing her capacity to wield it and this made it feel so real, so necessary and so tangible. This illusion was becoming the foundation of her impassioned being in the physical world. As its boundaries blurred she lost her hold on passionate being.

The winds of our fathers breathe freedom as the precondition for the burgeoning reconciliation of the body to its spirit, heart and mind. This reconciliation requires peace. The peace is carefully crafted by the nurturance of mothers, aunts and grandmothers. The men and women who were to inherit the skills of our grandmothers, mothers, fathers and uncles are all off balance. Siege precludes freedom. Siege is the absence of free upward and outward movement. It is a windless, directionless, breathless state of being.

The absence of peace is the enemy of time's illusion. Chronic strife bleeds the mind of its ability to indulge it. Nature abhors a vacuum. Marilyn needed some illusion to replace it. She could not face the depth of her agitation. She became dispassionate. It deluded her into believing she was at peace with the world. The illusion of peace cut into her belief in time, and the markers between the dream world and reality disappeared.

It sometimes happens that even wind retreats from its own passion. The whispered language of the wind softens, excuses, muses but does not inspire movement. Time stands still where there is no movement. The illusion of time is frozen by the space created by the inertia. Inert, the power, which is passion, looks elsewhere for expression. It searches for busywork and details to fill its eyes. Immersed in busywork, the body can no longer access its passion. Without expression, passion cannot be refilled. The body empties its compassion in tiny vessels of old voices — words repeated mindlessly by other busy workers destroying the illusion of time, creating dead spaces where no spiritual connection can be sparked up. Dead air space, a hot windless summer day, stagnation, tinder dry, waterless, voiceless, power stripped, parched, it vacuums the life out of those around it, pulling it from the centre to the periphery of the bearer's voice.

Westwind retreats when we lose our grasp of time.

ॐ   ॐ   ॐ   ॐ

Toronto is hot in June. Westwind sleeps. He refuses to waken until fall. It is as though the fight between warm and cold is so intense that, tired at the effort to push back cold, Westwind becomes comatose. The air is wet and thick in the absence of Westwind's cooling breath. It hangs about, an unwanted loiterer pressing against the body, blocking its urgent need to perspire. The pollution rises with the heat. It gives substance and colour to heat's thickness. Perspiration films the skin, mixes with the pollutants, creating a thin, sticky, inescapable dark sack over the exposed body. Marilyn tried to ignore the discomfort June in Toronto created for her. She moved as little as possible. Except for her frequent trips to the bathroom to wash the city mud off, she just sat and waited for her evening speaking engagements.

Gerri had an interesting selection of books, magazines and papers to read. Marilyn read, smoked and drank coffee and water by turns all day until supper, when Gerri would return to take her to the venue for her speech. The day crawled by without much mishap. Marilyn noticed early in the day that she was growing more and more agitated. The image of the man coming to take her for coffee later in the evening kept appearing on the pages of whatever she read.

Sometime around two in the afternoon she gave in to whatever it was that kept pushing up the picture of him. Fear. Right away she escaped feeling the fear by imagining the worst case scenarios about T.J.'s motive for offering to take her for coffee, and the shallowest of reasons for her acceptance. *Probably been too long since I had a man. Probably he's lots like other so-called political haunches. Probably his infamy goes hand-in-hand with taking advantage of a lot of womanizing opportunities and playing them out on broken-winged, lonely single Native women who are desperate to have some part of their dreams fulfilled, even for a few short moments. Maybe a lot of white women are just as desperate. We lead fairly loveless lives — at least it feels that way.* Marilyn picked up a pen and coined a few lines for herself in her tattered old travel journal. It carried over twenty years of scribbles from her journeys. She got suddenly curious about what the past years of entries looked like and flipped through the pages. The entries took her mind back to other trips, and the picture of the man and the morbid thoughts about loneliness and lovelessness disappeared.

Seattle, Washington, 1971

They are talking about an armed encampment — it sounds like a publicity stunt. I tried to make them see some sense. Weapons are not toys. The

American government is serious about protecting its interests. I'm heading home tomorrow. I am not ever going to pick up a weapon unless I plan to shoot someone. When I told them that, they all got strangely silent, like I was nuts. Lindy got her eyeteeth today. Another milestone. She should be through crying about it by tomorrow night. When we get home, we'll do something special.

It stunned her now to think that she could have written about Lindy's first tooth, killing, and the nature of publicity so glibly, without giving any one of them more weight than the others, as if there was no emotional distance between Lindy's teeth and killing white people. *Was I really that numb?*

Cache Creek, 1972

They're arming themselves here. I still don't feel like carrying a weapon I don't mean to use, so I told everyone I was leaving. Someone called me a traitor; that seemed to give everyone else permission to holler sell-out, coward, and so forth. Half the crew was hung-over. I feel so sad. I have to re-think this business of armed this and thats. I don't feel like I am afraid, or traitorous. I just don't feel like I am clear enough about my feelings to explain it to anyone.

It had taken her a year to feel curious about her feelings around killing. Why had it gone that way? What was to know? She remembered not feeling much of anything then. She read through her journal to see the journey, track it and make sense of it.

Ottawa, 1974

There are injured people everywhere. We barely managed to get out on time from the hellhole Parliament Hill and the caravan created for us. Some people got arrested; some of us got away. All of us are shaken. It all feels so unreal. Just six months ago, the railroad workers did the same thing — demonstrated on Parliament Hill. Nothing happened to them. Of course, they were all white and working — taxpayers, voters. It happened so fast: one minute we were full of ourselves, next minute we were just trying to find a way out from under all the clubs, cops. The white people were mostly CPC-ML behind us, blocking an orderly retreat. It almost seemed planned.

Unreal. Planned.

Mount Currie, 1975

The mosquitoes are horrific here. Sister and baby both are convulsive from it. I am almost hysterical from all the bites. There must be something our ancestors did to ward off the illness that goes with all these bites. Been interviewing people all day. Nationhood is on everybody's lips here. Tomorrow, we work in the gardens, then back to the city to raise money. Fund rejection has had a positive influence on the spirit of the Lil'wat people here. Dependence has to be the worst condition you can force on a human being, Mary.

"Gawd, I barely remember this," she whispered out loud. *I wonder whatever became of Mary?*

It was not a real question so she carried on.

Constitution Express train, 1980

The conversations are endless. The thinking here is not a bit cohesive. Everyone seems to have their own perspective, their own reason for being on this train.

She paused to remember the ride. Women with babies were nursing, feeding, changing and chatting. The faces on the train seemed so animated in contrast to her memories of the old village. Is that what it takes to uplift us, to spit in the face of the whole darn colossus somehow? she wondered.

Marilyn couldn't help but notice the gap between Lil'wat and the train ride. Five years. She had hidden from the world for five years. She remembered those years. In 1975 her husband had disappeared for the last time, never to return. She waited for him, just like her little girls did, sitting by the window night after night, peeking out and talking to herself about how tonight he would come back. She went to work each day in a numb stupor, returned at night only half-alive. All of them, Lindy, Catherine and she, tried desperately to will his return. Marilyn took to begging him to come back inside her head. She told herself that he left because she nagged him too much, complained about stupid little things, like the newspapers on the floor; she promised to be good, just please come home. It was so hard to mother the girls by herself. Now she wondered what the words of her daughters were on those nights when they all sat waiting, waiting, waiting.

Her mind took to retracing the growing anger inside her in those days of waiting. It seemed the more secret promises she made to him to do better if he came back, the angrier she got when he didn't return. There was no place to put the anger. It just kept getting bigger inside. The girls began to annoy her with their waiting, their endless questions about when he was coming back, why did he leave. At first, she tried to be hopeful, comforting, but that began to look and feel ludicrous. They looked so desperate, so hurt and so lonely. Marilyn hated seeing it. She, too, felt so desperate, so hurt and so lonely, and she didn't want to be reminded of it. After a while, she started telling them to shut up and go to bed. She winced at the sight of the two girls holding hands, scurrying to bed frightened, desperate and so alone now that Daddy was gone and Momma was so mad at them so often.

Her mind held her trapped in that morbid time warp until Gerri bounced into the room and filled it with her own excitement about the talk tonight. Everything was going to be just fine, the room would be filled with interested people, her friend would take them for coffee afterward and best of all, thus far all the sessions were beginning on time. Marilyn knew she was afraid now. He sounded so wondrous, so upright and so terribly sane, and she felt so mediocre, so hypocritical and so insane. She grabbed hold of Gerri's last phrase and clung desperately to it, trying to respond from someplace deep inside. "On time." This was a feat in Indian country. On time was rare. She managed to climb out of the trap her mind had clutched her in, but the effort tired her. She felt the tiredness someplace deep inside that seemed to be so old, so endless. She focused on Gerri. Time slowed. She shook her head and like a bubble popping, she got hooked into Gerri's enthusiasm, but only superficially.

Behind the mask of her enthusiasm there still was this agitation. After she renamed it, she was able to ponder it. It was Gerri's friend. The friend brought up the pathos of never having had anyone drive anywhere to hear her speak and take her for coffee. *Indian women have to be the most neglected women in the world*, she sighed.

Somehow this brought her to re-listening to the virtues of Salish women extolled by everyone around her while she grew up: Salish women are hard working. "Good worker" was the only compliment she had ever heard. She suspected this upbringing somehow opened the door to neglect. It made all of the girls work like driven animals, oxen harnessed to an invisible plough. Bucket after bucket of berries danced around her delicate four-year-old hands. Day in and day out, children and women all worked like maddened, mindless animals until overwork became normal.

She pictured herself laundering cloth diapers in the bathtub, wringing them out, hanging them to dry late at night on a clothesline, which rarely worked. On rainy nights after a full day of school she hung diapers across the backs of chairs, on door-ways, towel racks, the shower rod, even on the flat surface of the thing which served as a table. It seemed to her that she went to school in between moments of work. After hanging the diapers, she read furiously, legs shaking, her mind wrapping itself around foreign words as she finished her essays and dove into endless reports before the girls woke again at six. She shopped only on Fridays and Cat had to help push Lindy and the groceries home. She revisited the image of Cat, shorter than the handle of the stroller, leaning back to get the wheels up onto the sidewalk, while Marilyn pressed on the handle with her wrist, still clutch-ing three brown sacks of food, trying to give her a hand. Cat was so small; too small. Marilyn nearly choked.

This brought up the memory of herself heaving and sweat-ing over the task of cutting cottonwood trees and hauling them through the bush to home. She could see her three-year-old self trying to carry two logs, could hear her mom hollering for her to hurry because it was getting dark. Cougar will get you, she shouted. This generally got Marilyn's legs shaking and made the struggle all the more difficult to win. Where was Dad? This snapped her out of it. She knew where her dad was: he was buried in the old cemetery on her reserve. Tucked neatly away in his graveyard, he escaped the responsibility of child-rearing. She never bothered to visit him. She looked away from the window and blanked out.

§ § § §

They arrived at Marilyn's speaking venue. Gerri bounced out of the car, busied herself with grabbing things and was soon introducing people to Marilyn. Her friend was nowhere in sight. This worried Gerri. Gerri was proud; it would embarrass her to have insisted Marilyn meet her friend if he didn't show up. Marilyn felt relieved. When the speech ended, she stood at the back of the room talking to someone who looked homegrown. Turned out to be a relative from Sto: loh territory.

"What on earth are you doing here in Toronto?"

They engaged one another in friendly gossip about who was doing what to whom, et cetera, laughing and chatting by turns. Then the room seemed to stop breathing. It changed its whole feeling. *He must be here*, Marilyn thought. Everything slowed down. She turned to look. Directly across from her, hitching up his pants, was the biggest Indian she had ever seen. He filled the room with his presence. His head was massive and cocked to one side. His face wore no expression except a kind of mildly arrogant well-here-I-am look. Marilyn could suddenly feel her body, every inch of it. She could feel the muscle tissue contract, relax, feel her legs stretch as they moved toward him, feel the action her hips made as they moved her legs forward, feel her hands. She became conscious of her hands — lovely hands, graceful and expressive. She unconsciously counted on them to help her think, speak and draw difficult concepts from the corners of her mind and make them easily understood as well as irrefutable. Her hands were powerful partners in search of truth. It was this that gave them their grace and beauty, though Marilyn was altogether unaware of it; she just knew they were nice hands.

She introduced herself and smiled.

"Hi," he breathed the word out, "my name's T.J." Baritone, lyrical and smooth. The voice caught her off guard. It sped up the blood already pumping a little too fast. She breathed a long measured breath to try and slow her blood. Not fast enough. She felt her face flush. This annoyed her. His lips smiled an annoyingly triumphant grin. He looked as though he was deliberately trying to create the precise effect on her body that she was now experiencing. Smug rascal. Her eyes flashed. His eyebrows rose in response, then Gerri came over and asked if they had met. They said they had, and they all readied themselves to go to a restaurant.

The evening air was not as thick or hot as it had been earlier, though it wasn't quite as cool as Marilyn would have liked it. Outside, Gerri named the restaurant, laid out the plan to go dump Marilyn's briefcase with its unused speech inside, then trundle over to the café. T.J. filled Gerri in on the gossip from the crew that they had all come to know during the Oka crisis. He laid out the various political fractionating that was going on without much regard to how disarming this fractionation was, or how ludicrous given the general condition of powerlessness Native people were in. It never ceased to disturb Marilyn when she heard a Native man talking glibly about the divided condition of the political communities from which they both arose. She wondered if only women felt pained by it.

"The antis are having a field day now, what with the traditionalists split into dozens of groups. Civil war. We're going to have another civil war," T.J. said. This didn't seem to upset him.

"Kind of like the Xhosas and Zulus of South Africa. Apartheid is still in place and the victims are axing one another with all the rationalization and blessings of their leaders," Marilyn said. A moment of silence followed. T.J. cast a serious side-glance at her while she continued on. "Do you think the implosion that follows resistance gets worse each time we fail to count the gains and accord ourselves the compliment of a job at least partly done?" Her voice eased these words out slowly and with a careful softness. Marilyn got the feeling he was mildly taken aback by the thought and surprised at the question.

"Implosion?"

"Blowing inward, instead of blowing up."

"I know what it means." He cast her the sweetest smile she had ever received. She flushed again. Quit, she told herself. It was absurd for this to be happening to her now at her age. She had never blushed and flushed as a youth. For her entire adult life she took male flirtatiousness with a grain of salt. It wasn't modest to blush, and for the most part she was unaffected. He was still looking at her. She wanted to turn away. If she did he would know she had to look away. She didn't and her body carried on responding despite her explicit instructions to the contrary. Still smiling, he carried on, "I just never heard it put that way."

In the beginning, Marilyn didn't get it. She thought she did but the lines between truth and hope blurred. She fell in love with T.J.'s potential. The buttery voice and all her flushing and blushing, the sly smile felt so tacky, but like a furtive bird she approached him. *I'm in the middle of a cheap harlequin romance, that's all,* she told herself. She could actually picture how the words would fill up the page of a goofy love story. This helped to pop the feeling and gave her a chance to muster some control before they sat down in the café.

Some cafés are kind of frumpy. Plain booths made of cheap pine, thick benches covered with Naugahyde and wooden tables in the centre with no real artistic ambiance makes restaurants stout-looking and frumpish. The waiters in such places lack dynamism and character. They serve you because they get paid to and there is no question of whether or not they like the work. It was all they could get. They stay because they are scared to venture out again into a cruel job market without any skills to sell, and they have no savings to fall back on. Tips are sparse and it doesn't seem to matter how friendly they are to the customers, it won't get them any more tips than they get without having to make the effort to be friendly. Customers who go to frumpy cafés generally cannot afford to tip so they don't bother trying. If they do chance to catch the fancy of one of the waiters, though, they become one spoiled customer.

"So what else do you write?" T.J. asked as they sat down.

"Office policy and procedural manuals, reports, Indigenous nutrition guides, stuff like that."

"Sounds exciting." The sarcasm was not even veiled.

"Not as sexy as political propaganda or historical treatises, but it keeps me fed and on track." Her lips formed a pout. She was not accustomed to reacting emotionally to men. It felt strange. Must be the café. Her pout did not go past T.J. He leaned and breathed nearly inaudibly into her ear, "Better pull those lips in, you're going to make the ducks jealous." She wanted to laugh and cry at the same time. She let go a raucous raven-sounding squawk then settled into looking around the café.

℥ ℥ ℥ ℥

Walls breathe. They hold sound, speak to the spirit in the present, confuse pumping blood, alter brain activity. Scattered thoughts skip the process of rolling around the brain in an ordered circle designed to create rational being by passing through experiential brain banks, registering in unfamiliar parts of the mind, inciting fear. Fear speeds up the blood, triggers old emotions, hooks onto the past in a self-victimizing way without the benefit of deep experiential thought. Without direction, these bouncing thoughts move fear to near panic levels, driving breath to some places deep inside the body. In this state experience does not serve direction, it betrays, becomes a liability, paralyzing emotional movement. Emotions become strange, dangerous beings holding court inside the body, quite independent of the vessel in which they reside.

Walls holding sound repeat words fed them in random ways, in much the same way fear sparks random experiential victimization. There had been a lot of loves won and lost in this old café. Poor lovers quietly quarrelled, whispered romantic words, and engaged in illicit trysts full of lies and deceit. The whispers caught hold of Marilyn's internal voice, pumped up the phrases. Marilyn stopped breathing. Her eyes fixed on a spot beyond Gerri's face. She collected herself to halt the process that held her captive. The voices receded.

She stared at the Indians in the café. A lone man in the corner stared back. He seemed young. No, handsome. He stirred his coffee slowly, looking at her from underneath perfectly arched, teepee-shaped eyebrows. She wondered who he was. Their eyes met. He let a sweet smile play about his lips, and then she recognized him. He had been in the audience earlier. She wondered if he followed them to this place, thinking that maybe he'd join them, and then got shy. She wanted to smile back, but dared not. She felt as though she recognized him. Their eyes caught. He definitely recognized her. His eyes let go paragraphs, reminding her of how they had not really met. She had been one of those moments when stars permit men to be men in a star-nation kind of way. She choked on this and stopped looking at him. She scanned the rest of the place. From the broad range of her peripheral vision she peeked at him. He looked well satisfied.

There were a lot of Indians in this café. Well, three booths worth, which in Toronto is a lot. The sounds inside the restaurant matched the atmosphere — the ambiance, if you dared to call it that. The patrons' voices made a rolling chatter about two decibels up from the better eateries; you could hear the rhythmic clatter from forks and knives as they clacked against plates and the teeth of eaters who plunged various bits of food into their mouths. There was a heavy aroma of burger, fish and chips and toast and eggs in the air. T.J. ordered pie with his coffee and took a bite before resuming their conversation.

"Yeah, hunger and being off track sucks." This brought Marilyn's attention back to him. There was tiredness in his voice. She thought it might be the weariness of a man looking forward to the end of his working life, which he had to face without ever having had the opportunity to put away money for his retirement. It felt like it ran deep. There was probably more to it than that, she decided, but she couldn't picture what else could make him sound quite this weary. He finished his pie, rubbed his belly dramatically then quipped, "There we go, another two dollars invested in the old bread box. If I could just figure a way to get a return on the amount I invested in this thing, I would be set for life."

His mood shifted and with it followed a steady stream of stories rich with humour and filled with entertainment. Marilyn laughed till she could hardly breathe.

"Gawd, it has been ages since I laughed with a man." She choked up and the table got quiet. He was really studying her now. Westwind sneaked into the restaurant and rolled about the room, soft and quiet. He carefully felt his way about the surface of her body looking for a doorway inside. His breath caressed, wandered, stopped and searched for some fissure in the armour of Marilyn's stillness. His eyes lolled about while he seemed to wait for an opportunity. Her skin felt as though it had been touched by soft breath — Westwind's breath. Her skin wanted to free itself of its own version of Westwind's breath coming up from somewhere inside her womb, threatening to join the breath she imagined he had bathed her skin in. Her mind disconnected from her body. Her body sought liberation from the layers of old caution her mind seemed to hold tight to. The moment her mind disconnected, her skin took the opportunity to push through the cracks in the armour, opening up to Westwind's breathy presence. Once inside, her desire slipped gracefully from its drumhead prison, floated in and out of her cells at will.

Desire.

Westwind's lust-breath passion awoke her body.

Wind shapes breath. It determines being. Reliance on wind is hinged to origin. Westwind is Marilyn's father; East, South and North winds are his brothers. They are her first extended family. They all father Turtle Islanders in some way. The stillness of the lone survivor of that first carnage facing the newcomers halted Eastwind's connection to Turtle Island women but did not sever it. Eastwind brings first light, moving light, spirited light — the light that encourages being. Disconnected, Marilyn could not feel herself being fathered in the direction of free being. Un-free she cannot find peace in her varied emotional states. If she felt emotions she would react, sometimes badly. She did not trust her emotional expression to travel in any sure and reasonable direction. This made her fear any emotional expression. Fear which cannot be expressed finds its reaction in anger, hot or cold, smoldering and old. Cut off from Eastwind, Southwind's presence is felt only dimly. The dim hint of Southwind sharpens Westwind, which cancels out Northwind. Southwind brings wellness, soft warmth and nurturing. Northwind is active, brings with him the execution of the journey from light to health to passion, to action. If the breath of one is too powerful, the direction of the breath-holder becomes skewed. Too much passion leads to a life governed by lust. Lust is brainless, nearly emotionless, dispirited on its own. Lust is dangerous when disconnected from the characters our uncles and fathers all ought to shape.

The body in this state has its own memory to move from. No language is required for humans to express base desire. They only need to feel the hot breath of Westwind. Filled with desire, the body breaks discipline with whatever prisons the mind has set for it. Marilyn became aware that her hand was resting on T.J.'s thigh. She withdrew it with a snap like a burnt child. Where was she getting all this cheek? "I'm sorry," she mumbled.

She looked up. Gerri's eyes were round with shock. She was looking from T.J. to Marilyn and back. T.J. let out a satisfied, it's-all-right kind of sound and asked her when she was coming to town next.

"As soon as someone invites me," came too quickly.

"Do you do these speaks often?" He played with the spoon in his hand. His head was cocked to one side like he was strategizing about something far more important than the subject at hand.

"Yeah," she answered without too much pride. "I'm considered an expert on Indigenous feminine sociology." His eyebrows went up.

"Are you?"

"I don't know."

"Sure you do. In fact, you are the only one who really does know."

She waited for the rest. It didn't come. This remark threw her off somewhat. What did he mean by it? She hesitated to ask; instead she changed the subject.

"I'm in Winnipeg next."

"I make it out there once in a while. Got a few friends there." This started him on another roll of funny stories and quipping about the ridiculousness of some of our leaders. Marilyn realized he was conscious of how much she was enjoying his company. He looked at her every time he got her laughing. His face wore an arrogant Ravenesque expression, the one she had seen on his face back at Gerri's house before they met. She felt like he was playing with her. It was all so easy for him. Her body kept responding full throttle to whatever he did. *The feminists would have a heyday with this*, she thought. At the same time, she felt a curious desire to weep growing inside her. She misnamed it for herself: she called it the sad, lonely years of the past decade that kept playing a melancholy symphony underneath the gaiety of the moment. She persuaded herself that T.J. held the twisted desire of patriarchy's boy babies, who need to have Bluejay dancer's daughter approach, be rebuffed, fly back, lurch forward and finally crash on the shores of the very sea of love Bluejay conjures. The dance is born of internal hope, which the patriarchal dancer transforms into illusion. It took a lot of effort to hold the lonely music quiet.

She slipped back into the wind tunnel of her courting days with her first husband. There had been a lot of laughter in the beginning. It seemed to end with the decision to set up house together. It hadn't ended all that suddenly. In fact, it was so gradual she hadn't even noticed it. Now in hindsight, she realized it had been she who had tried to keep his spirits up as he slipped into longer and longer periods of moroseness. Eventually, the only thing that seemed to break up the periods of moroseness was his weeklong binges, which generally climaxed in some sort of violent drama. There was a lot of space between the binges but the rhythm of them, the regularity, never changed. Every three months or so there was a binge, a disastrous end, then a period of calm followed by a growing tension which culminated in another binge. She got so that she could feel the precise moment he was going to go to work and not return until he was broke. It was in his eyes. "See." Occasionally he was considerate enough not to take his entire paycheque and blow it, but just as often he not only blew the cheque but also lost his job. "Yeah. Violence and vagrancy are pretty big issues," she could hear her friend Gloria say after a particularly bad round.

If the rent was due, Marilyn went out and got another loan, which it took her a year to pay off. She screamed at him for days on end, and the whole thing repeated itself for about three years. At that point he took to drinking steadily rather than risk bingeing. It cost more in the end, but it was definitely less disastrous. Marilyn had to work, the girls went to daycare, and the family life drifted into a kind of emotionally oblivious repetition.

At this point, Marilyn quit being the resident cheerer-upper, as Catherine would so aptly put it nowadays. Some time following, Mat had taken to having affairs, disappearing for a week at a time and returning, job still intact and bottle still in hand. Marilyn had not even enough feeling left for him to be jealous. She plodded through her life as though she had to, not because she wanted to. That's when she took to nipping beer — during the weeks he took off. She would stare out the window apathetically wondering who he was with and when and if he would return. At first the girls tried to cheer her up, but eventually they gave up too. He always returned, at least until that last time. The apathy ended with that last disappearance when the weeks turned into months. Her desperation grew like a virus infecting and killing the relationship between her and her girls. What a life.

Her courses at university insisted that women from abusive families seek out abusive men. This all seemed so cruelly idiotic and simplistic. Secretly, she did not believe that. She knew that victims fill themselves with hope, twist it into belief, conjure reality from this belief, colour the shape of life in the mauve shades of hope-deluded being. It was all they seemed to have. *The hope is that you will find someone who is the absolute opposite of the father you left behind, unless he was kind and gentle.* She did not complete the process of thought she began. Bluejay was so gawky and colourful, so attractive; he stopped the process in her throat.

Courtship is a ritual of deceit, she decided. No one would come up to her and say, "Hi, I'm a dysfunctional jerk, would you like to be my victim?" If they did, she'd be gone in a minute. The ritual is a process of seduction: obtain trust, cultivate love and begin the betrayal slowly, waltzing from one minute to the next. Make the victim believe it's because she did this or that; make her swallow the blame. In much the same way the adult world forces children to take responsibility for acts of violence by adults, their words of violation. The emotions wrought on children are sometimes inspired by the parents' miscreant behaviour. Begin small; move slowly, until the victim is consumed by his or her own negation. When they are ready, let go the bottled rage full blast, refill the bottle, explode and refill it again. Confused, lacking voice, the victim is swallowed by fear.

Marilyn ran through her courtship years over and over, trying to see where the deceit had begun. Had she missed some crumb? No. Spirit gets hold of your own love for the world, seeks out the partner whose spirit can receive your loving expression, and binds itself to your desire. The courtship is ritual loaded with lies. It persuades the suspicious heart that yes, he is safe, he is kind; he loves me, wants me to blossom, cherishes my fire and honours my desire. Desire is about who we all are. It ought to inspire investment in one another, but it doesn't in and of itself. At some point you discover the emperor has no clothes; reality sets in. Once children are born, homes are created on the heels of courtship's powerful deceit and it's too late to turn back. The hints begin, the breadcrumbs drop, but the investment has been made; it needs nurturing and protection. You strive to care, to tenderly grow it, moment by moment. He eats up this tenderness; exploits it; shames your efforts; demeans your most sacred heart — your desire — until you no longer are able to muster belief in the dream, the hope or yourself.

The walls are bare, so are the cupboards. Marilyn's husband lay on the couch, one arm dangling over the edge. Lindy and Cat were standing at the table eating breakfast. He must have come back sometime after 2:00 a.m. He lay there, reeking of booze, taking up the space the girls needed to sit and eat. A hot fire started somewhere in her womb. The spatula was in her hand. She turned over another pancake, then stared at him for a moment. The heat swelled inside, filling her belly. She shook the spatula in his direction. The girls looked up. They must have seen the fire in her eyes. They backed away from the table. Marilyn lunged at him, swinging the spatula; he shuffled from side to side, crashed to the floor and cursed her as he awoke. He grabbed the spatula and swung back; Marilyn's nose bled. "Get out! Get out!" she shrieked.

"So where do you go when you tune out like that?" T.J. asked. Marilyn twitched. How humiliating. He had noticed that she had wandered off and he had the cheek to ask her where she had gone. She laughed self-consciously. Most would let you have that one, join the laughter and let the question slide in the joy of a shared joke, but not T.J. He was still waiting for an answer.

"Is that question rhetorical?" *Oh Christ, Marilyn, is that ever lame.*

"Nope."

Of course it wouldn't be, she said to herself.

"You really want an answer?" Lamer than the first, she couldn't seem to think of any intelligent way to put him off.

"Yeah." He slid along the yeah like it should have been obvious, like it was a given.

"The truth?" *Oh, gawd. That's it. My brain is completely out of gear.* She gave up on herself.

"That would help."

"Back in time."

"Ah," he stretched his words out like he was onto her. Where the hell was that coming from? She wanted to run and hide somewhere. He was prying. No one asks questions like that — it's plain rude. Her Salish sensibility disciplined the boundaries of her curiosity. If someone wanted to tell you something like that they did so without you having to ask. If they didn't, you could assume it wasn't any of your business, and since they didn't choose to tell you, you shouldn't ask. Questions should only arise around concepts, thoughts, never around personal data. He didn't seem to be the sort of fellow who would tolerate a "none of your business" response, however veiled it was. Sandwiched somewhere between her indignant internal monologue and his question which continued to nag her, she decided she would like to see him again, which meant she would have to forgo telling him he was rude and should mind his own business. Besides, he didn't ask anything more, so for the moment she felt safe.

Safe. She contemplated that for a moment. Not telling him anything more about where she went or what "back in time" meant was safe. From what? Him knowing. What difference did it make? It made her less vulnerable. To what? Her own feelings? Safe. Safe from her own feelings. Why wouldn't her feelings be safe? She stopped there. She didn't want to go any further down this road.

"Where're you at?" His voice was soft, solicitous, old and comforting. The burr left it. She could hear the original accent now. He used the back of his throat to form a kind of biting back vowel sound when he said his T's, instead of clicking his tongue like white people do. It formed a distinct accent. The rhythm of his old language required deep breath so it softened his voice as it gained melody when he relaxed into himself. Marilyn succumbed to the old familiar sound.

"I was thinking of safe."

"Mmm, the million dollar question. Do you feel safe right now?" She could hear Gerri suck wind. Marilyn watched her make that half-bent-torso-tucking movement (as though she were fixing to stuff an invisible shirt into some imaginary pant line) that Salish women make when someone foreign has crossed the line. *Don't go there*, Marilyn silently pleaded with him, *Don't ask*. She remembered something her brother used to say: "Just because some fool asks you a question doesn't mean you have to answer it." She decided not to say anything. She looked at him wordlessly. He met her look studiously, his eyes full of empathetic curiosity. He was as stubborn as she was willful. They stared for what seemed like minutes.

Marilyn was profoundly comforted by both the question and his respect for her decision not to answer it. To answer, she would have had to tell him safe was an internal question unless you were actually being attacked. She would have had to admit that at the moment she did not feel safe inside her emotional being. She might betray herself. In fact, she had a history of letting herself down. The question did tell her something about herself, however, and for that she was glad she had taken the time to answer it. If she hadn't, she might never have come to see what a sorry emotional state she was in. Having finished his coffee, T.J. pushed back his chair. "We should retreat to your place, what do you say, Gerri?"

Gerri looked suspiciously at him. "Okay." They busied them-selves tidying up the table.

"T.J., I'll get the coffee. You tip the waiter," Gerri instructed him as though this was some sort of usual ritual between them. The waiter hovered about collecting dishes.

"Don't bet on three-legged horses," T.J. told him. The waiter had to put his dishes down he laughed so hard. "Good one." T.J. had just made himself an indulged customer.

Marilyn loaded her things into the trunk and climbed into the back seat of the car. She leaned against the window and closed her eyes. T.J. carried on a conversation with Gerri. Marilyn drifted between the burr of their steady chatter and the hum of traffic.

§ § § §

Salish people always have been and always will be ... Line seven hundred and forty-two in her litany of oracy emerged from the spot where she had carefully tucked it. It came back to her in the same chronology as it had been handed to her. She played with this line for some time, drifting along the theoretical framework surround-ing the mental house she had built around the litany. *There are no external forces that can mar your internal sensibilities — not even death. Death is the delivery truck taking you to another eternal kind of spiritual life. You arrive there with all the truck and nonsense of your life intact.*

She shuddered, imagining herself arriving in the afterlife still feeling unsafe. The night sky was clear. From above she saw a star fall. She could not picture feeling unsafe in the spirit realm. Nothing can hurt you unless you are limited by physical being.

I must be imagining the possibility of hurt, Marilyn scolded herself. *After all, there is no real attack. No, the vulnerability is real, physical being or no,* she decided. The heart is about vulnerability. It strikes a fearsome chord, plays panic music, starts up a whole symphony of terrorizing sounds going on inside, replete with rhythmic drum tones pounding at your dignity. Dignity is spiritual; it tempers vulnerability; it depends upon spiritual belief. No Salish woman is permitted to violate her dignity or give anyone else permission to do so. Vulnerable people who betray themselves lack dignity. *I am lacking dignity,* Marilyn told herself. *How did I come to lack dignity?* She retreated from journeying to the end of the question.

ⓢ   ⓢ   ⓢ   ⓢ

Inside Gerri's house, the discussion skirted the outer edges of the issues that came up. No one seemed to want to tread into the realms of emotions any further than they already had. Marilyn found T.J. all the more interesting because of it — and less abrasive. Her body warmed to him. That place, that place that most enjoys the warming, fired up the spaces inside. She felt soft, languid, musing over the sensuousness of the night, how dark sometimes seems to just fall, its purple-black soft veiling the earth gently and deeply. Night can be so innocent, so revealing, so open, so closed, so welcoming and so unobtrusive in the moment. The heat no longer seemed to oppress. Toronto felt more familiar, reachable and tangible, as though it suddenly acquired a personality it had never had before. In the warm, moist heat Marilyn immersed herself in the physical pleasure of her body's response to T.J.

The night crawled by. T.J. no longer seemed so acutely aware of her. His eyes relaxed and looked in that ordinary way Native men do that disguises their emotional response to whatever moment is upon them. They laughed less intently. She found herself describing T.J. to herself. He was big — overweight, really, though this did not affect her the way she thought it should. His body movements looked so utterly graceful in contrast to his size. It was paradoxical. He had a way of touching one finger to his forehead when he had to articulate a complex thought. He leaned back into the words, one leg folded over the other, as though he was mustering the words for the concepts he was about to let go of from some place in the air just in front of him. It made him all the more attractive. His words spilled out uninterrupted, without the interjections that give speakers time to collect the rest of their thoughts. His mind seemed smooth-running, continuous and free of doubt. The subject began with Oka, moved on to the cigarette trade, touched on the efforts of the state to prohibit economic self-sufficiency among Native people historically, then connected the relevance of these events to the current crisis. T.J. seemed to be completely at home discussing political and economic theory.

He slid easily into the mistakes the traditionalists had made, the creation of millionaires, some of whom were unconcerned about creating a national economy from within the Confederacy. This coupled with the inability of the Confederacy to govern its people and the splitting of the nation's clans over non- issues were contributing factors spawning civil war, which now gripped the confederacy's villages.

"The Confederacy has fallen apart." The words dropped from T.J.'s mouth free of lament. It was just what they now faced. He ended his litany with, "We are stuck with the condition of knowing what we are against, but not what we are for." Marilyn's body now felt beside itself. She slipped into imagining what it would be like to roll around with him for a while — all that magnificent intensity, breathing different words, rhythmically, softly, seriously over her. His body with its great grace spilled its sensuality all over her.

He called it a night. She didn't want him to leave. "Are you staying with Gerri tonight?" she asked. She couldn't believe how cheeky this man was making her be. *No. No one makes you anything.* It was her body, her desire. She told herself it felt big only because it had been dormant for so long. It had been a long time — years, in fact. She could hear the seductive suggestion in her voice and didn't much want to engage in any fling with him. *I'm too old to fool around, besides I don't get to Toronto all that often,* she argued with her desire.

"No. I have a friend waiting for me."

Marilyn hoped this friend was not a woman. She thought not. He looked too lonely for that. He rose and strolled toward the door. Half-turning, he put out his hand to say, "Nice meeting you." Marilyn leaned forward and held him close, ignoring the hand. She whispered in his ear, "I'm from B.C. We don't shake hands." *My, he is a big man, isn't he?* she purred, stepping back, delivering the most luscious smile she could. She couldn't have been more hick-hokey if she'd tried. She wanted to kick her own backside. She was embarrassed. The only way she thought she could get through it was to treat it as though it was her normal old hick-hokey-bush-baby-kinda-self. T.J. looked at Gerri, full of surprise. His arms gestured — "What did I do to deserve this?" — and then he made a commitment to arrange to see her soon. *He must like hick-hokey*, Marilyn preened to herself.

ⸯ ⸯ ⸯ ⸯ

It was only after he left that Marilyn thought that his curiosity about her and what she did was patently thin. The evening had been taken up with laughter, a question about where she travelled, another about what else she wrote and several hours about the situation in Indian country — most of which was a monologue by him. In the dark, her restless, awakened body lay unsatisfied. She re-looked at the evening from this unsatisfied viewpoint. He hadn't even bothered to make an excuse for not listening to her speech. He had blandly announced he had been downstairs all the time talking to someone he'd run into. She hurt. Inside, a little razor cut into the goodness of the warmth he had inspired.

Gerri slipped off to bed some time after midnight, leaving Marilyn with her awakened being. Her mind drifted as far as it could from her body's reality. She thought about words and laughter. Words that sometimes began as jokes had become sage pronouncements. Old words unused and saved in this manner acquire false value, but at the same time they become valueless because eventually there is no context for using them. Saving words is another way to misuse, or refuse to use, time. She heard words she had saved and saved for this occasion, but now she couldn't place any value on them. "You are my breath" kept gliding overtop her words.

"You are my breath, my song, my wind" echoed like a chant in her mind between the lines of expository thoughts. Her propensity for analytic thinking made the poetic rhythm of breath phrases sound nonsensical to her. "You are my breath" floated soft as eiderdown inside her mind, ripped the significance from whatever analytic thoughts her mind came up with. "You are my breath, my wind, my song" sounded so old. Old words unsaid possess only false value. "You are my breath" The greater the expectation of the value of the saved word, the more devalued it becomes.

"You are my breath." She couldn't settle on any angle of perception to rationally consider the words marching about in her mind, pulling her first in the direction of breath, then thought, then breath and thought.

Sleep found her. It took her on a dream ride.

❦ ❦ ❦ ❦

Some dreams are like train rides into wind tunnels going nowhere — dangerous, breathy roller coasters in which the sound of the ride is magnified by the tunnel. The nowhereness of the journey robs the dreamer of sensory perception. The dreamer is never sure if he or she is really part of the dream. You awake feeling like you have seen a dream rather than been involved in one — like you had a dream.

In this dream everyone was talking. The movements were jerky, wasted, and mainly unnecessary. The people in the dream had familiar faces, yet their essentiality seemed to be unknown to

Marilyn. Acquaintance after acquaintance jerked and noised their way purposelessly from one end of the train to the other end while the train rode through tunnels of directionless, heavy, breathy travel. The train stopped. The noise died. Marilyn was alone on the train. Her body was rigid. The tunnel changed and she was back in that frumpy old café with T.J. This time she watched the meeting with great care and no concern for consequence, savouring the warming of her body, the melting of her walls. In her dream her breath was full, round and free.

The dream's end woke her. She peered into the dark. She tried to reorder her thinking, redirect her mind. Focus on the dream. "Meaning is so important," her great-grandmother interrupted. "Meaning is important, but expression is more important. In not expressing yourself, you lose meaning. When you lose meaning, you lose value. You may save your thought, but in the end the saviour is devalued. Eventually, the thought becomes valueless, like the holder. Speak, child, from the heart, from the mind, from the body, from the spirit. Speak, and speak from your essential self, your most ridiculous self, but speak — always remember to give wind-voice to being." Her great-grandmother sat at the edge of Marilyn's bed waiting for some kind of response.

Marilyn stopped breathing. It was dark. She hadn't turned on the light. Yet she could see Ta'ah sitting there, feet dangling, the rest of her body still. Marilyn watched as her grandma rose and reached over to play with Gerri's toilet things. She grabbed her nail clippers, twirled and twisted them. "What in the hell are these?" *This cannot be happening. Ta'ah is dead. She can't be sitting here.* "I know," Marilyn uttered aloud, "I'm still dreaming. I dreamt I woke up and found you here, Ta'ah."

"Doesn't matter. Still have to think about what I said," her great-grandmother replied, then disappeared. Marilyn reached for the light. Ta'ah was now definitely gone.

Damn, I think I'm losing it. Doesn't matter, she still had to think about it.

⑨　⑨　⑨　⑨

Marilyn awoke slowly, stretching and half-moaning while she did so. She was strangely satisfied and agitated by the night before. She slipped into her clothes and strolled into the kitchen where Gerri sat reading the morning paper. Gerri's anticipation of what all that was about last night was almost palpable. Marilyn ran a few lines inside her mind about the texture of the palpability and imagined herself asking Geri if she didn't want to put some of that curiosity in this here bowl and maybe share it around. Marilyn pictured herself waving a cutting knife and chunking off a piece of it and then popping it in her mouth. She could feel herself chewing hard before swallowing while she filled her coffee cup. After eating she would just sip the coffee elegantly. She looked at Gerri from the coffee urn for a while, but did not move.

"There is some strange freedom in dropping your defenses and floating on the tide of whatever emotions happen to be running," Marilyn finally said.

"There was a lot of electricity going on between you two last night." Gerri snapped the newspaper shut and set it aside. She looked askance at Marilyn and waited for her to explain.

"It has been so long since I laughed like that with a man." For no apparent reason Marilyn's voice choked up and her tears fell in a steady stream. Gerri's eyes opened wide. Marilyn fought to recover. Marilyn couldn't stop the tears. They felt so estranged from what she was feeling just then. She felt no sadness, and no desire to make any sound. She stared at the vapour coming from the coffee cup for a while. Finally she managed to retreat to her first thought: "I guess I'm lonely for it."

"For what?"

"Laughter, with a man."

"Hmm," she said. "You get a lot of that with that whole crew."

Marilyn's ears began to roar with an eerie, ocean-like sound. It was the same sound the sea makes when it gathers up the strength of deep water it will invest in Westwind's roar at earth and shore, calling it to change, to move the cold and make room for warm. "Move the cold, make room for warm" kept running around in her mind on the surf of ocean's roar. Her head twitched with the effort it took her body to arrest the sound and bury the words.

"You will have to kill the direction your breath is travelling and that is not possible," Eastwind murmured. It felt like the voice was in the room, was in her ear. Marilyn's body stiffened. She tried ignoring the voice. The voice repeated what it had said. She clutched at the cup. *Shut the fuck up*, she screamed to her mind. She told herself that she was imagining it. *Shut up, straighten up, and shut up.* She could hardly hear Gerri, who was going on about the guys she got to know during the Oka crisis, the laughter they engaged in when tension ran so high you just wanted to scream or kill someone. Their sense of humour saved Gerri and her friends from embracing pure hatred during that horrific summer.

In the sea's roar behind her ears Marilyn could hear laughter, a woman's laughter, vague and obscure at first, then slowly it gained volume and clarity. It was her mom's laughter. *Where was she?* Marilyn searched past the roar of the sea and the laughter. She was standing in the kitchen, the half door to the living room closed. She wasn't alone. *Who was there with her?* The image came up like a photo still being developed. Soon she could see herself and her two half-sisters standing there. Marilyn was bigger than the other two. She was looking through a crack in the door. All she could see were her mom's hands. The women in the village were canning fish and berries in preparation for winter. Among her mother and her three sisters they had only one canning kettle. None of the children were allowed in the kitchen, except Bobbie, whose sole job was to stoke the fire and stay put in the corner when he was not doing so. Sometimes the hot jars exploded. The women did not want the children to get hurt. Bobbie was the oldest boy and so he was an exception, like a man would have been. The women were helping her mother recount some story they all seemed to find hilarious. Marilyn found herself wishing she could remember it. She felt like she could use a laugh just now.

"Liff me up," Tina said. Marilyn did. In a moment she put her down satisfied.

"Liff me up, too," Trudi asked. She was the bigger of the twin sisters. Marilyn couldn't pick her up. She knew it. She tried anyway. She couldn't bear Trudi's sadness at not seeing her mom's hands like Tina and Marilyn had. She heaved up on Trudi. Trudi didn't budge. She heaved again; Trudi tried to help by pulling her-self up the half door herself. There was nothing to get hold of so this didn't help. She heaved again to no avail. Trudi knocked her hands away, sat down and huge tears escaped — soundless tears. Marilyn could feel her heart constrict. She tried to encour-age Trudi to let her try again. They did every day, all summer long. Marilyn never managed to pick her up high enough to see their mom's hands while she laughed and worked, but she kept trying day in and day out.

As Marilyn let the tears slip away the roar softened. She could hear Gerri still talking about her men friends. She could feel ten-derness in Gerri's voice, then she stopped talking. Marilyn didn't respond. She sat down. The tears dried up as quickly as they came. They sat looking at one another in silence for a while.

"Gawd girl, you got it bad." Gerri was referring to her and T.J., which was a light year away from what Marilyn had been think-ing about, but she let Gerri have her illusion. For a moment, Marilyn thought about telling the truth. Why not go ahead and tell Gerri she was gapping out? It wouldn't be that bad. Gerri might even understand. Marilyn studied Gerri and struggled to find the nerve to just face her madness. Her courage floated just out of reach. She wound up grabbing for it, then declined. Social workers are not supposed to gap. It was too dangerous to tell any-one the truth.

There was nothing more to say. The subject was finished. Gerri shook her head and smiled, then got up to make them something to eat. The moment shifted itself and the air got lighter. Outside the window was a big old oak. Marilyn stared at it.

The oak darkened; its broad leaves became cedar needles. The aromatic smell of the longhouse fire filled Marilyn's nostrils. There was a big man in the centre of the house. His voice boomed out some words about heroism and hardship and the year's toil in their village. Streams of tears rolled across his broad face. This started to make sense to Marilyn. As soon as he finished, a small group of woman started to sing. The song sounded like crying. Everyone joined in. The sadness sung like that felt so good. *Grieving helps,* she decided. *It clears the air.* She felt clear-headed. Clearer than she had felt in a long time.

She was falling in love. It was as simple as that. It was ridiculous, too. She and T.J. lived three thousand miles apart. They came from opposite ends of the colonial spectrum. It was an impossible love, filled with huge obstacles, not the least of which were cultural. He was a diehard traditional Six Nation's man; she was Salish. She wasn't sure how true to her ways she was, but she knew being around Salish people was so much more comfortable and comforting than being around anyone else. He seemed to understand the outside world. Everyone and everything that was not Salish confused and disoriented her. She tended to respond to everything non-Salish by pushing her ways forward and drowning everything in her path. It would be impossible to do that with this man.

She was falling in love. The phrase sounded so absurd. Falling in love. It had its own piteousness about it. It seemed crude and stupid to fall in love — what a ridiculous concept. English was so limiting. In her language you couldn't "fall in love." The expression for "I love you" was "You are my breath." Breath cannot fall;

it rises to touch the stars, the ancestors and the sky. Falling is what you do when love fails. *Why do these people say fall? Oh Christ, Marilyn, cut it out, you don't know this man from a hole in the ground. You have no idea what he does to stay alive. Well, bawling myself out is definitely not helping*, she decided. She tried using logic. She argued that she didn't know if he was seeing anyone else, had no idea how he felt about her. Certainly she had not a clue whether he was capable of any kind of relationship that would be remotely satisfactory to her. Logic was out.

She sank into the dream picture of what kind of man she had wanted and told herself that the likelihood of this man fitting the bill was slim. Still, she let herself feel the love come up, awaken her body, filter the thoughts and colour the memory of him. She let herself replay the conversation and rehear the smoothness of his voice and let its impact filter through this love.

There was nothing more to do. This love could never bear fruit. She could never uproot herself and transplant herself to foreign territory. She could not imagine he could either, so ensconced was he in the life or rather death of his Confederacy. She could not imagine loving him were he not ensconced in the life of the Confederacy. She was pretty sure his character hinged on the Confederacy. There was nothing more to think. This love felt so good, but it was a non-issue. It could never be realized.

She felt her way through the love that was being born inside; let it grow. *It can't hurt to feel it; just let it be*, she told herself. Her breath had gotten unbelievably calm and deep. It seemed so easy to breathe. It made her realize how laboured her breathing had been for so long. Her toes were wiggling in a shaft of sunlight, warm and cozy. She looked at them. She hadn't looked at her feet in so long. Her hands lay on her lap. They were small. Funny she hadn't noticed how small they were till just now. It was good to see them all there, her fingers and toes enjoying the warmth that was filling her up. *Love makes me stupid*, she realized, cracking up.

She felt so completely conscious of every part of her and so completely satisfied with herself that it startled her, made her see that she had not felt this way about herself before. Why had it taken so long, she wondered? The question didn't hurt. This surprised her. It should. Such questions usually did. No matter. Nothing seemed to matter but the feeling that was filling her up with immense peace and pleasure.

Even though she knew she could never realize the love she felt, she did not feel discouraged by it all. It was sad in a strange way. The sadness seemed distant, far away, irrelevant. It felt so good to know she was this capable of loving someone. It felt so good to know there was a real man for her to love. It didn't seem to matter that nothing would come of it. Her body was capable of longing for someone. She sat there enjoying the longing. Her body was excited at the thought of him. She sat and enjoyed the excitement. Finally, she giggled and smiled at Gerri, then threw up her hands.

"What are you going to do?" Gerri placed two plates of food on the table.

"There is nothing to be done. It is too ridiculous to even contemplate. The best I can do would be to persuade him to join me in having an affair. See him once in a while. I don't know. Right now I think I'll just content myself with knowing I can feel this good."

Gerri shook her head sadly. "He has little kids," she said. "He can't leave."

"He wouldn't anyway," Marilyn said with a smile.

The moment broke. Said out loud, this little piece of truth somehow seemed much more distressing to Marilyn than when it had sat inside her mind unheard and unarticulated. Now its volume seemed to call up the years of loneliness. She tired to remember when she had quit looking out the window for her husband. The day wouldn't come. It didn't seem to matter now. She had given up looking, but she had not recovered from the loneliness of being alone. She looked about. There were spaces between all the moments in her life, spaces between the memories, spaces between herself and every item in her house. It was a house filled with things she loved, but the house held no comfort, no spirit of love and protection for her. Right now she could see these spaces so clearly and they frightened her. Dread marched about. Dread and longing wound themselves together in a terrible rope of loneliness. She didn't want to go home. It was the first time she didn't want to go home. It was absurd. She didn't know this man, had not experienced any sort of love with him, and yet she was already beginning to fill up with the grief of loss.

"Are you okay?" Gerri held her fork still. There was food on it. She must have said something and Marilyn had not answered.

"His friend is likely another woman," she told Gerri.

"I don't think so," Gerri responded. "He would have told me about her. We are very close." A thin layer of challenge wrapped itself around Gerri's last line. It shortened her breath and tightened her voice. Marilyn paid no attention to the mental note she made of the voice change. It got filed somewhere in the back of her mind as she started to wonder what she was going to do.

"What am I going to do?" She was hardly aware that she had said this out loud. It was definitely not her usual behaviour to babble out what was actually going on in her mind. She felt a slight panic pushing at her belly. *Get a grip on your mouth.* She slowed her breath, felt it deepen, and then she sucked a huge gust of air, held it and let it go in a sweet, wistful sigh. Gerri heard it. "This love wants expression," she all but growled — and they both laughed. Marilyn's body was bursting with the need for its actualization. She laughed and then said, "Really I just want to roll around with him for a while — just one time. It would help if I hadn't waited so long."

"What do you mean by that?"

"Roll around? Come on, Gerri. You know what I am talking about — sex. Then I would have a memory to grieve. Something tangible would be lost. Right now there is really no love to lose — unrequited lust has got to be the worst."

"I don't think trying to engage him from that position is a good plan, pardon the pun," Gerri cautioned her. "He has principles about that sort of thing.

Yeah right, thought Marilyn, but she didn't dare say it out loud. Gerri was pretty defensive about her friend. Either he was a saint or Gerri was very naive. Marilyn declined to entertain either of these two options. Gerri was clearly worried about her. She didn't express her worry in so many words, but Marilyn saw it written on the softened lines of her face, in the curiously cautious tilt her face assumed as she gazed intently at Marilyn. Gerri's eyes were seriously questioning Marilyn's desire to see T.J. again.

No use thinking about it, Marilyn concluded, and she emptied her mind of the thought.

$ $ $ $

"A woman's voice is a smooth whisper well projected. There is magic in this voice. There is healing in the touch of it as the breath of her lets each sound float from her lips to wrap themselves around the listener. Its caress is carefully measured. Easing out heartfelt words can soothe the most troubled spirit." Ta'ah's voice floated back into Marilyn's life, wedging itself between moments of recollecting Saturday night's conversation, reminding her of the voice she longed to hear. The sounds made by her great-grandmother's English were so soft, so rhythmic they swooshed. Marilyn missed the sound. She listened to the memory of her old Ta'ah in the semi-light of her living room. The house was empty of people except herself and the sound of her great-grandmother inside her mind. It didn't feel lonely the way some houses do when they aren't full of people. Inside, her body felt full. The sounds Ta'ah uttered were textured with something — she tried so hard to name it — everlasting love kept coming back to her. Ta'ah had been dead for forty years and still she felt this everlasting love, this warmth, assurance, acceptance. No, it was not acceptance.

Ta'ah was not the sort of person who accepted behaviour unconditionally. She could stop a person from indulging the dangerous parts of their being. Marilyn chuckled at the recollection of the steely gaze that could freeze her to the spot when she was not happy with Marilyn's behaviour. She was clear, she was fair, but she was not accepting. There was challenge at every turn, but Marilyn had never felt inept in her presence. Everlasting love. There was never any hint of divorce in her behaviour, her language or her disapproval. "We are family. We are and always will be, without beginning or end."

Marilyn's breath slowed, her body thickened, her thoughts wandered in all sorts of directions and finally settled into a busy dream sleep. The curtains on the houses of her village relatives were closed, shutting out the day. The yards were empty of children and dogs. Strewn about each yard were odd toys. The earth underneath looked bald, about to perish because there were no children stirring up the dust or shifting her soil. The earth's breast was so bare that it frightened Marilyn. Marilyn hurried toward Ta'ah's house. The village was too silent. Its dead silence shook her. She hung her head trying to dodge the invisible insult this deep quiet delivered to her when she walked to Ta'ah's house on days like this.

She wanted to turn back. Run home. Go back and never return. *This walk is too far. The silence is too big, too deep and I am too small.* She couldn't turn around. There was no one at home. She had no idea where her mother and the others were. Home was black, empty and soundless. There were too many rats as company at home. Rats inspired terror and accentuated the largeness, the blackness and the emptiness of her mother's house. Rats made her feel much smaller than she was. The tension inside intensified. *Go home, go on to Ta'ah's, go home, go on, go home, go on.* She told herself she

loved the smell of Ta'ah's, the warmth and the feel of the place.
The familiar scent of Ta'ah's wood fire, the scent of food cooking,
the aromas curling and playing about in her kitchen compelled
Marilyn to speed her little legs up. She loved being at Ta'ah's, but
she hated the trek. The children were gone. "At residential school,"
her mother had told her.

The village didn't feel right. Marilyn thought she saw something
out of the corner of her eye. Her head snapped, but there was nothing there. She listened for it. There was only this deep quiet — this
residential school quiet, this dead silence surrounding her. She
remembered wanting to go to that school, to be with her cousins,
to be surrounded by voices with a familiar accent. She wanted to
hear words that didn't confuse. She asked her mom if she could go.

"Don't be ridiculous. Children don't make decisions like that;
you can never do what you want." Not going to the same school
as her relatives made her feel like she was not quite family. The
space between herself and her familial peers scattered her to
some edge, some place at the periphery of family.

She once tried to ask Ta'ah if she could go to school with her
cousins. "You are Salish. You do what needs to be done. White
kids grow up thinking they can do what they want; not you." She
had no idea what her mother or Ta'ah were talking about then.
Now, in her sleep, the words wrapped themselves in a cloth of
her own meaning. They fused themselves to her personal sense of
significance. She smiled as she heard them. They felt so old and
riddled with truth.

Marilyn spent most of her time with Ta'ah, even when the
children were home. It wasn't them she missed in her dream, but

the happy noise children inspire when the whole village is peopled. Everyone was lighter, gayer, when the children were home. In the absence of children, the village was covered with an unnameable bleakness that disturbed Marilyn's walk to Ta'ah's house. It disturbed her in a way Marilyn could not pinpoint. Even in the enlightened state of dreamspeak the words would not come. This terrible loneliness dogged her, haunted her and nagged her from childhood right through her marriage. The loneliness threatened to follow her into the transition between being mother and grandmother. She must name the disturbance or be maddened by it. It refused to be understood.

She inhaled the smoked salmon scent of her great-grandmother's living room. The smell rooted her to Ta'ah's voice. Ta'ah's words dropped from her barely moving lips. The words soothed her but they did not help clarify her thoughts.

"Ah. Woman. It is one of the few words in the white man's language that does not assault the spirit with the jagged edges of its sound. The word woman sounds so much sweeter to the ear than lady. This language has so many nasty sounds in it. The good part is white men never did wholeheartedly settle on the names they gave to life's beings. So they gave them many names. The trick is to choose carefully the names you use." Ta'ah liked the joke she found in this peculiarity of white men, and she laughed at it.

Marilyn was awake, still smiling from the dream of her great-grandmother. She feared losing memory of it. She bent forward as though this would help her to remember the dream. In the bleary state of being half-awake, memory eluded her and the dream threatened to disappear. Instead of remembering, Marilyn thought about her great-grandma from a superficial place. The memories weighed heavily on her these days. Marilyn decided the memories acquired weight because she had added so much interest to the accounts of her grandmother's words — maybe too much interest. She hadn't been using Ta'ah's words to govern her conduct or guide her life since childhood. It was as though Marilyn had been busy squirrelling them away for decades and now they were bloated with significance. She dragged them out of her savings accounts and paraded the swollen meaning the words acquired without thinking about what value they held now that they were so far away from their origin.

"Oh, shut up," she blurted out loud.

"What?" Gerri asked, a little perturbed. The car sped up. Marilyn had nodded out. She looked out the window, trying to locate herself in reality. She had no idea where they were.

"I must have been dreaming." Where were they? *I must have walked to the car. When did I get into the car. Have we been somewhere that Gerri is going to want to talk about?* Panic bubbled just under the surface. *Oh God, help me. Bastard is likely busy,* she thought.

"I hope so."

"Do you ever think about God, Gerri, about how busy He must be with all those people saying "Oh God" constantly?" Gerri looked dead at her. Marilyn smiled and winked. Gerri sighed, then laughed. The airport loomed ahead. The sun dropped from view as they pulled toward it.

§ § § §

On the plane ride back, Marilyn recalled the evening she'd spent with T.J. She re-ran the conversation in her head. Her voice softened. She regained the lyrical accent of her Salish origin. It sounded odd to her. She smiled. She had spent years schooling the lilt of accented Salish English out of her voice and had not heard it, even in her mind, for a long time. She wanted to call him, to see him again, but she had no way to reach this man except through Gerri. It didn't sit right with her.

Words stubbornly continued to journey, rootless, in her mind. It seemed as though they had been doing this for so long now without ever finding audible expression. They created silent spaces in her life so huge it seemed impossible to fill them. The treasure of words was hooked to passion somehow, and she knew it. They needed expression. They couldn't be expressed to just anyone, she rationalized. She had not felt this passionate about anyone or anything for years. It was as though her skin had gone to sleep.

Perfunctorily, she met people, men and women, month after month as they walked through doorways to clutch her hands, share touch or laughter, even the odd embrace. The impact of their presence had all been so ordinary. Not to demean the ordinary; it gets you by. The business of the ordinary took up most of Marilyn's life. It filled the nooks and crannies of her life with busywork. She no longer wanted it to consume her. She had no appreciation for the ordinary. She wanted to appreciate it, so she could exalt in the passion pushed up by the extraordinary. This last run of words made her feel sick.

Where am I going with all this? She looked around. The man beside her was reading. *Good, that means I didn't say it aloud.*

She tried to remember when she last felt passionate in the embrace of another. Her mind began to split. The fissure grew. She wandered first down one side of the fissure then down the other without realizing the seriousness of the split. The ordinary is medicine, like the dandelion, but the extraordinary is exquisite. Stones in their ordinariness joggle the passions, discipline the spirit creating wisdom from simplicity, but a diamond uplifts, encourages our ordinary selves to breathe from the rarified air in which the spirit of sharpness, beauty and strength resides. Human beings in their banality are wonderment en masse, but the beauty, the poignancy and elasticity of passion cannot be expressed to a mass without having passion's meaning dissipate.

The breath of passion has colour but no weight. These colours are dreamt. They are seen from the inside and used to repaint the world outside. What was grey cloud becomes a whirl of living puffs splashed with tender hues of soft, subtle pink, pastel purple, hints of magenta and skinny traces of pale blue. Colour takes on significance. The train carrying memory picks up new passengers, fills them with significance. Imprinted with passion's stamp, these passengers' laughter is textured with greater joy. Their sadness becomes compelling, their banality exciting. Passion drives curiosity. It cannot help it. It is as though passion and curiosity were wedded together.

Separated from the subject of passion, words become dull. Without curiosity humans cease to wonder about the smallest and most trivial things. So much so that the trivial gains importance because of the neglect that the dispassion of mundane living represents. Without passionate expression the world of the imagination becomes a series of discoloured paintings offending the inside so badly the viewer cannot see the reflection of material colours outside. Colours want dreamers to layer new colours onto the old ones. If new colours are not layered onto existing ones then the earth begins to appear as an unchanging, dull monolith. Humans who lose interest in colour lose interest in living.

I'm going mad, she told herself. *That whole diatribe sounds too much like I can't live without a man.* Her dispassion about her life was a sober light turned upon her life. The light weighed on her, diminished her.

In her dream-state, the memory-train pulled up. It was filled with men. They had all exploited the passion of some woman or other. Her work forced her to envision the exploited passion of other women over and over. Men turned women's passion into ploughshares, then harnessed the sweet love of women to haul them across rain-soaked sodden fields in which the only pleasures were those that men called into being, named and validated. Each woman's story buried her passion deeper. She felt her passion for T.J. sinking under the weight of the trainload of men.

You don't know this man, she cautioned herself. *My love is not a water tap. I can't turn it on and off,* she pleaded with herself. *Nor is it a tool for your victimization,* she responded.

"Be careful" ended the dream.

⚛ ⚛ ⚛ ⚛

Marilyn was shocked to find herself awake in a nearly empty plane. She shook her head, looked stupidly about trying to ground herself. She couldn't remember falling asleep or getting on the plane. The size of this gap was significantly larger than all the others. The lines between reality and dreamspeak were thinning, thinning so completely she was less and less clear about whether she was awake or dreaming. She tried desperately to appear nonchalant lest someone on the plane make note of her fright and address it out loud. The thought of having to explain her fright was more horrifying than feeling frightened. She sat in her seat next to a preoccupied man, fought a shudder, then opened her journal and began to write:

My youthful web stretched taut, barely holding the threads of me together, I barrel along, eyes wide open, heart too, grabbing ghosts from closets. I wrap myself around spirits whose yarn coils in twisted iron snakes of unbridled lust. I want to unbind the coil, snap the tension wire. I want to unlock demons that tighten the coil, pull the wire and cinch the twist. I open old wounded places — unbelievably soft; wires are stretched so tight they cannot feel me. I open smooth, sturdy thighs impassioned by bronze whose skin stretches over hollow cheekbones across vacant eyes, which are blind. I drown each moment in desire, scratched inside out by bronze men who empty out their manhood, spill it all over black webs of highway in directions complex and cold. I chase nightmares of confusion. I open full mocha-mauve lips, pulse across familiar terrain whose illusive velvet is encrusted with pale grey sand. My lips bleed, grow tender, bleed, grow raw, and bleed. They crack and dry for want of you. I try to leave the painful content of you, but with each good-time/not-a-long-time comes black-eyed wonderment.

Marilyn stopped. Her blood heated up. Her hands grew tense. Her lips curled. A half-empty coffee cup caught her attention. She grabbed it and smashed it on the table. It refused to break. She could hear a scream inside, feel the power of it, but she didn't want to let go of it.

I am unable to handle truth. I wander about chasing truth. I contemplate reality from a fearless and unbelievably peaceful direction. As soon as I get close I pull my own rug out. She watched as a tornado, a storm of images powered by lightning set fire to her body, her mind and her mouth. A raging inferno of fear lashed out at the ugly side of truth. The inferno turned to a deluge of water poured on the fire of any man standing near. Fear was her governess. This governess pushed to drive truth away. *I am afraid to love,* she admitted to her journal.

I am afraid to look at the love in front of me. I dodge it. I am swollen with fear. I wish I could say I believe in T.J., in me, in love. I feel so endangered — a victim of my own emotions. Somehow my body knows I put up this crazy wall made of circles of words I cannot hurdle — little circles of fire-branded words, which burn my insides and scrape away at whatever love still shapes itself inside me.

Her fear stood before her, naked. She moved to confront it, push up on it, lash out at it. She watched herself try to embrace it, respect the place it came from. She needed to cherish its origins — not the fear, but the place it began. She needed to see how joyful the original presence of fear had once been, how heroic and terrible was its journey. *Fear keeps us re-thinking, re-looking, evaluating life. It moves us to brilliance, to care and caution. Fear ought to keep us safe,* she wrote. She needed to see the beautiful beginnings of fear, but the absence of love was so terrible that it blurred fear's birth. She saw emptiness under the glaring light of her fear.

From in between the lines, as if through a fog, an image of a man appeared. She stared hard at him from some small place. Not a small place, no. It was she who was small. The man's face took on a shape; his eyes took on definition, his mouth curled into a knowing smile as he reached for her. She knew him. He picked her up, tossed her in the air; her laugh rolled out rich and sweet — free. "Oh gawd, its' my dad. I can't. I can't."

She watched as life painted her with an ugly brush. The paint went on thin, not quite translucent and just opaque enough to fog up and erase this memory of Eddy. The inferno of fear's fire came close. She tried to move away. It set root somewhere inside. The sparks, she had to remove the sparks, the brush, the logs, they were enraging the fire. People gathered in an angry circle. They threw logs at the fire. Her rage rose. The fire of her rage licked the edges of the circle of people. *What am I so angry at?* A face emerged, unrecognizable. *Where were you daddy? Why did you leave? That's a three-year-old's question*, someone scolded. She closed her eyes and fought to clear the strengthening memory of Eddy. Her mind refused to clear the picture from her field of vision.

Marilyn followed Daddy around the house. He fixed things. He built things for the house. He decorated and arranged the furniture. He hoisted Momma from a stepladder after she'd hung the curtains. She saw them exchange sweet knowing smiles, caught them engaging in touch when they thought she wasn't looking, magic touch, touch that made Momma smile all day and long into the night.

It was the first time Eddy had invaded her memory. He sat next to her on the plane, a slight grin on his face, and looked at her. She wanted to tell him that she was ashamed of not remembering him, of not seeing this before. *If you had known, Daddy, how much I loved you, would you still have run away?* she asked his ghostly image. They were now both sitting on her couch in her Vancouver apartment. She watched the scene in her townhouse as though there were two of her, one this tiny voiceless child and the other an aging mom. It was the older woman who spoke to her daddy.

If I had said the things I feel now, would you have stayed? Would you have been like all the others in my life, gauging me, judging me, lying in wait, ready to strike then desert me? Or was your one run at night a desire to escape becoming my tormenter? Eddy didn't answer. He moved from the couch and picked up his little girl and showed her a new world. He marched her about the house introducing her to each room of her home, and then he took her out into the front yard. The yard, the end of which killed him.

⑤ ⑤ ⑤ ⑤

Marilyn was back on the train, riding through her life. The train was part of the village picture. The tracks were right across the road from the highway. There was a porter on this train. He gave her an old brass medallion: faith, hope and charity, he said as he pointed to the anchor cross and rope embossed in the medallion. She giggled, twirled her feet and played with it. By the time the train rolled into Vancouver she had grown up. She was a teenager, looking in awe at the construction of high-rises. Her apartment with its table-less dining area stood stark and ugly in the light of her hope. She watched as she changed her hopes. No, it was more like she had given up her first hopes.

Hope had always lived inside her. Reality corroded it. She refilled herself with hope, and then reality corroded it, until she was weary of trying to remain hopeful. Now she felt hope gaining momentum again. Her hope was different in this dream. It was not pure like when she was small or young. It was connected to a whole list of "don't wants." She knew this list but didn't have a clue what she did want. The grocery list of "don't wants" was accompanied by faces — men she knew, men who worked either for government or for some Native organization, bureaucracy or the First Nations' governments themselves.

Just like that she was awake. She picked up her pen. Her journal was full. She dug about in her briefcase for paper.

She watched images of men she knew roll by overtop the scratching of her pen.

You left me small miracles. They fell fully formed and perfect from that impossibly soft place you had been. Creation rooted me to the concrete weapon you chose to scrape my insides, until leaving became unthinkable. The wire of you tightened. Her pen called up pertinent scattered scenes, then sorted them out in blue words scrawled onto the paper's smooth white surface. She ordered them up in accordance with what she didn't want. *Grew hot, wound itself in and out of my insides, round my neck. My neck shrunk to wire and the sight of my spirit's death terrorized you. You left while I waited like salmon-woman; waited for the razor you held to cut me loose to honour that place. Oh, that place. I ate cold stew from cracked plates on broken Arborite surfaces; scanned walls where you punctuated meaning with my mind. I cut my throat loose from this wire bondage, caress my own skin in dark solitude, but still I await your affection.*

Lover after lover initiated relationships with Marilyn with the line, "I don't want to get married or have kids." She was never sure of their motivation in saying this, but was still glad most of them did not get caught up in forcing the Cinderella syndrome on her. It never occurred to her till now that her attraction to their aloofness was connected to her dad's absence. There was a shallow callousness ensconced in their commitment to a hard shell of apathy toward her. She was appalled that she had been so willing to play the role of a romantic partner to men who did not think she was worth keeping.

She remembered talking to Sharon, a Winnipeg Native woman broadcaster.

"So. Can you tell who's with whom?" she challenged Marilyn at a local Native Expressions performance. They had just finished an interview about the Marsha inquest and were settling into an evening of meaningless gossip and fun when Sharon threw out the question.

"Sure," Martha replied with confidence. "The men are dating the women they are most markedly avoiding having any contact with. That means Rick over there is with that woman there, because they have not even looked at each other all night. Couples are sitting around tables and the men are talking to everyone but their wives."

When she quit laughing Sharon asked her what made her say that.

"I don't really know," Marilyn said seriously. "I guess I am getting cynical."

Sharon looked about the room and said, "But you're right; is that cynicism or painful realism?"

A gorgeous Lakota man was up next. He had on a slinky, crimson satin shirt that he wore buttoned only once, just above his navel. His hairless chest was a warm honey brown and his face had those flawless Lakota features you see only on postcard paintings of men from the past. His hair was big, long and silver, his face unlined — no chicken tracks around his sleepy, dreamy eyes. Big shoulders and thin hips completed the picture.

"Whoa, now, that's nice. He can put his backside to my fire anytime," Marilyn murmured.

"Ooh, you don't want him," Sharon said, waving her hands in dismissal. "I know him. He's from my reserve and he is a hopeless womanizer."

"Well, that's right down my alley," Marilyn insisted. "I just want to use him. I didn't want to keep him." A young man came toward her. He had recognized her from her national TV press conference. He wanted her to get up and say a few words to the group. Marilyn wasn't sure of the wisdom of that, mixing political activism around child apprehension with the largely country and western singing performances, but Sharon had said yes before she was able to decline. After the crimson shirt, Marilyn was called up.

She was unprepared. The audience was unprepared. She stared at them for a moment. Her mouth opened and the words just fell out: "Well. First of all, I want to say I have been divorced for a very long time. I really think it's unfair for handsome Lakota men wearing red satin shirts to get up here singing sad songs and reminding me just how long it's been since — well, I have forgotten the word to describe what it is I have been missing, it's been so long." She had their attention.

"Sovereignty, liberation, cultural revival are all words on the lips of men. I want to say, as a Native woman, keep on talking them words, but work to make them real. I need you to carry on singing for them, working for them, speaking for them. While you do, if you see us out there on the street, or in the courts or walking into the CAS offices, I want you to doff your hat, wave or just jump right alongside us, because without our women raising our children all the work of your generation will be dead by the next.

"I want you to remember, after the dance comes the love song, and sometimes after that come the babies. I want you to seriously consider whom you dance that dance with and really consider the consequences of that old love song.

"We need to have our babies on our side of the line. We, the women of First Nations, need you men on our side of the line in order to keep our children. We need your love and your support and I am not ashamed to ask for it."

There was a heady silence when she finished. Mr. Crimson stood leaning against the wall staring at her for a long time before he strolled over to the table.

"I want you to know your words moved me." He reached out, shook her hand, then left the dance hall.

"Wow, you must have done something, sweetie. That guy never leaves a dance hall clean and sober, let alone early and alone." This little scene convinced Marilyn of how fragile was the apathetic shell Native men wore.

She never saw the Lakota man again. She hadn't actually wanted to. She knew she could never hook up with a performing artist;

their lives were too vicarious. She needed someone who was rooted, rooted to some belief, someone who lived by some internal law she could not name. So many of the sixties' generation of politicos and intellectuals were hedonistic. They had come from virtual oblivion; invisible and unrecognized, they had leapt onto the world stage, the national stage, even the provincial stage, into the floodlights of power and privilege — and most had not yet recovered. Because they came from conditions of want and poverty, cruelly set beside opulence next door, they had insatiable appetites, which led them to indulgence. They could not seem to satisfy the their wants.

"I can't see one person being enough to satisfy another person," one man had put it.

"I can't see one man being able to satisfy me unless I'm the only one," she had replied.

"Well now, supposing I don't want someone quite that arrogant or smug," he smiled back at her.

"I would be curious to know why you believe my refusal to settle for less than I want is arrogant and smug." The dalliance with him had ended before it began.

She didn't want the sort of relationship in which each spied on the other. Nor did she want one in which they both wondered who each had been with, or the sort of relationship in which he stayed out until all hours of the night with whomever he chose, while she sat at home burning candles and waiting.

There it was again, the fucking waiting. She wanted to spit, to smoke, to just get off this damn plane. She broke into a sweat. Her body heated up; flashes of white-hot skirted across her neck. She was so hot for a moment she thought she was going to vomit. She reached for the bag in the sleeve behind the seat in front of her. Just as quickly as it began, it ended. "Oh gawd, not that, not meno-whatever-they-call-it." She didn't even know the name for it. "There is power in naming," she remembered. She realized she had never asked her mother about the process of ending the procreative period of her life. Why hadn't she? Well, maybe this was just rage. Her hands reached for a magazine. They were shaking. She would have to learn to live with it, she sighed philosophically, and then opened the pages. Ms. aging superstar was getting married again for the eighth time.

The article settled her and she took to looking out the window again, thinking about T.J. She would be in Toronto again. She was pretty sure he would be there when she came. It would probably be several months before she saw him again. That gave plenty of time to sort out what she wanted from the rest of her life. It was something she should have done for herself a long time ago. Now she didn't much feel like she could afford to put it off. She was oddly relieved he lived so far away.

Her mind was already back at work when the plane landed. She had decided to approach work differently. *I gotta gamble on these women*, she told herself. She knew the blueprints for therapy provided by years of university wouldn't help her to do that. She was painfully cognizant that there weren't many ideas about how to approach this without the textbooks, but she had a gut feeling that the key to sorting this out lay inside the women themselves. She made up her mind to trust them and her own smarts from here on out. *Elsie, I am going to let myself care.*

Part FOUR

༄ ༄ ༄ ༄

Some things make a woman tremble. The tremble does not always surface. It begins deep inside from some unnameable, unreachable place. It signals the body to proceed with caution, then alerts the mind to pay close attention to the world around her. She opens her eyes to any sign of bread crumbs that may create enough of a trail to assist her in tracking the source of the tremble and connect it to some experience that could help her to walk away from it, avoid it, or solve the problem causing it. The tremble is a felt thing, not necessarily a known thing. If her body is thick, crowding this unnamable place, dense, precluding her ability to reach it and read the signals the body gives off, she may not proceed with caution. She may barrel on through — an innocent detached from her own body smarts.

The tremble can grow, become a quake. A woman quakes when she knows that the rivalry between siblings is out of control. The nipping and biting has become persistent. In its persistence it accelerates, hurt accumulates, rage deepens, gains strength. The natural tensile stretch of the womb, the imagination and the mind shrinks like plastic, smothering all goodwill. Unabated, the rivalry becomes an ever-growing spiral of internecine war. This sparks the quake inside. All around the centre of the quake, life stills, grows quiet. Tepid is the blood pumping soft in the face of a coming quake.

The fight for our dead is a quake. Our living men are more like the men on the other side of the world. Men set the fires of Kuwait. Set the men locked into some kind of life-and-death game of sibling rivalry. This sibling rivalry sparked the Oka crisis. Likewise, the Xhosa-Zulu internecine war spawned greater chasms and more violence between themselves than between them and the bigots of South Africa. Now Ipperwash was raging and one young man lay dead. No one wanted to move. Not for the living. Dead people are innocent. They connect us to our past. They represent our future, but the living are the reason we are still futureless, despite our past. After the Ipperwash crisis, the Oka crisis, any crisis is over, the internecine war between siblings resumes.

Besieged from without, warring from within, the children of sky woman imploded and the earth quaked at the sight of it all. Everywhere these quakes were felt. Finally the quaking of Earth mother spread to the very core of her woman being. No one knew where their own quaking arose, but it was there. Earth woman wept, tried hard to relieve the quake going off inside. This quake is a stubborn one, born of female procreative tenacity and indomitable love. It refuses to quiet itself until it is spent.

In every village, town and home this quake besieged all our mothers' daughters. It rent their insides, shredded the present into strips of moments sandwiched between distant memories of the past and the mundane living of the present. Memories of loss after

loss after loss crowd the present. Violent memories of bodies flying through the air, screaming in the night, whimpering under the
slim, useless protection of skimpy blankets. Memories of the
intrusion of others whose intentions were mean, bestial, cold —
these memories sickened the bodies of the more stalwart women,
those who strode to the outer edges of villages under siege.

Finally, one woman faced the crest of Westwind's first breath
and uttered, "We're sick, we need to heal" — and a circle was
born. Westwind picked up her words, skirted them across the
land. In the tears of his mother's rain he deposited the sound. It
dropped helter-skelter on cities and towns, and ultimately
reached the ears of those who could still hear the rain from some
magical place of potential peace. Other circles were born. Other
women repeated the refrain, "We're sick, we need to heal." A
groundswell rumbled, pushed up from the fire raging at the core
of the earth, inspired by her quake, her destructive aftermath and
the image of total spiritual and emotional carnage, which the
state of siege had wrought.

Marilyn felt the quake. She could not see its origins. She
dared not search for any meaning in the face of it. The quake
stole moments from her a piece at a time. She would awaken
from these moments as though she had been somewhere else,
running away from something. She disappeared into the
moment's ghostlike passing through a sticky, invisible portal she
couldn't quite remember. In this portal she walked through the
wall separating past and present without knowing she had even
left. She could not be sure if she was in the present or the past,
the real or the unreal, the conscious or surreal.

Her Western education biased the way she looked at the world as she searched through her snippets of reality and pondered her experience. She dared not look at those moments pre-defined by white Western intellectuals as insanity, delusional, "schizo" ... At the same time she feared she was losing her mind. She stood on the edge of a precipice of barely sane emotions. She fought the images of completely chaotic spirit, heart and mind activity. She strode metaphorically from the edge of the precipice. It took huge effort. Her body moved as though it were constantly bucking the wind. She had already begun to feel tired from the effort this took.

If she had not become so biased by Western society's narrow perception of what constitutes reality, living beings and social interaction, she would have known that her body was moving as though it were bucking the wind because it was. If she had not left behind the science of her own people's holy knowledge she would have known a great gift was being born in her. Truth, earth truth, was visiting her. She had a place in which to search the moments of passing from the doorway of the physical to the world of the spiritual, but she closed the door to it, locked it away. Tenaciously and willfully, she refused to use the key to return to it in a conscious or sane way.

She had become a therapist long before the call to heal had rung its bell. It was a good job, an honourable way to earn a living. There had been no need for a personal commitment to her own wellness in studying the Western theories presented to her. No sense of urgency drove her to get the degree necessary to practice. She had no idea the quake inside meant seeing the breadth, depth and extent of emotional and spiritual destruction outside. Nor did she know that this quake inside all women held meaning for her.

She had just met T.J. He had awakened passion in exactly the way Westwind intended her to feel it. The ups and downs of going in and out of the present had been loosening the logical bolts holding her together for some time. She had been on this roller coaster for a long while. Meeting T.J. had been her only moment of respite from the violent ride.

She took hold of the relief of meeting him, drank fully of its gentle uplift, held tight to the momentary clarity it provided her. A doorway to light is love. Not white light, not purple light, but weightless light. The light was an easy, exciting, titillating light. Easy. Ease. Tease. To ease. Love teases the pressure of the moment into sheer joy. Passion carries blood, running hot with the fire of passion's promise, to the brain. It warms the chill of logic that recognizes the quake, the tremble, and the warning signals that deliver us to caution's door. Love hides the snake that forewarns us to search and research. The snake reveals doubt, helpful doubt, the wondrous doubt created by experience. Passion drowned Marilyn's natural doubt. The snake that creates genius inside our minds sat still in the flood of passionate blood. How could she know this passionate blood-pumping joy was itself delusional — that it veiled the quake, but did not quell it?

ⓢ ⓢ ⓢ ⓢ

T.J. knew this.

He came from a long line of grammas who birthed wisdom inside his body. He knew them. His grammas knew things, even before words shaped themselves. He felt things. This one old lady in particular visited his spirit. She called him, stilled his mind, and journeyed him through the inner spaces where storms dwell in the bodies of others without fear, without judgement. He had little fear of the quake inside women. He knew the quiet before the earth shook kept every living thing still. He knew the stillness was not terror. It was awe. When Earth mother's body opens up, the fissure of hot blood rushing here and there inside cracks her skin, sucking everything into her fire, cooking the layers of crusty garbage, cleaning everything in sight. In the aftermath of a quake, all Earth's children are left feeling joyously vulnerable if they are still alive.

He knew he would be shown the doorway inside the woman by the woman herself. He lay on his bed that night smiling. It had been a long time since sensuous passion for a woman had inspired such quiet courage in him. His senses were all alive. He could smell the fetid waste that is Toronto, know its origins and not be angry. Overtop the smell of decay wafted the scent of roses, their hips tart and medicating, their flowers, thorny and sweet. Cedar — elegant, smooth and powerful — and pine joined the roses and began to mend the wounds of yesterday. These scents overwhelmed the decadence of the city with its momentary, debauched lifestyle. The rose, cedar and pines are forever, while cities come and go, the old woman reminded him. Love is forever. Personal sickness is temporary. He slept, pleased with his own feelings for Marilyn. Marilyn — he even liked the sound of her English name.

Westwind has its origins in the bottom of the sea, where the mother of deep thought lives. Westwind is warm and unpredictable only to the human children who fail to understand he

responds to this woman who lives at the bottom of the sea. He
hears her. She processes the words of her mother from this place
of deep black dark. In ceremony she captures the spirit of life, the
fierce will of all survivors to enfold their life, fulfill the spirit of it,
enrich the heart of it and enjoy the passionate physicality of it.

Earth. She whispers her yearnings to Westwind. Westwind
brings lightning, sparks tears, fires the world with volcanic ash,
hurricanes of voices from the past, tornadoes of peaceful spirits
residing in the midst of chaos, giving humans hints of solutions.
Westwind does her bidding. He does not do this slavishly.
Westwind loves the woman at the bottom of the sea. He stands
and declares his passion for all to see. He remembers first woman,
the joy he felt, and he expresses it. His wind, his song, his breath
is a response to the woman at the bottom of the sea. Earth knows
this. She has mastered his language, knows how to call him forth.
She carefully nurtures his voice, encourages him to recreate the
voice the children of the earth need to hear to move forward.

Love calls forth the voice inside. T.J. and Marilyn could both
hear the song of love pumping out its powerful rhythms inside.
Both loved the sound of it. The waves of sound unlocked old
muscles long since permanently contracted. Within each old
muscle, the memories captured were let loose and they wafted
about, seeking release.

⚛ ⚛ ⚛ ⚛

Marilyn was barely in the door, her bags clumsily slapping her
legs, when she heard her daughter's voice piping into the answering

machine. She meant to drop the bags and run over to catch Lindy before her message ended and she hung up. She dropped her bags. Her legs refused to move. She stared into the dark hallway helplessly. "Hi Mom, it's us. How are you? Hope you had a good trip. Cat and I were thinking we might get together tomorrow night for dinner. How about it? Give me a call at home. Bye, love you." The dial tone sounded so lonely filtered through the dark.

Lindy had called. Not Cat, but Lindy.

Marilyn managed to flip the light switch before looking around at the apartment. She never tried to look at things in the dark anymore. It was a little too eerie. She put her bags in the bedroom then returned to the dining area where the phone was, stared at it for a few seconds, hesitated, then picked up to phone.

It was late. Lindy would still be up; actors never sleep. *I'm tired. It's just a call to arrange a date. Oh, quit, Marilyn, quit arguing with yourself.* She placed the call. Lindy chattered on happily. She had a new contract — as usual. She was excited, the director thought her beautiful: "Can you imagine, Mom? He thinks I'm beautiful." Marilyn tried to share her daughter's surprise, though she had been convinced since giving birth that her daughters were beautiful, much lovelier than she could ever be. The sad part was that she could not see much of herself, her face, in them. She faked it as she always did; it's a requirement of motherhood. Drag out the happy sounds in your voice if that is what you hear in the children. It seemed to fly with Lindy; she didn't ask her mom the perpetual "What's wrong?" every time she heard an off sound in Marilyn's voice. They set up a dinner date.

Click, quiet, then wind. The trees in the West answer the wind. They howl along, crying in the night with the rhythm of Westwind's breath. He never comes full force right away, this Westwind. Westwind creeps forward, eschewing love, singing lullabies through cedar branches — songs of sweet content just before he satisfies his sensual being. He caresses yearning. He arouses himself, stands straight up, then arches his back, opens himself up and from the great maw he creates, he rears disdain for those seduced by him. Westwind guards his crying carefully, hiding behind tongue-lashings of rage: renting trees, scoring earth in erratic, angry gashes. Bleeding, the soil cringes under the weight of Westwind's masked pain. Westwind dare not shed tears; dare not remember his lonely howling. Ungratified, he rests. He gathers energy, socks away his angry mask, begins to lull the fear he inspires.

Westwind is a man, virile and lovely, energized by his own inability to grieve the loss of first woman. Marilyn dared not breathe Westwind. She dared not raise her voice lest she too be consumed by her lonesome cries. She watched over her shoulder daily, ever on the lookout for the wrath of Westwind crunching back his eternal loneliness. She knew him without even knowing she knew him. She just knew him. She could see his moment rising. She recognized him, his look, in the eyes of human men. In T.J.'s eyes she saw the bodies of men from her past rear up invisible eyes filled with intent. Before it happened she knew it was going to happen.

T.J. is Marilyn's Westwind. He is a moment of awesome aliveness. He inspires oneness. His presence tugged at every cell, lined them up, opened her musculature. Light shot between each cell, blood rushed in, cleaned up old, toxic places, and restored breath inside every part of her being. Electricity vaulted between the newly opened pathways between each cell, recharging her body. She rose — stood up soft, supple and tensile, and for the first time she saw herself. Marilyn saw sinew and blood, muscle and bone. She saw metals, precious and sharp, twinkling in her own internal light. How had she gotten so dark, so breathless and rigid? She saw her lungs fill with air, saw her whole trunk expand, felt each minute particle of her dance rhythmically, heard the sounds of a hundred instruments, whistling, thumping, trilling and moaning inside. For the first time she felt strength: its powerful surge filled her up. She saw skin stretched smooth across cheekbones, which begged adoration; saw these cheekbones push up on her face. She felt her lips swell and looked right at them, loving the image of their fullness, their softness, satisfied by the way she knew they looked — a sweet, sweet pout playing about her gentle face — an old Salish pout.

The sound of familiar voices touched her. "Oh look, she's pouting," her auntie said as though it were another milestone. Laughter filled the kitchen. Momma picked her up, nuzzled her, pride texturing her laugh as she joined her sisters in marveling at Marilyn's ability to pout. Pop, silence, then wind. Wind tickled the trees outside, giggling wind, wind's purple breath soothing the skin of her old house, filled with women whose breath loved her being.

Somewhere in the night Westwind retreated to his lair. Things were going well.

§ § § §

Marilyn awoke feeling jittery. Her hands shook as she struggled to dress herself. Not even the shower relaxed her. She couldn't for the life of her figure out what was making her so shaky. *Focus on the small,* she told herself. Her mind ran through a mental inventory of the day's work, listing what had to be done to make her day's pay worth her employer's while.

She never had appointments after a trip out of town. A report on her journey, the workshop, the response, et cetera needed to be done to satisfy her board that she should have gone all the way to Toronto. The board was convinced that these trips were good public relations for Indian control of Indian children. It left a bad taste in her mouth but she had long ago given up arguing with them.

The idiots still believe you can actually control children, she mumbled, almost tripping as she stumbled into her pants. *What the heck was I dreaming about? she wondered to herself. Oh gawd, the financials have to be ready Tuesday.* That meant she had to get the documentation ready for Janet today. Normally she would either have gone in early or stayed late. Today was also Elsie's weekly appointment. She was generally careful not to set up appointments on the day she had to prepare for any kind of report. She hadn't paid attention before she left, so today was going to be trying.

Elsie came for her afternoon appointment right on time. Marilyn watched her during the session. She marked her hand movements. Elsie's voice tones intrigued her. She noticed for the first time there was something awry about Elsie's total being. It

puzzled her. Her mind flipped through her reference texts, her file
of psychological disorders and their symptoms, but she found
nothing to describe the being presented by Elsie. It was as if she
were apathetic, but not quite; disconcerted but not quite; uncaring
in the moment, yet deeply caring over the long haul. Her breath
was shallow. Her shoulders folded in when they weren't shrugging
a vague "I don't know." She gave Marilyn the impression she was
trying to shrug something in rather than out or off.

"How did you feel about being left in the park?" Marilyn
asked. Elsie shrugged in. She looked at her hands and murmured,
"Bad. Georgie hurt his balls. He was in the hospital. What if
something had gone really wrong?"

"I don't want you to think about Georgie. I want you to flip
back and think about you, alone in the park. What was your body
feeling?"

"Cold" was all she said. Cold. Marilyn sat straight up when
Elsie said it. There was a hint of challenge in Elsie's eyes — that
was it. Most of the time Elsie's eyes looked flat — dead. Lifeless
eyes. Marilyn's mind shot back to her Momma staring out the
window on foodless days. She could hear herself and the other
kids asking if there was anything to eat. Her mother answered a
flat no. Elsie didn't have that deeply depressed, vacant stare,
though. Marilyn pushed back on the memory, which seemed to
want to just hang about like some old painting. Her memory was
intruded on by the sensibility of her education. Words tumbled
about the painted memory. She seemed to be standing in the
middle of the fracas this created. Elsie's ability to answer her questions and at the same time have the same flat eyes of her Momma

intrigued Marilyn. Cold. Cold was some sort of key. She picked it up and decided to run with it. The decision popped the picture; she was back in the room focused on Elsie. She went after whatever was behind the door called cold.

"Were you cold a lot?" she said, softly without much interrogative rhythm in her voice.

"Yeah."

Marilyn wondered if chronic cold is a symptom of an emotionally disturbed patient. She couldn't find the answer, decided not to ponder it too much and moved on. Some little whisper told her to stay curious about Elsie's cold.

"Picture yourself cold," Marilyn said. Elsie looked at her oddly. "Close your eyes," Marilyn continued. Elsie obliged her. "What do you see?"

"It's dark."

"Where are you?"

"In my room, the blankets are heavy. It's so cold I can see my breath." This made no sense to Marilyn. If was dark, how could Elsie see her breath? Still, she opted to accept this and push on.

"What else do you see?"

"Jenny is next to me. Her feet are cold. I don't like her touching me when her feet are cold like that, but I don't say anything." Marilyn thought it interesting that Elsie spoke in the present whether the event she was referring to was in the past or present. Maybe it was for Elsie the difference between active and inactive. She mimicked her by staying in the present tense with her.

"How old are you?"

"Not very big," was her answer. They started to play a game,

Elsie explained, a game designed to warm them up quietly. Marilyn wanted to know who made up the game. Somewhere in the lull of Elsie's recounting she asked her.

"I did." Elsie opened her eyes. The eyes gave no impression that they acknowledged what she had just said of herself. No pride registered. No response to her small accomplishment. Everything about Elsie was entirely too matter of fact.

"That's pretty smart," Marilyn ventured tentatively.

The shrug-in motion. *No value,* Marilyn murmured to herself. *She has no way to value herself, so self-appreciation is impossible. At the same time, she shows no signs of a sociopath except as regards her neglect of her children. How odd.* Marilyn's mind raced. Unable to internalize the other world's culture, yet divorced from her own, Elsie had no way to value herself. Of course, Marilyn knew hundreds of Native intellectuals who ascribed to the concept that Native values were destroyed in residential schools. She used that line herself in her talks, but until this moment, it had no clinical significance for her or her clients. Everything tumbled out so logically. Colonization is such a personal process. Culture is so intensely personal. There must be something about us that never quite gives up that never quite can be completely erased, but at the same time over a hundred years of cultural dismemberment has to surface in some intensely personal way. In the absence of our own cultures we would naturally develop this not quite completely valueless, not quite completely apathetic, not quite completely uncaring self. Elsie's persona seemed to live on the periphery of herself somehow, as though she were on the outer edge of her own life, unable to fully participate in it.

"What nation are you from?"

"I'm Indian." There it was. No-name-brand misnomer, undefined from within, numbered and identified from without, just like the Jews before the concentration camps murdered them. Jeezus, maybe none of us are all that disturbed; maybe this is all just a consequence of conditioning.

"Indians are from India. We are from Turtle Island. We each have different Nations. For example, I am Sto: loh. What are you?"

"Oh. I'm Ojibway."

"Do you know anything about Ojibway ways, traditions, cultures, songs — anything?"

"No." Elsie stared at her hands.

"Neither do I," Marilyn quipped with excitement. Elsie laughed. The light came into her eyes.

"That's two things we have in common," Marilyn said, and Elsie giggled. "We like beauty shops and we don't know anything about Ojibways."

"Have you ever seen the photographs taken of your place the day they took your children away?" There was an edge to Marilyn's voice. Her own anger, she guessed. "Do you want to see them?"

"Do I have to?" Elsie wrung her hands.

No, but it might help, Marilyn thought just a little coldly. "No," she said. Her voice sounded so deeply tired, as if every cell was weighted with fatigue. Marilyn decided to quit pushing Elsie. "Let's call it a day."

Elsie turned to look at Marilyn before she closed the door. Her body registered puzzlement. She almost looked as though she wanted to ask something. She said nothing, however. She went out, closing the door deliberately, slowly, gently, as though she was desperately trying not to cause the air to stir. Marilyn wondered about that. *Scared to move the air. Afraid of living breath. Ooh, that is powerless.* She began writing progress notes: *Elsie's movements are entirely too unobtrusive and thrifty, sometimes the body language contradicts her voice tones; sometimes even her words don't match the body language.*

She stopped writing. She felt like she needed to know something about the Ojibway. She needed to know when Elsie's movements were responses to her own dysfunction and when they might be ordinary Ojibway body language. She called the local Native Friendship Centre, told them who she was, and inquired about Ojibways. The receptionist didn't know anything about them either, but said, "You have one working in your building, don't you?"

"Randy?" Marilyn asked.

"Yeah, that's his name. He runs the employment services for Native people in this city. I guess Eastern Natives are the only ones out here who know about working," she laughed. Marilyn did too, though she didn't really get the joke. Maybe Randy could give her some clue about Elsie's body language. She called him and arranged a lunch date, making sure he knew it was business, not pleasure.

She needn't have bothered, she learned when she met him for lunch. Randy, oddly enough, was in love; even more odd, he was in love with his wife of eighteen years. Never mind. He helped Marilyn and as a bonus she got to know another man. She made a friend, the first one in — she hesitated to calculate the answer. Back at her office she began an action plan for Elsie. It had been a trying day.

"Thank goodness trying days go fast. Pressure speeds up all activities and the clock ticks so mercifully quickly that you hardly notice how painful the pressure was," she said out loud to herself as she swung into her Burberry, packed up her things and readied herself for her date with her girls.

Westwind licked at her heels. Faces blurred by. Traffic hummed and honked along. Marilyn smiled every time an Indian face jumped out of the blur. Halfway to the car she chuckled quietly. She realized she did not really see the foreign faces in this city. *Actually, I don't look at these people at all. Like when I was at college.* She remembered her college days, walking into the cafeteria with an Indian schoolmate, not seeing any other Indians and saying, "Nobody here." Both she and her mate cancelled out the other eight hundred or so students in the cafeteria like blank cheques. As a child, she had hated being invisibile in the eyes of white people. As an adult, she preferred not to see them. *Life is so ridiculous.* Click, snap, the seatbelt was in place and she swung out into the traffic.

ⓢ ⓢ ⓢ ⓢ

The girls were to meet her at the Red Lobster. Marilyn was early for once. The maitre d' behaved as though he was glad she had arrived. It embarrassed her. He reached out to grab the menu. She thought he was trying to shake her hand. She noticed the hand about when he decided she wasn't going to shake. She pushed hers forward as he pulled his back. She snapped hers back so hard it whacked the podium behind her, knocking the rest of the menus over. Both of them bent over quickly to pick them up and they knocked heads. They both jumped up apologizing. Marilyn couldn't decide whether she wanted to laugh or cry.

"Tell you what," he said. "Let's start all over." He stood at the maitre d' podium. He stepped back and introduced himself then led her across the room, politely waiting to see what she would do with her hand. By this time she just wanted to be out of sight and out of mind. The girls arrived just as the maitre d' was about to locate the table.

"Mommm," Lindy growled.

"Mo-om." Catherine said it like a happy question, a pleasant surprise. Marilyn slipped her arms around both girls and their chatter fogged the maitre d' and erased her embarrassment. She wished she had been seated when they walked in. She remembered many other dinners, sitting in a spot where the doorway was visible, waiting for them, watching them slide through the front door as though they didn't really walk but rather glided along ripples of air, so graceful were they. Their hands cut beautiful images of their words into the spaces around them, drawing sweet pictures to accompany their smooth Salish voices. Their steps were so carefully measured, sweeping their graceful bodies, their delicate hands gesturing while their lyrical voices trilled out with soft murmurs. Marilyn didn't care what they talked about — she just liked watching them. They were so beautiful, so stunning, that they drew attention. Marilyn liked to watch other people take note of them. She liked seeing them walking and talking and gliding through the door toward her.

Tonight she missed it. She had this godawful feeling everything was going to go wrong. Both girls listed what they had been up to in the week since they'd dined, then they wanted to know how the trip had gone.

"I met someone," she blurted. *What the hell was she saying? Met someone.*

"Hard to do in Toronto," Lindy teased.

"Lindy," Catherine scolded. Lindy responded by making a face.

"Well, surprise me. Come on, Momma. Tell us — male or female?" Lindy asked.

"Lindy, of course he is a man," Cat replied.

"Can't assume that nowadays, Sissy," Lindy said.

"A man." Marilyn was beginning to get annoyed: at herself, for bringing the subject up, at Lindy for making so light of it, at Catherine for taking the time out to make Lindy behave when she made a joke of it. She felt her lips tighten. Time drifted. She was thirteen, looking in the mirror. She was cute, no matter what them white boys said. She liked her face: full lips, big half-moon eyes and clearly defined eyebrows. She returned to the mirror image of herself this morning. Her face had changed. "That's it." She had no idea she'd said this out loud.

"What's it?" Both girls looked at her, mild concern on their faces. The lack of context for her words concerned them more than Marilyn could know. She had to say something. As a mother she had so many years' practice of covering truth in respectable clothes before presenting it to her daughters that just telling them the truth seemed too simple, too implausible. She quickly tried to think of some respectable falsehood. "Time," she replied, "Time is slippery in the cold, dark water. It floats." She had not intended to say this at all. It just rolled out. She watched Lindy's eyes first narrow, then grow wide, then register doubt, side-glance Cat, and then look nearly normal. Cat betrayed nothing but curiosity. "Days slide into nights, into dark without much notice. Light is thin in the cold. Dark is all pervasive, deep black. Sunshine passes through very little of the surface. Distance rather than time becomes the standard measure of being. The difference between moonlight and sunlight is negligible — except you can swim farther under the light of the sun, enjoy the swim longer. It seems warmer because distance becomes more possible."

Christ, someone has hold of my mind and is pulling words without meaning out of my mouth. She stared at the girls. Their returned stares indicated she hadn't said the last line out loud. "Great," she said out loud. She couldn't seem to stop the words. They spilled unconsidered into the space between them.

Marilyn fought so hard to forget her nightlife; her dreams fell wasted and useless to her days. "What the hell am I talking about? Where is all this coming from?"

"Yeah." Lindy's voice was rich with her attempt at an emotionless response.

"Well, ladies, what'll it be?" Thank God the waiter arrived so the conversation Marilyn had just initiated could die unnoticed.

"You got a drink called sanity? I could use a little." Marilyn winked at the girls.

"Make that three. We could actually use a lot." Lindy responded quickly. They laughed.

"I was thinking of this woman, a client," Marilyn explained to her daughters. "She puzzles me. Cold, time, distance, lack of value for herself — she has all that without really being disturbed.

You know she's not a sociopath or anything. Somehow the answer lies in our poetic loss of the above." Marilyn suddenly felt exhausted. Some little ball of anger fired itself up as the fatigue grew. She wanted to tell Lindy not to be so concerned. She wanted to tell them that the words came out of her as strange and bereft of meaning to her as they were to them. She wanted to tell Cat not to jump on a guilt trip whenever she read annoyance in her mother's voice. Cat grabbed her hand, tried to comfort her. Marilyn wanted to jerk it back, tell Cat she wasn't the centre of Marilyn's damned world. She need not be so conceited as to assume she could fix Marilyn's annoyance. She wanted to holler at both women that her annoyance did not even have a remote connection to them. She wasn't sure it had any direct connection to herself. In fact, she had no idea what it was connected to. Instead she swallowed, smiled, and accepted the comforting looks as graciously as falsehood could muster. *Another dishonest meaningful moment in a whole string of them,* she muttered cynically to herself.

The weariness grew. An old, breathless, windless snake crept inside, filling up her body cell by cell like a virus leaping as it reproduced from nucleus to nucleus. It consumed all her energy as her body gave it life. She needed to talk to someone. To T.J. But she had no number for him. She wanted to have just one conversation with someone in which deception was not the main course. Desire has weight, she told herself. It is a living being. Fed, it grows. Hungry, it demands food. If the subject of desire is not present, the body will substitute by screaming for sweet foods. Desire is what makes humans so chaotic, she decided. Chaos. Off rhythm. Eating and being off rhythm is chaotic.

Eating is not a rhythmic movement for the body. Sweet foods create the greatest chaos inside the body, just like desire. She dared not look at the girls, in case she had uttered all the foregoing seeming nonsense out loud.

"So. What're his intentions?" Lindy asked.

"Intentions?" Marilyn asked. She had no idea what the question meant.

"Is there an echo in here? Intentions. Yeah. What are his intentions?" Lindy repeated.

Marilyn threw up her hands, looked from her fork to her knife, back to her plate, around the room and said, "Intentions? Well. We only just met. He gave no indication he had any intentions about anything." There were too many pages between the question and any possible answer, Marilyn decided. She was interested in him. Whether he had expressed an interest in her was at best unknown. The signs were too vague to just ask, "What are your intentions?"

"Momma, you didn't ask." Cat sounded disappointed. Lindy looked at her from under eyebrows, which clearly meant to tell Marilyn that her miscreant behaviour began with not getting a handle on this right in the beginning.

"Did you ask him if he was ever married?" A rush of blood, a pull of powerful tension and the picture changed. The Red Lobster disappeared. They were all three of them standing in a park. They were lost. Catherine was grumbling, "Momma you have to ask someone for directions. We are back at the same spot we were just a minute ago. You have to try to remember where we live." Marilyn was a little tipsy — drunk, really. She dared not talk to anyone in case they noted this fact and decided to exploit her or her daughters. How do you tell a five-year-old that you don't walk up to a stranger half drunk and start up a conversation. What if he was a jerk? What didn't occur to her then was the maturity of the five-year-old scolding her mom. She saw it now. Their world was upside down from the beginning. Cat was more often the responsible person in this little trio, and she and Lindy took turns being the naughty children. The table pulsed to the rhythm of blood pounding in the back of her head.

The waiter arrived, interrupting her memory and offering an escape hatch to responding to Lindy. His voice brought Marilyn back in the room. How long had she been gone? *Long enough for Lindy and Cat to notice,* she thought. *I'll tell them I'm tired. Work has me stressed out. I'll tell them more about Elsie.*

Lindy ordered food without taking her scrutinizing eyes off her mother.

"You're impressive," Marilyn teased. Lindy gave a slight toss of her beautiful face, lifted her perfectly arched slender brows and Marilyn carried on. "You just read the menu without taking your eyes from me and did a perfect pass to Cat without looking at her at all." The waiter agreed. "It was impressive." Lindy did not look at him nor answer. Cat jumped in to fill the dead air space that Lindy's silence threatened to create.

"Yes, well, our Lindy is very impressive, thank you."

Marilyn wondered first when Lindy had gotten this rude, and second, why Cat cared. Secretly she wished Cat didn't give a good goddamn.

"Nice dodge, Mom," Lindy remarked cryptically.

"No. I didn't ask his intentions. I was too busy looking at his beautiful brown body."

"Touché," from the waiter.

"Was I talking to you?" Lindy said in a fake Brooklyn-style accent. The waiter laughed. Wrong move. Cat caught Lindy's arm.

"Lindy," Cat warned without letting go of her arm. Marilyn thought Cat knew Lindy was not kidding. The waiter blushed as he too figured out Lindy was serious.

"Yes," Lindy snap-drawled to Catherine. It was clearly a threat. Cat slowly let go of the arm.

"Did you know, Catherine, that's twice you've done that?" Marilyn asked. The tension around the table was thickening.

"Twice what?" Cat asked.

"No, you don't, Momma. You're not worming your way out of this one," Lindy jumped in.

"First, it is only 'worming' if the business you're trying to climb out of is dirty. Lust, passion, is not dirty business. So, I am not trying to worm my way out of anything. In fact, I am trying to worm my way back into my own business without dragging my daughters with me." Both girls gave each other inquiring looks. They took the wind out of the sail Marilyn had started to ride, but she persisted with a little less push. "That's twice you bawled Lindy out, Cat. I remind you I'm the only mother here. Second, she is a grown woman entitled to her own ways, so you are wasting your breath. Breath is a precious thing — not to be wasted. Last, no one has the right to govern a Salish woman's relationships with anybody." The words spilled out feeling slightly foreign, like some voice was compelling them other than her own. The words felt old.

"Well. That was a pretty good bunch of shut-me-up lines," Lindy uttered when she had recovered enough from the shock to say something. Cat looked hurt. In one swoop Marilyn felt like she had demolished the arc of the bridge their relationship had been standing on, and she was powerless at this moment to rebuild it.

"Does that mean a change of subject is in order?" Lindy offered, slowly sipping her soup.

"There's a plan," Marilyn whispered softly.

"So and how about them Jays?" Lindy quipped hollowly after the obvious inability of anyone else to fill the dead air space.

"Why don't we go back to the man I met and stay away from whether I was responsible about having met him." Somehow it didn't seem so bad to talk about it anymore. The current discomfort between them seemed worse.

"Oh great. Let's go back and chat up what got our heads bit off in the first place. Yeah. I am about right for another verbal spanking. How about you, Cat?"

"Touché," Marilyn said. Her voice had no breath.

"Maybe we could begin by having you draw the lines of demarcation around whatever boundaries you would like us to respect. After all, if we don't know what is our business and what is not, it is hardly fair for you to bully us when we cross some line we were unaware existed." Cat's logic was impeccable. The can of baby snakes opened up. The snakes crawled in every direction, wriggling, hurrying away from Marilyn, threatening to escape before she could name them. It was too much. She collapsed. "I don't know what got into me, I am so sorry."

"Momma, are you trying to say we are all adults here and we should each and severally respect whatever choices we make independent of all the rules you set up for us for the past two-and-a-quarter decades?" Snake one. Lindy was going after them all, one at a time. Lindy got hold of it, turned it on its belly and read the thing in a totally different manner than Marilyn saw it.

Snake two. Neither girl had ever dared challenge their upbringing and now they were trying to get Marilyn to abide by her own rigidity. She wondered if her rigidity appeared as cruel and ridiculous to them and as it did to her now. She could not reconcile herself to herself. "I suppose that is what I mean."

Snake three: this was going to take her places she didn't want to go back to. She knew it and didn't like it.

"So this means all those rules weren't such a good idea after all." Snake three. Marilyn caught this last snake. It was heading for the wooden spoon. She saw a pair of scared little beings standing in a half-lit hallway, clutching one another's tiny hands desperately, bravely trying to face the threat of the big lady they loved. They shook, hoping against hope that this lady would find enough love for them to stop her from swinging that spoon. Worm four. Guilt-driven, Marilyn could not erase this picture, could not justify it.

"Could we not talk about this?" Marilyn whispered.

"Oh. I can't speak for you," Lindy responded, "but I can certainly discuss this."

"Yeah," Cat said. "Unless you have some giant with a wooden spoon stashed under the table, a giant who is mean enough to make us behave, we'd best work on the basis of agreement. I may be wrong here, but it seems agreements are negotiated between free citizens. And of course, we are more willing to discuss this than you imagine." Cat — quiet, well-behaved Cat — had found her tongue. Worm six. More quiet.

"Okay," Marilyn stammered. "I had that one coming for a long time."

"Does that mean the spoon was not such a good plan to begin with?" Cat squeezed out the words written on snake seven without breathing. All movement arrested itself. Both girls stared at Marilyn.

Marilyn's breath darted out, sucked back, stopped, danced tentatively forward and stopped again. It was playing games with her and the worms were reacting. Each change of breath led them to change direction. A whole lot of mucous gathered in her throat. "Yeah" came out thinly, swimming across the mucous. Nobody moved. Movement might disturb the depth of truth being uttered here. The waiter was back. He looked between the statuesque women and waited with the platter of drinks. It brought them all out of the well they had sunk themselves into to consider the moment. They looked up at him at the same time. He arched his brows and dropped the drinks like he sensed being there was not such a good idea, and then he left.

"Oh gawd," Lindy murmured.

"I think I'm going to lose it," Marilyn muttered like a home-less bag lady talking to herself over her shopping cart.

"Not here, Momma," Catherine pleaded. Marilyn read the assumption of responsibility in Cat's last remark. It was unbear-able. Something inside wanted to snap. Some tension wire made of years of knowing Cat would always assume responsibility for her mental state stretched itself tight. It was more than Marilyn could bear.

"Why the fuck not here?" Marilyn said too loudly.

"Why not?" Lindy responded, slowing her voice down as though everyone at the table knew exactly why not. Then Cat answered Lindy's question.

"Because the wounds are too deep, the blood clotted around them too thick, the people here too uncaring and there are just too many words wrapped around it all. Let's go to your house, Momma. We'll finish it there." Cat's hand clutched a fork. She gently pushed the peas about her plate. Cat's voice had no push. Lindy's eyes stared off into nowhere. Her eyes filled with tears, voicing the distance this moment had travelled before it bore this terrible poisonous fruit. Marilyn had not realized Lindy was voiceless until this moment. All those years of silence around the wounds made this remark ring so loud it filled the room even as Cat was only able to whisper words. The walls, the chairs, the wooden floors echoed the soft insistent sound of Cat's words. Memory after memory of the fragile-looking Cat girding up her loins, thrusting out her chest and delivering steely words behind which Lindy stood staring painfully into space floated above the table. The pictures danced a crazy dance of love, of fear of Momma's hateful eyes, of Cat's endless Raven spirit, of Marilyn's hateful eyes, of Lindy's fear-filled eyes with their pleading looks, fingers twisting, and Marilyn's inability to stop the train driving them all to destruction. The shock of all this reality rooted her to Cat's solution.

"Good idea. After supper. Shall we do a secret group hug?"

"A secret group hug?" Lindy's voice sounded as though the respect she generally wrapped around her language for her mother had been sanded away.

"That's when we all hold hands, then you let the feeling in your hand make a circle around your body, like you're being hugged. Then we eat. Go to my house after, talk and have a PJ party, listen to some stupid music, tell dumb jokes and stay up too late." *Secret group hug? Where did she get that? Never mind,* she told herself, the air was beginning to soften and relief was in the offing.

"Why not? It's Friday." Both girls looked somewhat perplexed, but neither dared go back to their former conversation.

They mumbled their way through dinner making the usual comments about the mussels, salmon and shrimp, sighing at the delicious spread before them. The girls seemed excited at the prospect of having a pyjama party with their mom, but Marilyn began to dread it from the moment she suggested it. Maybe she was too hungry for them. Secretly, she wanted more out of life than she believed it was possible to receive. She was so hungry she risked starvation rather than acknowledge and honour the food she received. She tried to enjoy one bite at a time, savour the flavour, stretch the moment and hold onto the feeling long after it was over. She had not had much success with this approach.

She remembered a contest she and her sisters used to engage in. They were all so hungry. Jell-O was so rarely served. When they did get it, they competed to see who could eat it most slowly. Trudi always won; Marilyn always lost. She would start out well, then the hunger for it would create such a huge anxiety she'd wolf the last two bites. She grew anxious between meals, imagined terrible things for want of them. Worried about her daughters constantly, but was starved for words to express the worry. Maybe she was so hungry between bites that she could not bear sharing the goodness of their presence with them, could not relax and be comfortable with the world they created around her and just enjoy being alive. Maybe she was recreating this condition of chronic hunger over and over like Wild Woman. Whatever the reason, her hunger was so big she envisioned herself eating her daughters up in one bite. Maybe Wild Woman was a warning to mothers who withheld the precious food of emotional joy. Maybe the story is about the joy that they need to give to their children. Maybe mothers get so hungry, they are no longer able to engage their children or themselves except in relationships tainted by the same mystical, spiritual cannibalism.

The rest of the meal was reasonably uneventful. The waiter didn't bother much with their table after that first round. This suited them. They ate, paid and left.

Inside the house the girls busied themselves getting snacks and futons ready for the party. Marilyn watched the chaotic preparations, amused by the productive disorder of the busywork, observing it from some place not quite rooted in the moment. Little instructions between the two young women, "Get the dip ... the chip bowl ... We need napkins," got her moving about and joining the business without engaging her mind much. She appreciated that. Her hands gripped the chip bowl incognizant of its smooth surface. She leaned into it to smell the white corn chips inside. Nothing. She was standing in the middle of the kitchen staring at the can of utensils when her eye caught sight of the wooden spoon. It swelled in size, filled the corner of the kitchen, terrorizing her. The girls were already spread out on the floor atop the futons, crunching back potato chips. She put the white corn chip bowl down, shook her head and moved to the can. She remembered spending hours decorating coffee cans with Southwest design upholstery cloth — expensive cloth from Belgium.

"Go figure," she said to no one. The cloth created useful art she could not appreciate. She reached for the spoon.

She entered the living room tapping the spoon in her hands. The women stopped eating. They watched warily. Lindy looked ready to react. They stared at the spoon at an odd angle, as though not able to look at it head on. Breath stood still for a moment. No words entered the air space, but the paragraphs of emotion dividing them were hidden in this one small gesture with an old spoon — and they all seemed to know it. Marilyn slipped slowly to the floor and snapped the spoon on the way down.

"I should have done that years ago," she said. Both girls wept soundlessly. Marilyn gathered them up just as she would have years ago had someone else delivered the blows. She held them and whispered words of comfort. Their cries grew big. They sounded so old, so small and so big at the same time. Finally, Lindy grabbed the broken spoon and snapped it in half again. Cat tried hard to break the other half one more time. She couldn't. Instead she stabbed the futon laughing and crying at the same time. Lindy's voice snapped out laughter like Raven called up joy after a funeral feast. Marilyn joined them. Cat cracked a joke about not being able to break the spoon.

234 $ LEE MARACLE

Their laughter came out squeezed between tense, still-nervous vocal chords. It gained volume as the fear floated up and out. The laughter under the fear rose full round and pushed up by rivers of rain. Somewhere in the laughter Marilyn realized she wasn't hungry for them at all, but for herself. She hungered to express love to them in the way she felt it. She had always felt the love. She had just never been able to push through the thick, sticky web of stillness her love seemed to be captured in to express it. It felt as though her love for them, for life, had been squeezed small, dense, and encased in some crazy wrapping that kept her springing in subtractive directions. It was as though every human act led to some unchangeable, impossible connection to the human condition her people were consigned to. Every joke told became someone laughing at her. Every question became an assault on her dignity. Every alone moment became part of the dire loneliness. Her life had not been that bad. It was her inability to enjoy it with had been too small. Crazy.

She saw her slender, youthful body tense, ready to spring, rise to whatever assault she imagined was at hand, on guard constantly like a threatened cougar. She felt caught in some sort of strange process of creating ghostly enemies with the world. She searched her vocabulary for a name for this feeling. There wasn't one. "Enemification" should be a word. "To enemify": the feeling of enemification wrapped itself tightly around her love, shrunk it, and precluded any sort of expression of it. Across the old mattress of her bed, men whose names were lost floated, their touch, rich with stubbornly impossible promises, lingered. She wanted to march them back, back to a time when sand did not paper old paths or scrape young insides. Back to a time when wires did not whirl around her thin neck. The wires were snapping now. Small and unexpressed, the feeling of love had grown dense, compacted. It submerged itself under the ever-growing feeling of war inside. Her whole body engaged itself in trying to experience the antagonism physically. She needed an enemy. She needed someone to punish. It was this strange condition of search and destroy, make war on something, which had locked her up, governed her, given her permission to make war on her daughters. She wanted to go back to a time when laughter, blushes and touch spoke star dreams, coaxed warm sounds gently from her body to be bequeathed to these two when they really needed to hear warmth in her voice.

Sometimes breath hides. On entry it can slip past anticipating vocal chords, which quiver excitedly at the prospect of creating sound. It seems to be able to wrap itself in a thin skin of protection. The ball of breath slides in total silence between strings that normally vibrate and bring language to emotion. If the breath is balled up and still, when it does move it moves too quickly to connect with voice's source.

Marilyn could feel her breath play delicate touch songs on her lips. Breath rolled out, caressing the inside of her mouth. As breath approached the back of her mouth, her throat constricted too tight to embrace breath, to free it of its skin. Panicked, her throat jerked, grabbed breath and hurled it past the strings, anxious to make sound, lest breath commune with chords to recreate old memories too dangerous for her voice to greet.

Throat sent breath flying to a tiny purple ball of sounds hidden somewhere inside her body. Below her belly? It all happened so quickly she didn't see where the ball was; rather, she could see the ball suspended seemingly nowhere. Her belly was numb, too numb to feel her breath.

Of its own accord breath flew past secret doorways, small closet spaces in the body where old memories piled up, still, serene and mute. Throat need not have worried. Breath dared not address these doorways, dared not open them. Breath knew the clutter of memory was dangerous. All of them grew dense and hid within the innumerable layers of Marilyn's enemies. Enemies of the Sto: loh remain forever ostracized. Marilyn would have stopped her breath before opening herself to the tower of memories. The memories coiled themselves between skins of fear stretched taut as breath approached, threatening to open them up. They sat paralyzed in crazy knots. Breath knows these layers of memory and fear, fear and memory are really wire webs posed to ensnare should the doors be moved, the knots untied. Breath meanders past them, considers them occasionally, nonchalantly, as though they don't really belong inside Marilyn's body.

Breath is a woman, warm, soft and passionate. She has no time for the snaky explosion unleashing memories from between the sheets that fear creates. Breath adores courage and hides from fear. Breath is wind. Breath begins as man.

Marilyn felt breath hiding. She felt breath's adoration of courage, watched while breath shrank from the closet spaces of fear-filled memories. She watched breath enter. She felt her roll around her mouth in a lazy kind of way, felt her throat grab breath, jerk it past those vicious strings that always threatened to yard open the doorway to her closets of fear. The closets were full of memories held hostage by fear. Her voice strings might weaken when breath slid slowly past them. It might open the strings. How could this be? she wondered. No, it isn't the strings that rope the doorways — something else does that. She stared at the purple ball hiding inside. Something inside the ball wanted to look in the closet. Somehow the ball agreed to hide breath, keep it from singing across voice; at the same time, something inside wanted to peek at the little piles of memory and commit them to Marilyn. This commitment would force Marilyn to engage them, face their ugliness. *What makes you think they are ugly?* she heard herself ask. Marilyn moved on to travel along the pathway to desire without answering the question. She wanted to know what was inside the purple ball.

This want, this desire, had a pulse, energy, and some sort of push to it. She couldn't name the thing, couldn't identify what it was that made her want to see it. She had no idea that the memories were the same as the ugly knots in the closets. Breath herself did not seem to care. It was as though breath picked the images, tied them into knots, prohibited them from getting loose, arrested them before they brought themselves to full voice recall. Breath did this, but not of her own free will. *Whose will was holding all this together?* Marilyn wondered overtop the images. She could feel something directing breath to hide. Breath hid at the direction of this something. Marilyn's voice joined breath, turning it all into a strange conspiracy of silence.

Voice. That is what they called it. These people who were now bent over her. The closets grew locks. She placed them on the doorknobs to the closet spaces before her ball of breath could reach them. If she could not see inside the closet, she would not want to unlock her voice, give breath to them. Left to her own devices, Marilyn's breath travelled in treacherous directions, disentangling the complicated threads of self-deceit breath spurned into a big ugly key unlocking all that fear. The memories covering the fear spilled all over the floor of the room. They jumped into scenes, formed their original shapes, disorganized and out of order. The dark room where night no longer was a living, breathing dream-state of spiritual repose seemed only to brighten the scenes spilling, shaping and threatening Marilyn. Night died again in this room. Again? Pieces of Marilyn split away from the moment, became a gallery of audience members who chose not to participate in her life just then.

Nerves. Her nerves helped to kill night. She watched it perish. It perished like any living thing. One moment it was alive — a velvet, soft, invisible being, spawning comfort, catalyzing wondrous pleasant dreams. The next it lay agonizing, life dripping from its velvet being. The next it was dead. Somehow the rawness of her nerves stripped free of protective covering had murdered night.

It happened so fast. Thin slivers of sound made by nerves communicating terror to her entire body pierced the room. Exploding, they forced blood to pump hard and fast. Everything heated up. Breath shot here and there, looking for Marilyn's voice. Then fear, ugly and lifeless, enveloped itself around the moment, captured her spirit, covered it with a skin of deep purple hues which protected its purity but denied Marilyn access to its impetus, power and governance. The slivers of sound burst into her light. The light reversed itself, retreated to the purple ball. Breath helped the fiery sliver retreat. The blood rushed helter-skelter, pounding against tensed veins, constricted first by shock, then pain. Fear retreated to the spaces between the molecules whose movement was slowest and least essential to the process of aliveness, pulling memory and images of reality along with it. In the midst of the explosion of memory cutting through its imprisonment, pain and shock, a whisper came to Marilyn across breath's pathway. "Shhh."

Where is this sound coming from? Marilyn wondered now.

"Who is telling you to shush?" *Someone else must have heard it and thought it was me,* she said to herself. Marilyn could barely recognize the voice that asked the question. This voice belonged to her, to family, to self, yet it was not her. It must be Lindy or Cat or some other family member — the chords, the melody, the rhythm were so familiar. It sounded timeless in a curious kind of way. The timelessness made her feel forever alive — floating in space above time. Forever being has no beginning and is without end; it is about being. It comforted and encouraged her. She felt safe.

"Don't talk," some other voice rasped out, punching holes in her safety. It seemed to throw the feeling away from her body.

"It'll be worse." This voice was familiar too. Who was it?

"Be still," said the voice. She didn't intend to move, so this set of words threw her off.

"Open your mouth." She shut it. Clenched her teeth around the sound of the order.

"Who's there with you?"

Marilyn could not tell. The figure rasping out orders was blurry. It was as though she was looking at something through dark moving water. Some splinter of herself was standing offside as it happened. Each happening seemed to occur in some wedge of a circle in which she was at the centre, except for this sliver of a self. Her sliver self seemed to be some mystic engineer without physical or emotional presence — a strange being with a long-distance framework for considering life, but without any urgent need to participate in the consideration. A contemplative self who could engineer her life but chose not to.

At first the voice sounded deep, hoarse, as though breath were playing tricks with it, performing the role of some imagined character inside it. Breath can do that. Marilyn knew it could. She had worked with breath before. Her body had danced in meadows of flowers amid green cedar saplings. Rain sprinkled cool water across her skin while breath concocted voices of fantastic individuals who existed somewhere inside her mind and came to life at her instruction, then retreated at her will.

She listened to the voice. The sound seemed to be coming from a being whose body she could not see — a shadow, a silhouette, active and faceless, standing on the periphery of the memory she was immersed in. She wanted to retreat from the memory, step outside it, get some kind of command of it. Her feet remained planted inside the memory. Breath seemed to be making the voice happen all on its own. She could feel her mind whisper to her voice, *Why are you making ugly sounds like that?*

These aren't the words I want to hear, she told her breath. *Make a different voice. Say something else. I didn't ask to hear this.*

Blood sped up, veins constricted, the voice in her head scurried to the centre of memory, grew faint as it concentrated itself in a cacophony of unintelligible rasping hard sounds mixed with squeaks of fear. Her mind chased it. Breath came out of hiding, joined the chase, grabbed the sound, pulled it into the purple ball, then went back to its hiding place. The purple ball grew denser, gained weight like a stone. This stone of sound hung suspended, unable to untangle itself or order up the pieces of words that spiralled into a tiny speck of truth she dared not voice.

Marilyn tread softly in the wake of the storm passion naturally presents. Passion requires reckless gestures, violent emotion to suppress it, to temper it in the absence of the elder brother winds. Marilyn's body knew this. Her mind did not know it, but her body did. Her body, this conservative keeper of the history of pain and doubt, of consequential memories, of action and reaction, so thoroughly useless when disconnected from the mind, heart and spirit, rallied itself even while her swollen lips indulged their sensual imagined pleasure. The muscles of her hips contracted, pulling her abdomen shut, locking the soft, sweet place that is passion's journey's end. Her rib muscles pressed hard on her rib cage, blocking deep breath, satisfying breath, enlivening breath and spirited breath. "Shut down," the body commanded. And those old fatiguing memories of consequence had shut down the fire rising in Marilyn's body.

She woke with a start. Her hand touched her thymus.

Why am I sitting up? She paused and searched the room. She recalled her dream; for the first time in weeks she had not dreamed of the girls. She was relieved. For a long time she had felt as though she were sliding over some edge, losing time, really disappearing into some other place.

Marilyn thought of T.J. He inspired oneness, but it was not for his presence that her cells cried out just now. It was not for him that the light inside shot between each cell. Her blood desired family. It pumped out a desperate hunger to clean old toxic places. It screamed for the restoration of the magic breath between herself and her children. She knew this breath. She breathed wonderment all over them when they were born and for almost two years afterward. She wanted it back. It was her breath she wanted back, not theirs. She was anxious to open the old electrical vaults, which would open her up to her own pathways. These vaults held the charge that would renew her body.

⑨ ⑨ ⑨ ⑨

Westwind rose to the edges of the sky. In the deep purple black he sang a salmon song. Eastwind joined him. Northwind waited patiently on the edges of Earth's skin. He would be needed here soon. Southwind played about Marilyn's lips. She needed him now.

In his retreat Westwind left behind the courage to dream. Old images returned of bodies threatening home, arms swinging randomly, connecting with flesh, tissue, tears. *My tissue*, Marilyn told herself, *my muscles receiving blows, mingled with my desire. My desire is tearing. Need tears at desire. Need be damned.* She opted for another swing on the bungee cord of desire. Quenched it. Pushed up on it. *Come desire, follow despite the blows, and swing fearfully from this cord.*

The cord is bound together by some other's desire. Desire to stretch backward into someone else's time. Someone else's standard.

Standard rope, cord, measure, distance, time, behaviour. Standard light, weights, strength, average, standard weapon, standard. The bungee cord breaks. She awoke determined to murder the standard she had inherited, not the relationship she desired.

ᔥ ᔥ ᔥ ᔥ

Marilyn had slept too long. Jumping up, she grabbed at shoes, leapt across the room over the girls, snapped pants and blouses from the hangers and knocked over something in the closet. Mustn't be late.

"What're you doing, Mom?" Lindy rolled over and leaned on one arm.

Marilyn started, did a half jump turn, tripped over her, still only half in her pants. She stumbled, saved herself from falling and finished dressing. "Going to work. Hopefully I will find some dignity on the way there before I arrive."

"On Saturday?"

"Saturday?"

"Yeah. Saturday." Lindy looked around. "There goes that damned echo again."

"Oh, well then. Maybe, I am just getting dressed. Yes. I am just getting dressed on Saturday, in some kind of a hurry, for no reason at all." She sat slowly on the chair, stared at Lindy, trying to decide whether to laugh with relief or cry with shame. It was unbearable to realize she did not know what day it was.

"You're in trouble, aren't you, Mom?" Lindy let it go like a gentle invitation to talk about the trouble.

"Yeah."

"Been gapping?" It came out sweet and easy, like it was no big deal. "Seeing anyone about it?" The tone of her voice was genuinely curious and free of challenge. "Or are you going to?" Casual, like it didn't really matter one way or another.

Consequences. Marilyn knew about consequences. If her Board of Directors ever found out she had to see a therapist, she would have to resign. If she didn't see a therapist, she would go slowly insane. She knew it. She wanted to tell someone how serious all this was for her, but she did not want her children to play the role of confidante. Yet there didn't seem to be anyone else. She wondered how she came to be so isolated over the years. How long had it been since she had seen some of her friends? When she started work she had friends here in the city. They'd drifted apart. It had been a couple of years since she had called on anyone but her children. She hadn't made friends with any men for a long time. Randy's friendly daily gestures had been invitations that she never responded to. *I'm such a fool*, she thought.

"It's more than just a few sessions I need. If they find out at work, I'm dead." Somehow some new wind had come up inside. She realized she had options. She had money in the bank, grown children and she could find friends.

"You own this place, don't you?" Lindy asked.

"Yeah. Do you think I should sell it?" Nothing seemed important just now. Some sort of foggy pressure lifted. The fog had colour and shape. Marilyn watched it as it rose and passed through the ceiling of her apartment home. Marilyn had a new car, an RRSP, an apartment, money in her savings account — she was a woman of means. She decided to apply for extended sick leave. Plenty of social workers do it all the time. Maybe she wouldn't have to sell anything, but she didn't feel like her things were all that important anyway. She could sell them without too much concern.

"Noooo. I was thinking you don't need much to live on if you don't have to pay rent every day, just your upkeep fee. How big is it?"

Marilyn thought about the size before answering. She had two rooms: one was an office, the other her hobby room. It had been six years since she bought the unit. She hadn't been in her hobby room for two years. It was too big. She had a small upstairs with a guestroom. "Three bedrooms and the guest room."

"I meant the upkeep fee."

"Oh, $75 per month."

"Take sick leave and rent out the spare room upstairs. Go to a treatment centre that deals with early childhood stuff from a cultural perspective. Most of us just hurt. Being Indian hurts, Mom."

They stared at each other. She wanted more than to heal her past. She wanted to mend all the bridges burnt between them. Now or never, sink or swim.

"It isn't just about me. It's all of us. I want to mend the bridges between all of us."

"Go to the centre. Come back and we can all begin with disclosure and our choice of a family counsellor." It all seemed so simple.

"Yeah. That's what I'll do. What about you, do you really care for the place you're living at now?"

"No. But I am planning on moving in with Cat."

Cat didn't bother to remove the blankets covering her face.

"Before you make any plans for me, I'm pregnant. I plan on keeping the baby."

The air split. The wind of Marilyn's problems changed direction. Baby? Grandmother — this meant she was going to be a grandmother.

"I guess I had better hurry and grow up then," she said barely out loud. Words sometimes crack walls inside. Cat's words blew up the cylinder Marilyn had locked herself inside. She watched it shatter. Tears, laughter and crazy statements disconnected and without much meaning bubbled up from the wall's pieces, ending with: "We have to go shopping."

The shattering of the wall ordered her mind. She realized she was not hungry for a man at all, but hungry for her daughters. She wanted to set things right, but now this impulse didn't have an emotional grip on her. Time would resolve it – and maybe it would take some effort too. Cat's wall-busting "I'm pregnant" opened the doorway to something else. Marilyn remembered her own great-grandma. She chose to relay the memory to her daughters.

"This is Marpole," she said to them.

"Yeah," they drawled. They knew that.

"I remember being small, standing with Ta'ah at the river's edge and asking where it went. She answered: 'To the sea, to the salt sea air. To the ocean of love we all swam through before we arrived here.' I asked her what it looked like. 'Ah, my girl,' she said, 'like nothing you have ever seen. The ocean is vast, deep and at the bottom lives a woman — the mother of hidden being, of thought. She helps us to think deeply before choosing, to consider carefully before acting, and to see broadly before naming.

And the smell of her is so sweetly encouraging.' Is it far away, I asked? 'Too far for you to walk now,' she answered, 'but not so far for a grown-up.' When I grow up, I said, I want to walk to the end of the river. She smiled. 'That's good,' she said. Why? I asked. 'It is your first dream. It is a good dream. One you can realize. If you do, you will forever be courageous.'" Marilyn looked at her daughters. "I'm tired of my fear. Do you want to walk to the river's end with me?"

"Yeah," they answered softly.

"I have a feeling you are going to go anyway," Cat said.

"Yeah."

"Okay," and they rushed for their clothes, shoes, socks, and snacks and out the door they went.

❦ ❦ ❦ ❦

They chattered as they strolled in the morning sunlight. No cars were about. It was Saturday. They reminisced about the dykes, the berry-picking.

"Funny," Marilyn mused.

"What?" Lindy said, slipping her arm through her mother's. Marilyn felt the strength of her daughter's love. It was not as familiar as she would have liked it to have been, but it was exquisitely more wonderful than she had imagined. Southwind skipped about her heels and she imagined she heard him chortling with joy. "The memory of berry-picking doesn't seem to hurt anymore."

"Oh. Oh. Don't even go there," Cat guffawed. "I still have scars." They burst out laughing, recounting memories about climbing the dikes, slipping off, getting torn up by the thorns. Then they recalled that first taste of blackberries, how it inspired breath, made you feel like you were going to live again.

"Dolly lives on the north arm of this river," Lindy offered tentatively.

"Who's Dolly?" Marilyn asked.

The scent of guilt competed with the sweet smell of bog and salt sea air. The sounds of their careful breathing interrupted the river's roil as it greeted the sea. Marilyn clutched Lindy's arm trying to reassure her that whatever she said was okay. The girls glanced at each other.

"Dolly," Cat cleared her throat, "is like our other mother. She is a seer, a healer who helped us to find ourselves when we were teenagers. Oddly enough, she helped us to carry on loving you, despite all the memories. Memories of hurt, of absence, of your dead eyes, of no Daddy, of waking up and knowing you were hung over, knowing you hid your boozing. Memories of praying you would stop and just love us."

The biggest snake was out. Marilyn felt light and weak at the same time. The tears rolled out. She felt ashamed that her girls had fought so hard to continue loving her in the face of hurt. It was a good feeling, this shame. She let it sink in. It was the shame of knowing there was no excuse for what she'd done. It felt good to know she had never wanted to excuse herself. Underneath the old snake lay her memory of praying for change. It felt good that she had won that battle. She knew it wasn't enough, but she had fought for herself and won. She could do it again.

"How come you changed and our daddy couldn't?" Both girls

wept quietly as they walked. Marilyn had no answer. Instead she told them the story of the double-headed snake.

"Sometimes we swallow the snake. She nests. Pretty soon there are so many snakes of doubt inside that the doubt eats us up. Empty, the spirit swallows anger and shame. Maybe he swallowed too many snakes."

"Not good enough," they both answered. The river lolled a mile wide now at the last bridge to the north arm. The bog's Labrador tea hung pungent, obscuring the scent of blueberry and blackberry. Every now and then the tea stepped back and the smell of bog fruit surged forward, like her daughters somehow.

"Yeah," she answered. "He was some piece of shit, don't you think?"

"Yeah," they said.

The sun danced red-gold and huge on the horizon. They murmured comments of awe for it. "You surprise me sometimes," Cat offered tentatively. "I didn't expect you to agree Dad was a piece of shit."

"How come? Shit has a value," Marilyn said, barely able to hold back a laugh. "It grows the best mushrooms and roses. Look at you. Maybe I have a vested interest in trying to understand him. I was a piece of shit too. I decided one day there was nothing wrong with being shit one day, unless you have two legs, in which case you ought to try to be a human. But first, I had to accept that I was a piece of shit. I don't know if that makes any sense, but it is what inspired me to stop whaling on you. Through it all, the two of you became these two lovely roses — a little thorny, but oh so lovely."

Dolly's house came into view. Marilyn had no idea where she wanted to go with all of this. Dolly sounded like some old person from around the turn of the century. Marilyn was a social worker heading for the twenty-first century without ever knowing what was sandwiched in between the hundred years that separated one century from another. It didn't matter just now. The house was modest and small, like her great-grandma's. Then she remembered something else Ta'ah had told her. It was a love story. Two men fought over a woman. She told them not to, that it wasn't up to them anyway. They didn't listen. She lamented and complained to a lake, salting it with her lament. The lake spoke to her. Told her to get them to come there and have a canoe race. She did. They came. They paddled out onto the lake and it swallowed him. "What did you do that for?" she said. "Sometimes to go forward you have to go back to the beginning."

Dolly's house would be a kind of beginning for Marilyn and her girls.

About the AUTHOR

~~~~~~

Lee Maracle is a mother of four and a grandmother of four who was born in North Vancouver, British Columbia. She is a member of the Sto:Loh Nation, and a nationally and internationally acclaimed author of fiction, non-fiction and poetry. Her published work includes *Sojourners and Sundogs* (Polestar, 1999), *Ravensong* (Press Gang) and *I Am Woman* (Press Gang). Her work is studied in universities in Canada, England, the US, Germany and France and she teaches English Composition at the University of Toronto. Lee Maracle is also a respected advocate for social change and is committed to justice and cultural freedom for all peoples.

MORE FINE FICTION FROM POLESTAR AND RAINCOAST

Sojourners and Sundogs • by Lee Maracle
One book combining two of Maracle's best-loved works of fiction: the novel *Sundogs* and short fiction in *Sojourner's Truth and Other Stories*. "[Maracle] is an original warrior, the consciousness of an age." — Joy Harjo
0-88974-061-5 • $23.95 CAN • $19.95 USA

Pool-Hopping and Other Stories • by Anne Fleming
Shortlisted for the Governor-General's Award, the Ethel Wilson Fiction Prize and the Danuta Gleed Award. "Fleming's evenhanded, sharp-eyed and often hilarious narratives traverse the frenzied chaos of urban life with ease and precision." — *The Georgia Straight*
1-896095-18-6 • $16.95 CAN • $13.95 USA

What's Left Us • by Aislinn Hunter
Shortlisted for the Danuta Gleed Award. Six stories and an unforgettable novella by a prodigiously talented writer. "Aislinn Hunter is a gifted writer with a fresh energetic voice and a sharp eye for the detail that draws you irresistibly into the intimacies of her story." — Jack Hodgins
1-55192-412-9 • $19.95 CAN • $15.95 USA

Some Girls Do • by Teresa McWhirter
In prose that's as sharp as broken glass and shot through with poetry, Teresa McWhirter unlocks the extraordinary subculture of urban adults in their twenties and early thirties. "Realistic dialogue — heavily peppered with slang, swearing and esoteric pop-culture refrences — contributes to the novel's over-all believability. The humour and wordplay alone mark McWhirter as a writer to watch." — *Quill and Quire*
1-55192- 459-5 • $21.95 CAN • $15.95 USA

A Reckless Moon and Other Stories • by Dianne Warren
A beautifully written book about human fragility, endorsed by Bonnie Burnard. "Warren is clearly one of a new generation of short-story writers who have learned their craft in the wake of such luminaries as Raymond Carver and Ann Beattie ... Her prose is lucid and precise." — *Books in Canada*
1-55192-455-2 • $19.95 CAN • $15.95 USA